Praise for Valerie Burns and her Baker Street mysteries

TWO PARTS SUGAR, ONE PART MURDER

"Snappy dialogue, a well-drawn supporting cast and an irresistible canine companion all add delicious flavor. Gulp this book down or savor it, but consuming it will guarantee a sustained sugar high."
—*The New York Times Book Review*

"With a one-of-a-kind heroine and a plot that's just as addictive as checking Instagram, *Two Parts Sugar, One Part Murder* is a fresh take on the cozy genre. I couldn't help but root for influencer Maddy Montgomery whether she was trying to solve a murder or just not burn the cake. The Baker Street Mysteries has already become one of my favorite series! #MorePlease."
—Kellye Garrett, Agatha Award–winning author of *Hollywood Homicide* and *Like a Sister*

"A lively series launch, with an edgier heroine than the baking-framed novels by Jenn McKinlay and Joanne Fluke."
—*Booklist*

Please turn the page for more praise!

"Valerie Burns sweetens the pot for cozy mystery fans with this debut in her new series. City transplant Madison Montgomery finds her small-town tribe and new strengths in a delicious story of baking, backstabbing, and murder."
—Maddie Day, author of the Country Store mysteries

"Everyone is a suspect in Valerie Burns's entertaining new mystery, filled with surprising twists, suspicious characters and a mastiff named Baby who will win your heart. Top that off with humor and delicious recipes and you have a delight of a cozy."
—Valerie Wilson Wesley, author of *A Fatal Glow*

MURDER IS A PIECE OF CAKE

"This fun culinary cozy mystery is the perfect beach read."
—Modern Dog

"Burns proves that a girl and her mastiff can't be defeated."
—Kirkus Reviews

A Cup of Flour, A Pinch of Death

Books by Valerie Burns

Baker Street Mysteries
TWO PARTS SUGAR, ONE PART MURDER
MURDER IS A PIECE OF CAKE
A CUP OF FLOUR, A PINCH OF DEATH

Books by Valerie Burns writing as V. M. Burns

Mystery Bookshop Mysteries
THE PLOT IS MURDER
READ HERRING HUNT
THE NOVEL ART OF MURDER
WED, READ & DEAD
BOOKMARKED FOR MURDER
A TOURIST'S GUIDE TO MURDER
KILLER WORDS
BOOKCLUBBED TO DEATH
MURDER ON TOUR

Dog Club Mysteries
IN THE DOG HOUSE
THE PUPPY WHO KNEW TOO MUCH
BARK IF IT'S MURDER
PAW AND ORDER
SIT, STAY, SLAY

Published by Kensington Publishing Corp.

A Cup of Flour, A Pinch of Death

VALERIE BURNS

Kensington Publishing Corp.
www.kensingtonbooks.com

KENSINGTON BOOKS are published by

Kensington Publishing Corp.
900 Third Avenue
New York, NY 10022

All Kensington titles, imprints, and distributed lines are available at special quantity discounts for bulk purchases for sales promotion, premiums, fund-raising, educational, or institutional use.

This book is a work of fiction. Names, characters, businesses, organizations, places, events, and incidents either are the product of the author's imagination or are used fictitiously. Any resemblance to actual persons, living or dead, events, or locales is entirely coincidental.

To the extent that the image or images on the cover of this book depict a person or persons, such person or persons are merely models, and are not intended to portray any character or characters featured in the book.

Special book excerpts or customized printings can also be created to fit specific needs. For details, write or phone the office of the Kensington Sales Manager: Kensington Publishing Corp., 900 Third Avenue, New York, NY 10022. Attn. Sales Department. Phone: 1-800-221-2647.

ISBN: 978-1-4967-3827-1 (ebook)

ISBN: 978-1-4967-3824-0

First Kensington Trade Paperback Printing: August 2024

10 9 8 7 6 5 4 3 2 1

Printed in the United States of America

A Cup of Flour, A Pinch of Death

CHAPTER 1

I blame the Admiral. Being raised by an admiral in the United States Navy who dragged me to military bases all over the world meant that when I hear a loud explosion that sounds like gunfire, I duck and take cover. I expect explosions, gunfire, and even drone attacks when overseas, or on a military base during training exercises. I don't expect to have to crawl under a desk in my home in the peaceful lakefront town of New Bison, Michigan—Population 1,600. But there was an explosion. One loud bang and then smaller, rapid-fire bangs, like a machine gun. I leaped from my chair and dove. It was a reflex action, like kicking your leg when a doctor hits your shin with a little rubber hammer. Stop. Drop. And roll. No, wait. That's what you do for fire. What is the mantra for when you're under attack? Stop. Drop. And hide? Whatever. I glanced up and saw my two-hundred-fifty-pound English mastiff staring at me. His head was cocked to the side, and he gave me a puzzled stare.

"Baby, come!" I ordered.

English mastiffs can be stubborn, and Baby was no exception, but he had been well trained by my great-aunt Octavia and rarely refused a direct command.

"Baby, come!"

He sighed and inched closer.

When he was within reach, I grabbed him by his collar and tried to pull the massive dog under the desk with me. It was an effort in futility. He wouldn't fit, but I felt a certain amount of comfort just holding onto this muscular beast.

I pulled my cell phone from my pocket and quickly dialed my roommate and friend, Sheriff April Johnson.

"April. Someone's shooting at the house."

"Are you serious? Who would be shooting at you? Are you sure?"

Before I could respond, there was another explosion. Fortunately, April heard it.

"OMG! I'm on my way and calling for backup. Where are you?"

"Baby and I are taking cover under the desk upstairs. I—"

"Maddy? Are you home? I came to drop off a few . . . What the—"

I recognized the voice. It was Leroy Danielson, the head baker at my bakery.

"Leroy, take cover! Someone's shooting and it's not safe!" I yelled.

"What's going on? What's Leroy doing?" April yelled. "I'm sending a squad car to the house."

Despite the carpet, footsteps pounded like a platoon on the stairs. Was it Leroy? Or, had the shooter taken him out and come in search of more victims? I looked around for a weapon. Unlike my dad, the Navy Admiral, or my boyfriend, the ex-Army officer, I didn't know how to defend myself with a paperclip. The only thing within reach that might be slightly useful as a weapon was my wireless keyboard. I slid the keyboard off the desk, and climbed out from underneath. I hurried behind the door and wielded it like a Louisville Slugger.

My first clue that the intruder wasn't intent on murder was Baby's reaction. He stood up and faced the door. His tail wagged.

The door opened and Baby trotted forward, got up on his hind legs, and proceeded to give the intruder a face wash.

"Yuck! Baby, off." Leroy stuck his head around the door and caught sight of me.

I lowered my keyboard and tried to hide it behind my back. "Is the shooter gone?"

"What shooter?" Leroy asked.

"Didn't you hear the gunshots?"

"Gunshots?" Leroy thought for a few moments and then a smile broke out on his face.

"Yes, shooter. Look, I know what gunfire sounds like, and I heard gunshots."

"Come with me." Leroy turned and headed downstairs.

Alternating between tiptoeing and clutching the back of Leroy's shirt, I followed him downstairs and into the kitchen. My normally pristine kitchen looked like a war zone. Bits of white, yellow, and brown shrapnel were everywhere. "What the—"

Leroy walked over to the stove. "Were you boiling eggs?"

"Yes. I promised April I'd boil five dozen eggs for the Easter Egg Hunt at the police station."

"So, you put five dozen eggs in a pot together?"

I nodded.

"How long ago and how much water?"

I glanced at my watch. "An hour."

I could barely hear the sirens from the police cars over Leroy's laughter.

April burst through the door with her gun out and ready to fire. She was followed by Officers Al Norris and Jerrod Thomas from the New Bison Police. She quickly assessed the scene and then lowered her weapon. She pulled out her radio. "False alarm."

Normally, Baby would have greeted April with love and affection, but he was too busy devouring the remains of the exploded eggs that were covering every surface of the kitchen.

Leroy pulled out his camera and started videotaping the chaos.

Experience told me that I'd never get the phone away from him before he had the catastrophe documented and making its way through cyberspace.

"Just when I thought I was getting a handle on this cooking thing . . . this happens." I stared at the ceiling.

Six months ago, I couldn't boil water. That was before I inherited a bakery from my great-aunt Octavia, and had made significant progress. Thanks to lessons from Leroy and the recipes Great-Aunt Octavia left me, I'd even won the local baking festival. But, as my other assistant, Hannah Portman, often said, "Pride comes before the fall."

After April got over her anger and frustration, she laughed at me, too. "Maddy, I can't believe you left five dozen eggs in a pot to boil for over an hour." Hilarious cackling followed.

"I was revising the Baby Cakes website and I must have gotten distracted. I forgot." I grabbed a broom and swung it overhead to remove the exploded eggs and shells that were stuck to the ceiling, light fixtures, and walls like glue. Interesting that my most humiliating cooking experiences all involved eggs. "Eggs are my nemesis."

Leroy and April took rags and helped with the cleanup, but they didn't make a lot of progress because they kept bursting out laughing every few minutes.

Leroy's cell phone dinged like a bell-ringing Santa in front of the Salvation Army at Christmas from people who loved the video he'd uploaded. As a social media influencer, I'd long ago tucked my ego away in a closet. Sadly, the more humiliating a video, the more views. When my ex-fiancé, Elliott, was a no-show for our live-streamed wedding, and I was left at the altar in humiliation, I went viral and got the highest number of views

I'd ever gotten. At the time, I thought my world was over and wondered if I'd ever be able to show my face online again. What a difference a few months made. Six months later, I was scraping eggs off the ceiling, but thanks to Great-Aunt Octavia, I owned a house, a bakery, and a two-hundred-fifty-pound English mastiff. I had friends and there was Michael. I grinned at the thought of how completely different my life was now and how much happier I was. *Thank you, Elliott.*

Baby stopped eating eggs and stood on his hind legs. He tilted his head to the side and listened. After a few moments, he went to the back door, barked once, and wagged his tail.

I opened the door without waiting for the peal of the doorbell or a knock.

"Is that some type of sixth sense?" Michael stood with his hand poised to knock.

"I've got my own alert system." I stepped aside to show him Baby.

Normally, Michael Portman was ruggedly handsome with dark skin, light gray eyes, and a five-o'clock shadow. Today, that shadow was set to nine o'clock and when he kissed me and nuzzled my ear, I felt an overwhelming desire to scratch.

I pulled away and gazed into his eyes. "You look awful."

"Thanks." He pulled a piece of eggshell from my hair and glanced around the kitchen. "What the heck happened?"

"Don't ask and don't change the subject."

He had to work to keep from grinning. "Let me guess, egg mishap?"

Leroy showed him the video and Michael tried hard not to laugh, but he failed. Soon, he, April, and Leroy were all chuckling like they were at a comedy show. I can't be the only person who'd ever exploded eggs before.

"Come on, Baby." I tugged his leash, but a large mound of eggs took that exact moment to fall off the light fixture and he was determined to devour it. Normally, I would have worried about his consumption of the shells, but according to Google, eggs and the shells were a good source of protein, whether cooked or raw.

After a bit more laughter, Michael wrapped his arms around me and hugged me close. "Hey, Squid. I'm sorry."

After graduating from Princeton, Michael spent four years in the Army. He'd been an animal care specialist, which is where he discovered how much he loved working with animals, so he went back to school to become a veterinarian. As the daughter of a Navy admiral, we often exchanged friendly quips.

"Don't call me Squid." I gave his chest a light tap.

He mumbled something that brought heat to my cheeks and then he kissed me and the heat moved down throughout the rest of my body.

"Ahem. Now that the active-shooter situation has been neutralized, I need to get back to work." April cleared her throat and passed her rag to Michael. She gave Baby a scratch and then left.

"I need to . . . um . . . head out, too." Leroy dropped his towel on the counter and headed for the door.

"Wait. What did you come by for?" I asked.

"I picked up a box of supplies. I left them in your car. Oh, and I almost forgot." Leroy reached into his back pocket and pulled out his phone. He made a few swipes and then held it up so I could see the pictures he'd taken at his baking class.

"Wow. Looks like a full house."

"The class was full, and so was the overflow area." He shook his head. "I can't believe people pay money to sit and watch other students learn to bake, but you were right."

"Who's that man?" I used my fingers to stretch the photo and pointed.

Michael and Leroy looked over my shoulder at the photo, but both shrugged.

"No idea," Leroy said. "Why?"

"No reason. I've seen him hanging out near the bakery a lot lately."

"Maybe he just likes your buns." Michael winked.

"And on that note, I'm out of here," Leroy said. He and Michael fist-bumped before he left.

Michael reached for me. "Now I have you all to myself."

I sidestepped and turned to him. "I think we were talking about how tired you look."

"Really? I don't remember that conversation at all. I thought we were talking about something completely different." Michael sat on one of the barstools that was around the massive kitchen island and propped his chin with his hand.

"The reason you don't remember the conversation is because you're so tired you can barely think straight."

"Who me? Tired?" His argument might have carried more weight if he hadn't yawned.

"Michael, you've been working like a slave, and you're wearing yourself out."

"Business is good." He shrugged. "Besides, I love what I do, and my patients need me. Why is that bad?"

I leaned across the bar and looked into his eyes. "I'm glad you love your job, and I know your patients love you, but I've grown rather fond of you, too."

He caressed my lips with his finger. "Really? I had no idea."

I stood up and prepared for my second attack, but he preempted me. "Maddy, I know I've been working a lot of hours, and you're right."

"What?" I cupped my ear. "Is that a G.I. admitting he was wrong?" I joked.

"There's a first time for everything."

I took a dishcloth and swatted his arm, but he was too quick for me, and he grabbed the end of the towel and pulled me around the bar and onto his lap. He kissed me thoroughly.

When we came up for air, he held me close. "Okay, Squid. I really have been listening, and you're right. I've been putting in a lot of time at the practice, so I'm thinking of bringing in a partner to help out."

"That's great."

"In fact, I was hoping that you and I could spend a lot more time together. In fact, I have been meaning to ask you something. I— "

My phone pinged, and I glanced down to see that Leroy had sent me the photos from his cooking class. I stole one quick look at the first photo and then returned my attention to Michael, but I was immediately yanked back to my phone.

I picked up the phone and swiped the photo to enlarge it and gasped. "No. No. Heck NO!"

"Excuse me?"

"Of all the people to make their way to New Bison, Michigan . . . It can't be . . . There's no way that witch would dare show her face here . . . at Baby Cakes . . . It just can't be."

He looked at the picture on my phone. "Who is she?"

"Brandy Denton. And if I see her in my bakery, I'm going to kill her."

CHAPTER 2

I gritted my teeth and did a couple of laps pacing from the stove to the bar around my kitchen. "That fiancé-stealing, two-faced shrew has a lot of nerve showing her face here."

"Ah . . . Brandy Denton. She's the girl who—"

"Who pretended to be my friend while she was stealing my fiancé? Yep. That's her."

Michael stood his ground in front of me and grabbed me by the shoulders. "Actually, I was going to say isn't she the one who saved you from marrying the wrong man."

Something in his voice sent a shiver down my spine. *The wrong man. Is he implying that he is the right man?* My voice froze, and my mouth forgot how to form words. All I could do was stare dumbfounded. Eventually, I nodded.

"Then, I'd say we need to thank her. Maybe I should pay her a visit and tell—"

"Oh, no you don't. You stay away from Brandy Denton."

"Nobody can steal someone who doesn't want to go."

"I know."

"And for the record, I'm not Elliott and I'm not going anywhere. He might have been crazy enough to let you go, but I've got more sense than that." He wrapped his arms around me, and electricity shot through my body.

He kissed me and I forgot about Elliott, Brandy Denton, and exploded eggs until his phone rang. He swore and pulled away.

I took a moment to catch my breath while he answered. I only heard one side of the conversation, but I could tell it was an emergency.

"I can be there in about fifteen minutes. Keep her warm and calm." He disconnected and turned to me. "I'm sorry, I— "

"It's okay. Drive safely, and text me when you get home."

He kissed me and then pulled away. As he hurried out the door, he mumbled, "I definitely need to get help."

The house was eerily quiet and darker after Michael left and the empty void wasn't just in the house. The emptiness was inside me.

Baby stopped eating exploded eggs and stood up. He had eggshells on his nose, and a large piece of the yellow yolk was on the top of his head.

I took out my phone and snapped a photo and uploaded it.

#CleaningUpTheEasyWay #ItsRainingEggs #EggsAreMyNemesis #BabyLovesEasterEggs

He gave himself a shake, flinging drool around like tinsel on a Christmas tree.

"Ugh." I got the Lysol wipes from the cabinet and gave the kitchen a thorough cleaning. Another thing I would never have done six months ago. I glanced down at my shorter and less blinged-out nails. I still got a manicure every two weeks, but instead of the dramatically long claws that I'd worn most of my life, I now wore my natural nails in a clean French manicure that allowed me to cook, clean, and type.

I glanced around at my clean, sanitized kitchen with a sense of pride. Another surprise. I enjoyed cleaning. I loved seeing something dirty sparkle. Plus, it didn't require a lot of thought or decisions. I still struggled with making decisions. All evidence of my egg debacle was completely gone, so I put away the cleaning supplies.

My stomach did a few flip-flops and I felt jittery. I didn't think I had enough caffeine that day. It took a lot of caffeine for me to get moving. I didn't even remember touching my fourth cup. I glanced at my watch. I had time.

"Come on, boy."

With no more eggs to eat, Baby moved to the dog bed I bought for the dining room and stared at me with an accusatory look. *You could have left some of those eggs for me.*

I ignored the look. "Let's go for a ride."

He lifted his head but still didn't budge.

"Okay, fine. I'll get a Red Eye, and you can have a pup cup."

At last. The magic words: *pup cup*. Or, in his case, a full-blown mountain of whipped cream in a cup. Baby stretched and then slowly climbed down and ambled to the back door.

I was still adjusting to my new SUV, a Rivian R1S, a gift from the Admiral. When I first came to New Bison, it was winter, and I hadn't planned to stay, so I'd left my sports car at home and rented a car to get me around until I could go back to the warmth of California. Fortunately, the lady behind the rental car counter ignored my request for a sporty luxury vehicle and put me in a Range Rover. After a short time with a two-hundred-fifty-pound dog who drooled like a faucet, I bought it. After he destroyed the inside of the vehicle and broke a window to get to me when he thought I was in danger, it had to be put out to pasture. Most of the time, Baby was a giant goofball, but when he went into protection mode, he was as tenacious as a Navy SEAL.

I smiled at the realization that my change in vehicles mirrored the same changes that my life had taken. I'd gone from a social media influencer intent on living the life of a reality television star to that of a baker and business owner. My new Rivian R1S wasn't close to the same level of luxury as the convertible I'd driven in L.A., or even the Range Rover with its soft leather seats and wood dashboard. My dad thought I'd lost my mind when he saw the Rivian's *vegan leather* seats. In other words, fake. Or, what Michael's grandmother called *pleather.* Still, it was an all-electric SUV that had all-wheel drive, perfect for Michigan winters. Lots of space for hauling around baked goods, supplies, or two-hundred-fifty-pound English mastiffs. However, the key selling feature for me was the pet-comfort mode. Similar to Michael's Tesla, pet comfort kept the air-conditioning and radio going while I ran into a store so Baby could remain cool and comfortable without me having to crack the windows. For most people, lowering the windows even a small amount could make it easier for thieves to steal a small dog or even your vehicle. In Baby's case, being able to keep the windows up was a safety feature for anyone with ill intent who got too close. Plus, I liked the interior cameras that allowed me to watch him on my phone to make sure he wasn't eating the dashboard or ripping the stuffing out of the seats.

The drive downtown was short. Of course, given the size of New Bison, it didn't take more than fifteen minutes to drive anywhere. I pulled into my parking space behind Baby Cakes Bakery. One look at the sign Great-Aunt Octavia placed behind the building still brought a smile to my face: OWNER. DON'T EVEN THINK ABOUT PARKING HERE!

I got out of the car and held the door for Baby, who climbed down with grace and then meandered over to the dumpster that was next to my parking space and hiked his leg. I unlocked the back door and turned off the alarm that the Admiral insisted I install. Despite my arguments that New Bison was safe, my dad disagreed. The fact that two people were murdered and found inside the bakery hadn't helped my argument. The facts were against me. The Admiral was a man of decision and action when confronted with facts. After a thorough rundown of the victims that just *happened* to be found in the bakery, he presented me with choices: move back to California, where he could keep a protective eye on me; hire an armed security guard to patrol 24/7; or get an alarm system and learn to shoot a gun. At twenty-eight, I didn't need my father's approval. However, years of struggling to make decisions and a Navy admiral who excelled at making snap decisions in an instant had meant that I'd relied on his decisions far longer than I should have. I still struggled with making decisions, but lately, I'd learned that when the decisions mattered, I didn't hesitate. To the Admiral's disappointment, I chose to stay in New Bison, run my bakery, and keep Baby. However, my dad did know a thing or two about security, so while I'd resisted firing a gun for over twenty years, I acknowledged that an alarm system wasn't a bad idea. Between the Admiral, my ex-Army boyfriend, and my best friend, the sheriff, avoiding the gun had taken a lot more effort than it should have. We compromised on a Taser. After I accidentally tased the Admiral when he tried to teach me how to quickly draw it out of my purse and prepare to use it, he conceded that perhaps I wasn't ready for a gun.

Baby Cakes Bakery was in a brick building on the corner of Main and Church Streets. The block-long brick building was the home of four businesses. The business next to Baby Cakes had once been a hardware store owned by the town's previous mayor. However, after Mayor Rivers's death, his wife, Candy, converted the hardware store into Higher Grounds Coffee and Tea Shop. I first met Candy Hurston Rivers when she was a server at the local casino. Considerably younger than the late Mayor Paul Rivers, she wasn't a Rhodes scholar, but she was kind and brewed a mean cortado.

Leroy had left a box of supplies in my car when he stopped by the house. I carried them inside and was greeted by the sweet aroma of sugar, vanilla, and chocolate. I took a deep breath and allowed the scents to infuse my soul. I placed the supplies in the pantry. I took a moment to admire the space and the neatly stacked items that now lined the room after our renovation.

Woof.

Baby didn't share my joy at seeing the neatly stacked items and paced the kitchen as though looking for his pup cup.

"Fine. I'm coming." I closed the pantry door and snapped on his leash.

We walked out the front and went next door to the coffee shop.

Despite the fact that it was almost eight at night, there was still a crowd, and Candy was busy behind the counter. Too busy to talk. So, I turned to the ToGo shelf she'd set up near the door. If you downloaded her app and paid online, you could bypass the lines. I was considering adding something similar to Baby Cakes, but Hannah felt there was a benefit in making people see the other delicacies and inhale the wonderful aroma. More often than not, customers came to Baby Cakes for one specific item but couldn't resist the racks of yummy treats or the smells. The smells got them every time. Very few people possessed the willpower to resist a buttery croissant or a dozen thumbprint cookies. Hannah may not know much about social media, but she knew people and the power of a flaky pie crust.

I found the box with my name that had a large Red Eye with a double shot of espresso and an even bigger cup with Baby's name, which I knew was full of whipped cream. I grabbed our items and turned to the door. Baby was excited for his pup cup, so he wanted to get outside as much as I did.

"Why if it isn't poor Madison Montgomery."

I froze. I'd know that nasally whine anywhere. *Breathe. Hold. Exhale.* I turned and plastered a fake smile on my face. "Brandy Denton."

CHAPTER 3

Brandy ran toward me and flung her arms around my shoulders. From her big peroxide-blond hair to her fake nails, fake eyelashes, and Botox-injected lips, Brandy Denton looked as though she'd just stepped off the screen of one of the *Housewives of . . .* shows. She did the French *la bise* cheek kiss without touching me while making a loud smooching noise. When her lips were near my ear, she whispered, "My, how the mighty have fallen." She pulled back, flashed a big smile, and flipped her hair over her shoulder. She looked me up and down, as though she were judging the prize heifer at a state fair. "Are you okay? You look horrible."

I gritted my teeth. "I'm doing great, actually. Never better."

"Are you sure? I've never seen you look so . . . well . . ." She waved her hand to indicate all of me. Brandy's big hair, extra-long lashes, and big gestures were drawing attention. Few people in New Bison had seen anyone like her, and she stood out like an English mastiff in a pen full of Chihuahuas.

"I'm doing great. I've got a great job. A wonderful dog. And a wonderful man in my life. So, things are going well. Of course, I'm still online a lot, which must be how you found me." I smiled. "How are things with you and . . . what's his name? Ethan? Elliott?"

Brandy frowned but quickly buried it. "We broke up. I have no idea how you were able to endure his arrogance for as long as you did, but then I guess when you're in love, you overlook annoying little things like that."

Hmm. She and Elliott broke up. "I had no idea he broke up with you. What a shame. You two were so perfect for each other. Are you okay?"

There was a flash in her eyes that indicated I'd landed a blow. *So, Elliott had dumped her.*

Brandy rolled her eyes and waved her hand. "Oh, we both realized it wouldn't work out. We weren't together nearly as long as you two. I guess I was lucky to have caught on to what type of man he really is so quickly."

Okay, score one for Brandy.

We glared at each other for several seconds, but Baby had had enough. I was holding his pup cup. He stood up on his hind legs and gave the side of my face a lick.

"Ick. That must be *Baby.* I'd heard you'd gone to the dogs. I guess it's true."

"Baby, down." I said a silent prayer when he complied and turned to Brandy. "What brings you to Michigan?"

Brandy shifted from one thigh-high black leather Jimmy Choo boot to the other. *Darn it, those boots are amazing.* I forced myself not to notice that I was wearing my Pyer Moss Sculpt sneakers. Something about the way Brandy avoided eye contact made me wonder what she was hiding. "I just wanted to see for myself if the rumors were true."

"Rumors? What rumors?"

"That you were about to sign a contract for a reality television show based on your life living in rural America." She flipped her hair. "I heard you pitched it as Paris Hilton meets *Green Acres* or some such nonsense."

"Where'd you hear that?"

"I'm friends with a friend of Kim . . . you know, Kardashian. My friend told me your social media was getting noticed and the producers were looking for something . . . different." She scrunched her nose as though she'd just gotten a whiff of a skunk.

"Well, I can assure you that nothing could be further from the truth." I grinned. "So, I guess your friend of a friend can tell Kim that the rumors are false." I waited a beat before adding, "I guess that means you'll be heading back now, but it was definitely good to catch up. The next time you're in town, be sure to call, and we'll do lunch. Sorry, I don't have more time, but I'm really busy." I smiled.

"Oh, I think I'll be sticking around for a while." Brandy pulled out her phone and snapped a picture of me. "I want to make sure to see all of the sights of New Bison. Plus, I'd love to meet that new beau of yours. He looks positively scrumptious. Ta!" She wiggled her fingers and sidled past me toward the counter.

I stood staring at her back for several beats.

"Excuse me, Maddy?"

I snapped out of my nightmare and focused on the man standing in front of me. "Chris. I'm sorry. I didn't mean to block the door."

Chris Russell had been Great-Aunt Octavia's lawyer. Now, he was mine. There weren't a lot of options as far as lawyers go in New Bison, but so far, I didn't have many complaints. He hadn't had to do much from a legal perspective, but the town had credited him with saving my life. Although, between my handy cast-iron skillet and Baby, I had the situation well in hand.

Chris Russell reached around and opened the door and held it for me and Baby. Once outside, he turned to me. "You seem distracted. Does it have anything to do with your friend?"

"That woman is *not* my friend." I took several deep breaths. "Sorry, she's just someone I knew before."

"I see. Well, I hope you two have a good visit . . . or not." He shook his head and walked away.

Woof.

"You're right. I shouldn't let her get to me." I took the lid off Baby's supersized pup cup and held it so he could lick all of the whipped cream.

In seconds, he had consumed the contents and was licking the sticky foam from his nose.

I tossed the empty cup into a nearby receptacle and started walking. Downtown New Bison wasn't long, only about two blocks of retail shops, but it was a quaint and picturesque resort town located right on the Lake Michigan coastline.

Next door to the coffee shop was Tyler's Knitwear, which was owned by my friend, and now acting city councilman, Tyler Lawrence. A small café and a used furniture store that the owner referred to as "antiques" completed the block. On the opposite side of the street, there was another brick building that housed a shop with soap, candles, and essential oils, a bookshop that had been owned by my late great-aunt Octavia's beau, Garrett Kelley, a boutique specializing in women's clothing, and a custom jewelry store.

In early April, it was still light at eight in the evening, so I continued my walk. I was frazzled and angry with myself for being frazzled. I'd allowed Brandy Denton to get under my skin, and she knew it. *Darn it.*

My favorite walking path took me in front of the Carson Law Inn, a mansion built by Beauregard Law, New Bison's oil tycoon. Law had one child, a daughter he named Carson.

Scrumptious! How dare she.

My phone rang, and a quick glance pulled up Michael's picture.

"Hello, Beautiful."

I smiled. "Hey, are the animals of New Bison safe?"

"I can't confirm that all of the animals are safe, but New Bison's bovine population has increased by two."

"Twins! Isn't that unusual?"

"Yeah, and it was tricky, but both calves and the mom are alive and well."

He spent a few minutes talking about the difficult delivery. Pride dripped from each word. He truly loved his job, and I loved that about him. I loved a lot of things about him. In fact, I loved Michael Portman.

He yawned.

"You sound tired."

"It's not so bad until I sit down, but I'm going to take a shower and crash." His voice was muffled as though he had just pulled his shirt over his head.

"Have I told you lately that I think you're scrumptious?"

"No, but I think you're pretty scrumptious, too." He spent a few minutes telling me some other thoughts he had that brought heat up my neck. By the time I'd walked back to Baby Cakes and got into the car, I had to turn on the air-conditioning, and it had nothing to do with the red eye coffee or the exercise.

"Give me twenty minutes, and you can tell me face-to-face exactly how scrumptious you find me."

I laughed. "I thought you were tired?"

"Tired? Me? Must be some sailor you were thinking about. Army GIs don't get tired. Haven't you heard our motto? 'Always Ready.'"

"That's the Coast Guard." I chuckled.

"Whatever. Still applies. I can bring all of my scrumptiousness over in ten minutes."

"I still need to make five dozen boiled eggs for the Easter Egg Hunt, and apparently you can't just put them all in a pot together and boil them for an hour. So, it's going to take some time. Can I get a raincheck? Tomorrow? You get plenty of rest. You're going to need it."

He swore. "Five minutes. I can be there in five."

I laughed and disconnected. I glanced at Baby. "What?"

He refused to make eye contact and instead glanced out the front window as though he were embarrassed. Not for the first time since I'd met him, I wondered exactly how much of my conversation Baby really understood.

CHAPTER 4

"What are you doing?" April walked into the kitchen and stared at pots filled with eggs and ice water that were scattered on every flat surface.

Sheriff April Johnson was nearly six feet tall and one of the most stunning women I'd ever seen. The fact that she was wearing a uniform and packing a gun meant she was gorgeous with an edge that I knew men found sexy, no matter how much she tried to downplay it.

"Making the boiled eggs I promised for the Easter Egg Hunt."

"I gathered, but what's all of this?" April spread her arms to encompass everything.

"According to Google, it takes twelve minutes to make perfect hard-boiled eggs."

"Have you never heard the old adage that a watched pot doesn't boil?"

"Urban myth. I've watched these eggs like a hawk." Alexa, Siri, and the timer on the oven all went off at the same time, and it took a few moments for me to silence everything.

Baby rolled onto his back and put his paw over his face.

I took the last batch of eggs to the sink and filled the pot with cold water and ice.

April leaned over my shoulder.

"That stops the eggs from continuing to cook. I had no idea that they would continue to cook even after I turned off the stove."

April leaned against the counter and stared at me. "How many batches did it take before you figured that out?"

I ignored her for a few moments before answering. "Two dozen."

"So, seven dozen fails altogether?" Her lips twitched.

"I prefer to say that I found seven dozen ways *not* to boil eggs."

April burst out laughing.

I stretched.

"Thank you. You didn't have to do this, but I really appreciate it, and I know the kids will be so excited."

"My pleasure." I glanced around at my handiwork. "Now what?"

"Nothing. I'll take it from here." She fidgeted with a dishtowel. "Leroy's going to help me dye them tomorrow." She avoided eye contact.

I stared at my friend.

"What?"

"I didn't say anything."

"Your silence screams louder than a siren on a fire truck. Spill it."

"I think it's great that you and Leroy are *finally* hooking up." I chuckled.

"Hold up. There's no '*hook up.*'" She used air quotes to emphasize "hookup." "We're just friends. We've always been friends. He's a baker and a nice person, and he offered to help me dye the eggs using natural ingredients."

"Natural ingredients? What's natural about dyed eggs?"

"He swears we can create some beautiful colored eggs using cabbage, onions, and beets." She shrugged. "We advertised all-natural Easter Eggs, and we've got a ton of parents who said they're coming. You'd be surprised how competitive the Easter Egg hunt market is. Last year, we only had five kids come to the police station. The winery had over two hundred kids. The members of the force didn't even come. I spent two whole days trying to find all those eggs and still didn't get all of them until they started to rot. Then, you just had to follow your nose to find them." She scrunched her face and held her nose.

"I had no idea. What's the big deal with Easter Eggs?" I asked.

"It's not the eggs or even the kids. It's all about getting to the parents. I have a friend who works at the winery, and they said they sold close to twenty thousand dollars in wine."

"Ahh. I get it. It's the additional sales, but . . . the police department doesn't sell anything."

"No, but the parents vote, and this is an election year, and we need new equipment—bulletproof vests, body cameras, new high-tech guns, all the stuff that bigger cities get from taxes. In New Bison, extra money for police and schools has to be put on the ballot and voted on. Plus, yours truly is up for re-election."

"I had no idea. But you're a great sheriff. You don't have anything to worry about." I gave her a reassuring back pat.

"Ha. In the past six months, we've had two mayors murdered, plus my husband was murdered, and there are still folks around town who believe that I was somehow involved. Or, that I put someone else up to it." She blushed and turned away.

"Ah . . . so that's why you've been so distant to Leroy."

"I haven't been distant, but—"

Baby hopped up from his sofa and gave April a nudge. When she turned, he stood on his hind legs, wrapped his paws around her shoulders, and gave her face a lick.

"Aww, Baby is such a good boy," April said. "Too bad more men aren't like him."

"I'm sure you could find a man who would lick your face." I laughed.

"You know what I mean. He's just so loving, and all he wants is a little ear scratch."

"Wait. If you're dyeing eggs tomorrow, does that mean you're not going to the tea at the Carson Law Inn?"

"I wouldn't miss that tea for anything. Carson Law is supposed to be back in town from Paris, and I can't wait to see what she's going to wear."

"She's a milliner, right?" I loved fashion and haute couture, but I wasn't really into hats. Preparing for my first tea at the Carson Law Inn helped me discover an entirely new world with hats. There wasn't a milliner in New Bison, so I'd reached out to my stylist at McMullen Boutique in Oakland. She sent so many cute hats, I couldn't pick one, so I ended up buying five.

"I've heard that people pay thousands for Carson Law's hats to wear to Ascot, the Kentucky Derby, and, well, anywhere that fashionable hats are worn. I wish I could afford one."

"You have not adapted to your new financial state," I said. "You're rich. You could buy whatever you want."

April's late husband had been shady, underhanded, vindictive, and rich. Before he was murdered, he intended to leave April one dollar and a worthless diamond mine in Alberta, Canada. However, he died before he could take some of the property out of April's name, leaving her a couple of pieces of real estate, including Garrett Kelley's bookstore, which she planned to rent to Leroy's mother, Fiona. The Rucker-Merkel

Diamond Mine didn't contain diamonds, but instead contained ammolite, one of the rarest gemstones on the planet.

"I'm not rich. You and I both know Clayton never intended for me to profit from him in any way whatsoever." April folded her arms across her chest.

"He may not have intended it, but he gave you that mine, and those ammolites are yours, and you've been offered a small fortune for the mine."

"I don't want it. I wouldn't know what to do with all that money anyway."

"I can help you with that." I grinned but quickly got serious. "However, I understand your reluctance. Anyway, what are you wearing?"

April shrugged. "I don't know. I have a blue suit. I guess I'll wear that . . ."

I shook my head. "You can't wear a business suit to high tea."

April frowned.

"Come with me." I grabbed her hand and pulled her to my bedroom and to the closet. I squinted and gave her a good look. April was thinner and taller than me, but depending on the way the dress was cut, I knew she would be able to wear it.

I pulled out a dress that was ankle length on me, but I knew would be tea length on her. It was a navy-blue silk A-line dress with a full skirt and a fitted lace overlay bodice with a bow in front.

April's eyes lit up, and I knew we'd struck gold.

"Try it on, and I have the perfect navy-blue Philip Treacy cocktail hat that matches the dress." I pulled out the hat boxes and held up the small silk hat with a thin, ornately tied blue bow.

The dress fit April like a glove, and I could tell by the way she caressed it that she loved it.

"This fabric is so soft. It feels amazing."

"You'll need to sit for me to put this hat on." I walked toward her with the small blue fascinator hat.

"What in the world is that?" April stood up and backed away from me.

"It's a hat. Well, technically, it's called a fascinator."

"How am I supposed to wear it?"

"It has a comb and a band." I showed her the underside and assured her that it would stay on.

She glanced at it skeptically, but the small tear-shaped hat matched the dress, and they would look great together.

It took a bit of manipulation, but I got the hat on, and she stared at herself in the mirror.

"It looks great, but don't you think this is a bit over the top for tea? I look like I'm going to a wedding."

"Nope. I read about Carson Law. She loves haute couture and vintage clothing. In every picture I found of her, she was wearing a dress like Jacqueline Kennedy or Audrey Hepburn from *Breakfast at Tiffany's*."

"What are you going to wear?"

"I'm still trying to decide." I reached in the closet and pulled out two dresses. "I'm deciding between this classic Isabel Sanchis dress that I absolutely love and this vintage Elie Saab appliqué."

"Both dresses are amazing. So, let's see them on. I haven't played dress-up since I was eighteen and still doing the pageant circuit." April sat down carefully on the bed and crossed her legs at the ankle.

I slipped the purple Elie Saab cocktail dress on first. It was a tea-length A-line dress that was sheer, with appliqués strategically placed for modesty.

"Va-va-voom. That is so risqué."

I swirled in front of the mirror, examining myself from all

sides. "All of the important parts are covered, but you can see the outline of my legs. I wonder if New Bison is ready for that." I extended a leg.

Then, I tried on the Isabel Sanchis.

"I like both dresses," I said. "Which one do you think I should wear?"

She tilted her head to the side. "I think you should wear that one to the tea. I like both of them, too, but you look so sophisticated in that one. Not that you don't in the other one, but that Sanchis dress makes you look regal, like Grace Kelly in one of those Alfred Hitchcock movies . . . A Black version with natural hair. That other dress, that Saab, is sexy. I think you should wear that one when you go out with Michael. Where on earth did you find these?"

"Bridal shops." I felt my cheeks getting pink and turned away quickly, but not quickly enough.

"Bridal shops? Is there something you want to tell me?" She wiggled her eyebrows.

I hesitated a few moments. "I've had most of these for several years. They were part of my trousseau."

"Oh, Maddy. I'm so sorry. I opened my mouth and stuck my big foot inside. Forgive me."

"It's okay. I'm over Elliott." I waved away her apology. "When the Admiral finally accepted that I didn't intend to move home, he had my clothes sent, and I've been going through them and found these." I glanced at myself in the mirror from every angle.

"They're beautiful."

"Normally, I would never be seen in public in a dress that was more than one or two seasons old. In fact, I was going to donate these to charity, but . . . I don't suppose it matters. It's not like anyone in New Bison will know."

"I'd be surprised if anyone in New Bison had ever heard of

either of these designers, let alone that they would know what *season* the outfits were from. If you like it, then does it matter if it's a few seasons old?"

I turned back to the mirror and avoided eye contact with April. There had been a time when the season an outfit, purse, or shoes came out absolutely did matter to me, but that was before.

"I don't want to pry, but things between you and Michael seem to be going pretty well. Do you think you two are serious?" she asked with a lilt in her voice.

I hesitated.

"Never mind," she said hurriedly. "Don't answer that. It's none of my business."

"It's not that. It's just . . . I don't know. I *think* things are serious, but it's hard to know. If you'd asked me that question a month ago, I would have said absolutely. When we're together, he acts like he's serious, but lately, he hasn't been around very much, and I can't help wondering if maybe he's gotten bored."

"That's crazy. He's been working a lot. You can't think he's seeing someone else," April said.

I was quiet and April came around and turned me so I was facing her and couldn't avoid looking her in the eyes. "Maddy, you don't think that. You can't think that. Michael would never . . ."

"Cheat? I didn't think Elliott would have cheated, either."

"Michael isn't Elliott."

"I know, but I've been thinking about things a lot because I am serious about Michael, and I never thought I'd fall for another guy again. I certainly never thought that I'd think about marriage, not after Elliott dumped me at the altar. I didn't love Elliott. I know that now, but I didn't have a clue that he didn't love me. We'd been together for years, so I thought we were both on the same page about our future together. Even though I didn't love Elliott, it still hurt. My feelings for Michael are a million times stronger, and I don't want to make the same mistakes with him that I made with Elliott."

April hugged me. "Oh, honey. I'm sorry."

After a few minutes, we pulled apart. April got a tissue from a box on my nightstand and then handed me the box.

"I'd better take off this dress before I ruin it with all my blubbering." April removed the dress and got into her own clothes.

I followed suit but placed the Isabel Sanchis dress over the closet door. We sat down on the bed.

April took my hand and gave it a squeeze. "What exactly is it about Michael that has you worried?"

"I can't put my finger on one thing. He's always very sweet when we're together. It's just that, lately, he hasn't been around as much as he was. He's canceled dates several times in the last few weeks, ever since the Admiral left."

"You don't think your father scared him off, do you?"

I thought for a few moments and then shook my head. "No. Michael doesn't scare easily. Besides, they actually got along well. They spent a lot of time talking about the military, sports, cars, and . . . I guess male bonding." I smiled. "I thought they got along well."

"Is that everything?" April stared hard into my eyes as though she were trying to read my soul.

"I can't stop thinking that I should have seen the warning signs with Elliott. There had to have been signs, right?"

"Usually, but—"

"I read an article in a magazine about how to suspect when your man is about to dump you." I hurried to the nightstand and found the magazine. I turned to the article and showed it to her.

"I don't think Michael is about to dump you. He seems like he really likes you."

"Yeah, well, I thought Elliott really liked me, too. It says that if your man cancels dates, it can be a sign. Michael canceled two dates in the last two weeks."

"Wasn't one of those nights when he was up for twenty-four hours delivering a horse for that farmer in Watervliet?"

"He wasn't delivering a horse last Thursday."

"What happened last Thursday?"

"He said he had to go to Chicago, and even though I hinted that maybe we could go together, he never invited me to go with him." I gave her a knowing look.

April thought for a few beats, but then she shook her head. "I don't care. I don't think Michael is about to dump you. But if you're worried, maybe you should talk to him."

"Maybe . . ." I took in a deep breath. "That's the worst part. There's one part of me that wants to be prepared, but there's another part of me that wants to just enjoy the time we have together and stop worrying about *what if.* Then there's a part of me that thinks I should dump him before he dumps me. And another part that just wants to curl up in a ball and cry."

"That's a lot of parts." April teased and then hugged me. "I'm sorry. I know you're worried, and I don't mean to make light of it."

"It's okay. I need to think about something else. I need something to get my mind off it."

We spent a few more minutes discussing hats and fancy teas.

Like most of the males in my life, Baby wasn't into fashion. He slept through the fashion show, but when he sensed we were heading to the kitchen, he sat up, tilted his head to the side, and listened. After a few moments, a deep growl made its way from his belly up to his mouth.

April and I froze and turned to stare at the mastiff.

He leaped to his feet and tore from the room, down the stairs, barking and drooling.

"Stay here," April said. She patted her holster and pulled out her gun and hurried downstairs after Baby.

CHAPTER 5

I hesitated a split second. The reality that I was alone changed my mind about staying upstairs alone. I looked around for my Taser and realized that I'd left it downstairs. Another glance around showed me that the only weapon heavy enough to do any significant damage was the trophy I'd won at the New Bison festival. I grabbed it and headed downstairs after April and Baby.

By the time I got to the kitchen, the back door was open, and the house was empty. I exchanged my baking trophy for a cast-iron skillet that I'd used in the past with great results.

Outside, Baby barked, but I didn't hear anything that sounded like a lion ripping apart a gazelle, a sound I'd never forget from my many travels.

"Baby, come!" April yelled.

In a few moments, I heard galloping as if a pony were coming into the house. I lowered my weapon. April closed the back door and locked it. Then, she and Baby came into the kitchen.

"What was it?" I asked.

"By the time we got outside, I heard tire tracks, and then

that was it." She shrugged. "It's getting warmer. It was probably just kids taking a shortcut down to the beach. Miss Octavia used to find them making out there all the time in the summer months."

"Why don't I believe you?"

"You've got a suspicious nature." She grinned at me but quickly got serious. "I don't think it's anything to worry about, but I'll have the guys increase the patrols around the house."

It took a few cups of tea and a dozen thumbprint cookies before my heart stopped doing the macarena in my chest and my hands finally stopped shaking.

April went downstairs to sleep after ensuring that a patrol car would drive by every hour until six. I felt a little guilty knowing that I had a two-hundred-fifty-pound dog for protection until I remembered April was packing heat. I took Baby and my skillet upstairs and locked my bedroom door.

Within moments of his head hitting the pillow, Baby was snoring and drooling next to me without a care in the world.

It took me a bit longer. I tossed and turned until the covers were a knot around my legs and I had to kick to get free. Baby opened one eye at all of the movement but was snoring again before he closed it.

The next day was Easter Sunday. It would be packed with kids dressed in their Easter outfits and adults who came to church only once per year. However, I planned to go to church. I wasn't a particularly religious person, although since moving to New Bison, I'd found that attending church had a great many benefits. Religion and church were a central focus in many Black communities. Whenever I moved to a new community, finding a church was a great way to meet people—Black people. From there, I learned the places that were safe and the places to avoid. I learned where to go to get my hair styled. Where to buy Black hair care products and where the best places were to get soul food. Once I knew where Black people congregated, I had a sense of safety and well-being. It was like the "Black Table" at college. Most universities had one, and my alma mater, Stanford, was no different. If you went into the cafeteria, there was one table where most of the Black people sat. You didn't need to know anyone else at the table to sit there. It was an unspoken understanding that all were welcome. It was a safe place. Church was the same way. Over time, I'd noticed that the institution itself seemed to be losing some of its dominance. However, the older generation attended religiously.

First Baptist Church of New Bison was similar to Baptist churches in practically every city I'd ever lived in the United States and abroad. Great-Aunt Octavia had been a member of New Bison AME Church. The Methodist church wasn't quite as lively as the Baptist, so when she wanted something livelier, she went to First Baptist Church with Miss Hannah. I tried both and had to agree that the Baptist church was much more interesting. Not only was the choir amazing, but the women got dressed to the nines every Sunday, so it was right up my alley. Plus, Michael was Baptist. Miss Hannah said I needed to come and "stake my claim" to him. *Was that why I attended church? To stake my claim?* Ugh.

If staking my claim was truly my goal, I was sorely disappointed. Michael sent a text early in the morning that he got called out in the middle of the night and wouldn't be at church. When I was over the disappointment, I offered to pick up Miss Hannah.

Michael's grandmother, Mrs. Hannah Portman, was in her sixties. She had been my great-aunt Octavia's best friend for more than fifty years. When Hannah had been diagnosed with dementia, Michael gave up his veterinary practice in Illinois and moved back to New Bison to take care of her. Still in the early stages, Miss Hannah continued to come to the bakery every day she was able.

She said don't B late. Wants 2 get her pew B4 Sister Thelma

I grinned. Miss Hannah had been having a silent feud with Sister Thelma Alexander for a particular pew that both women considered their personal property.

BRT in 15

I'd grown quite fond of my sassy baker and hoped that regardless of what happened between Michael and me, she would still be an important part of my life.

"I hope nothing will change between Miss Hannah and me, even if Michael and I aren't together. I'd miss her." I turned to Baby. "You'd miss her, too, wouldn't you?"

He yawned.

"Yeah, I know. You're tired of hearing about me and Michael."

I let Baby out and then led him back to the bedroom. He climbed back up into the bed. I gave him his peanut butter treat and turned the television onto his favorite show, *Absolutely Fabulous* or *Ab Fab*, a 1990s British sitcom he used to watch with Great-Aunt Octavia.

Miss Hannah was waiting outside for me, so I didn't get a chance to see Michael. I drove to the church and dropped my charge at the steps of the church and then parked.

By the time I found a parking space and made my way inside the sanctuary, service had started. I spotted Miss Hannah standing and singing while the Praise and Worship Choir got the congregation in the right state of mind for the sermon. She'd managed to beat her rival to *the pew* and was settled in and smiling. No one glancing at that angelic face would know the cutthroat pew strategy that went behind that smile.

I took my place next to Miss Hannah on the pew, which

served multiple purposes. First, it said that while I may not have been born and raised in New Bison, I was accepted. I wasn't an outsider. I belonged here. Second, even though Michael wasn't there, it sent the message to all of the other single women in the church that he was not available. I was accepted by his grandmother. Family.

I glanced around at the angelic faces in the predominantly female gathering. First Baptist Church had a diverse group of churchgoers. The vast majority of faces belonged to people of color. However, sprinkled throughout the congregation were people of different shapes, shades, and economic positions. Prominent members of the local community attended service here. The church also had an extensive outreach program designed to help everyone from students at a nearby college to disabled veterans and the homeless. It was one of the things I liked about the church. All were welcome. I also saw many familiar faces. Most patronized Baby Cakes Bakery at one time or another. However, there was one face that looked familiar, although I couldn't recall why. When the minister asked for "all heads bowed and eyes closed," I felt a gaze searing into me. I opened my eyes and squinted in time to see a pair of blue eyes staring at me. At that moment, I remembered why he looked familiar. He was the man in the photo Leroy took at his recent cooking class. His was also the face I'd seen several times over the past week at the bakery.

Our eyes locked. I wasn't vain, but I'd grown up on a naval base surrounded mostly by men who stared, flirted, and *hit on* me. I'd grown accustomed to stares and had become adept at interpreting and responding. With one glance, a raised brow, or a smirk, I could indicate my appreciation or rebuke the starer with ease, but this wasn't that type of look. This look searched my face for an answer, but I had no idea what the question was. After a few moments, he broke off the eye contact, turned, and hurried out of the church. After a moment of hesitation, I grabbed my purse.

"I'll be back," I whispered to Miss Hannah and turned to follow Blue Eyes.

I sidled out of the pew and headed for the door. I almost made it, but the pastor had started to pray. Praying was one of the few times when people were expected to remain still and reverent without leaving. Sadly, the back door of the sanctuary was being guarded by Sister Sylvia. Sister Sylvia was the head usher. A tall, grave woman, she took her ushering duties seriously and manned that door like a member of the military police. Lacking only the rifle, Sister Sylvia delivered a stern look that halted me in my tracks. She held up a finger and pointed to a nearby pew, indicating that was the place I was to wait.

For a split second, I contemplated ignoring her and pitting my strength against hers. After all, I was younger, and my upper body strength had improved as I'd learned to knead and work with dough at the bakery. Plus, over the past few months, I'd grown more physically fit with quicker reflexes, as I'd been forced to prevent calamity by corralling Baby from time to time. I felt confident that if push came to shove, I could take Sister Sylvia.

Sister Sylvia lowered her chin, raised a brow, and gave me a stare.

Was it just my imagination or was her brow raised in a "Go ahead, make my day," *Dirty Harry* stare?

Wait! What was I thinking? I couldn't possibly be contemplating getting in a tussle with an usher in church! Geez! It didn't matter how stoic and stern she was, this wasn't the time or the place. So, I forced a smile and stepped toward the pew she'd indicated.

The minister finished praying. I hopped up and headed back toward the door. Sister Sylvia stepped to the side and held the door open.

I flashed a smile that bounced off her like water from a duck's back. Sister Sylvia wasn't fooled. Just like my eighth-grade math teacher, she was a mind reader, and she'd read mine.

Outside, I looked around, but I knew it was too late. Blue Eyes was gone.

CHAPTER 6

The last thing I wanted was to face Sister Sylvia again. Service was in the home stretch and would be over soon, so instead of going back inside, I walked to my car. I spent a few moments contemplating what I would have done if I'd caught Blue Eyes. What would I have said? *Why have you been at my bakery or my church?* That was lame. Baby Cakes was the only bakery in town. Plus, our baked goods were darned good.

I pulled in front of the church to wait for Miss Hannah.

I didn't have long to wait.

She chatted, kissed, and hugged friends, waved at anyone she missed, and then got into the car. "Whew! Step on it. I can't wait to get out of these shoes, and my girdle is cutting off the circulation in my legs."

I choked back a smile and pulled away from the curb. "You know, you can skip the girdle. I didn't think women were still torturing themselves with those anymore."

"I see these young women with their fat giggling and rolls of cellulite like cottage cheese, and I just can't do it. I prefer to have all of my bulges and bumps hidden, thank you very much.

I wasn't raised to let it all hang out like young people do today."

"You don't have to let it all hang out, but you also don't have to be uncomfortable. Modern technology has improved significantly."

"Hmm. I let one of those clerks talk me into one of those newfangled underwire bras and I've never been so uncomfortable in my entire life. You can keep that new technology." She pursed her lips.

"I'll admit underwires aren't my favorite, but you really should consider Spanx. They're amazing." I glanced at her out of the corner of my eye and could see the skepticism on her face.

"We'll see. Anyway, what were you thinking trying to get out of the sanctuary when Sister Sylvia was manning the door?"

I paused while I slowed down to take a tight corner. "Have you noticed anyone hanging out in the bakery lately? A white male with blue eyes?"

She paused. "I don't think so. Why?"

Good question. There was a man hanging out at the bakery. So what? Maybe he just liked thumbprint cookies.

I shrugged. "No idea. I've just seen him around a lot, and, well, I was curious."

I pulled up to the house and had hoped I'd get to see Michael, but his truck wasn't there. That usually meant he was working. Sigh.

"It doesn't look like Michael's here, but you're welcome to dinner. I ain't got nothing fancy, just baked chicken, snap peas, carrots, smothered cabbage, and I made a few egg tarts for Baby Cakes."

"Thanks, but April, Baby, and I are going to high tea at the Carson Law Inn."

Today was a good day. Miss Hannah seemed to be doing well, so I helped her inside and then headed home.

I got home with plenty of time to spare before I needed to get dressed for tea. I opened the door to the bedroom to let Baby outside to take care of business.

Normally, I could open the door and Baby would find a tree, hike his leg, and be back inside before I could get my jacket on. Plus, he was so well behaved that I stopped putting on his leash. Today was not that kind of day. Baby lifted his head and caught a scent. His body tensed, and I watched as he caught sight of a squirrel who had been exceptionally impudent with him just the previous day.

"Baby, nooo."

He ignored me. As if in slow motion, my two-hundred-fifty-pound mastiff took off like a large lumbering pony while I stood yelling for him to return. At the last minute, the squirrel looked up and saw Baby approaching. With what I can only describe as a look of fear, he scrambled down the stairs of death.

My property was perched atop a bluff overlooking Lake Michigan. At the back edge of the property, wooden steps allowed access to a private beach below. The stairs were old, rickety, and didn't look the least bit safe. I was fairly confident they could hold the weight of the squirrel, but Baby's eighth of a ton was another matter entirely.

I ran to the edge of the bluff and leaned down over the edge.

Baby had slowed down but was still rushing down the stairs.

Looking over the edge, I thought my mind had begun playing tricks on me. At the foot of the stairs, I saw a woman's body, sprawled on the sand, facedown.

That's how Great-Aunt Octavia died. She fell or was pushed down these same steps. That's when my nerves got the best of me, and I let out a bloodcurdling scream.

CHAPTER 7

"Maddy, are you okay?"

I was sitting on the ground. Baby sat by my side and licked my face.

It took a few seconds for me to catch my breath and come back to the here and now. Great-Aunt Octavia was dead and buried. There was no way she could have been lying at the bottom of those stairs. I shook the cobwebs out of my mind, gazed into the sad soulful eyes of my companion, and flung my arms around Baby's neck.

"Whew! Are you okay?"

I looked up and saw Candy Rivers staring down at me.

"Candy? What're you doing here?"

"Thank God you're okay." Candy sat down on the ground next to me and took several deep breaths. "I was trying to work on my tan, but you screamed and scared the poop out of me."

"I scared you? I looked down the stairs where Great-Aunt Octavia fell and saw a body . . . well, I thought it was a body . . . I— "

"Oh, honey. I'm so sorry." Candy flung her arms around

my neck. "I didn't mean to scare you. I was just trying to get a little sun. I hope you don't mind. Miss Octavia used to let me use the stairs to go down to the beach. I just didn't think you'd mistake a pale white woman for Miss Octavia . . . besides, she's dead."

After a few moments, we both burst out laughing. I finally pulled myself together. "I know it's crazy, but I've been terrified of those stairs since I heard how she died. I guess my brain was just playing tricks with me."

Daisy, Candy's own mastiff, must have been down on the beach, because after a few moments, she joined us. At a mere one-hundred-sixty pounds, she wasn't nearly as large as Baby, but the two mastiffs were best buddies. After making sure I was okay, they started a game of chase on the bluff.

"Is Michael going to the Carson Law Inn Tea today?" Candy asked.

"No. He's supposed to be helping with a pet adoption event today at the Humane Society."

Candy stared at me. "You look like a woman with man trouble. You wanna talk?"

"Not really." I had no idea how she knew I had "man trouble," but I certainly didn't want to talk about it. Nevertheless, that's exactly what I did. Sadly, I have a habit of oversharing when I'm nervous. I didn't even know I was nervous until I started talking and couldn't stop. I told Candy about Michael's late hours and canceling dates, and I didn't stop to breathe until I'd shared all of that along with my fear that he was bored with me.

"You poor thing." Candy wrapped an arm around my shoulder. "I know exactly how you feel. Well, maybe not exactly but close enough. You're insecure."

I turned and glanced at her as though she'd revealed the secrets of life. "I *am* insecure."

She nodded. "I used to feel the same way about Paul. He

was older than me and a politician. I barely graduated from high school. I used to wonder what someone like him could possibly want with me." She chuckled.

"Well? Did you ever discover what it was?"

She gave me a look that brought color to my cheeks.

"Oh."

She shrugged. "I think Michael really likes you, and the two of you have so much in common. You're always joking about the military, and you both love dogs. Plus, you're not like me. You graduated from college. You're smart. You own a business and—"

"Candy, you're smart, too."

She shook her head.

"You *are* smart. How many women your age own their own coffee shop?" I asked.

She paused for a few moments and then shook her head again. "That's only because Paul left me the hardware store."

"Right. He left you a hardware store. New Bison isn't a large town, but a small hardware store can't compete with the chain hardware store that just opened on Red Arrow Highway and the big-box home improvement store less than fifteen minutes away. He was struggling, and you recognized that. You were smart enough to realize that the town didn't have a high-end coffee shop, and you were smart enough to open it next to a successful bakery with an owner that is addicted to cortados." I stared into her eyes.

She chuckled. "Well, I suppose. I never looked at it from that side."

"You know Great-Aunt Octavia left all these notes and videos all over the house for me. Some of them were just funny stories. Some of them were comments about the goings-on in New Bison and her conspiracy theories, but there was one that was just a note of encouragement. She said that if things got tough, I shouldn't worry because she had faith that everything would be okay. She said she knew that I didn't know anything about baking, but that I reminded her of her mom. That would have been my great-grandmother Willa Mae . . . or is it my great-great-grandmother? Oh well, whoever. She said her mom only had an eighth-grade education, but she was the smartest person she ever knew."

"Wow. That's saying a lot. Miss Octavia was so smart. She graduated from college and knew a lot about chemistry and baking and everything."

"She said her mom had something she called 'Mother Wit.' She knew when to plant and when to harvest. She knew a lot about plants and which ones to mix to heal and which ones were poison. She made all of their clothes and knew a ton of things that no one ever taught her." I gazed at Candy. "I think she must have been a lot like you. You may not have graduated from college, but you're smart. You found that tunnel that links Baby Cakes to your store. Plus, you know how to make one of the best cortados I've ever had, and that's saying a lot."

Candy grinned. "You really think so?"

"I do."

"I've never met anyone who can drink cortados and Red Eyes like you. Speaking of coffee, I saw that woman yesterday. She's the one that . . . well . . . I read about in your social media posts."

"Yep. She's the one."

"Well, you just say the word, and the next time she comes in Higher Grounds, I might just mistake the sugar for the salt when I make her an Americano."

"No you don't. Just because I don't like Brandy Denton doesn't mean that I want you to ruin your reputation. She may be a horrible friend, but she has a large social media following, and the last thing I want is to have her criticizing my friends and ruining your business. I just wish I could figure out what she was doing here."

We sat and watched the waves crash against the shore as our dogs frolicked like two goofballs until they were exhausted and lay on the ground next to us. It was a peaceful moment. I'd traveled around the world with the Admiral, but nothing was quite as beautiful as the waves across Lake Michigan on that sunny April Sunday.

"I love this view." April pulled her knees to her chest and wrapped her arms around her legs.

"Me too."

Staring at the water had a calming effect, and before long, I had forgotten about Brandy Denton and blue-eyed strangers. I was here sitting on my own property with my dog and my friend watching the waves. It was a beautiful day, and I was happy to be a part of it.

"Well, we better go. I've got to get back to work." Candy turned and opened her mouth but before she could speak, her eyes grew large and she screamed. "Daisy, noooo!"

I turned in time to see Daisy and Baby flop down on the ground and roll around. I recognized that roll. Baby had found his favorite *eau de parfum*: deer poop.

Candy and I rushed to the mastiffs, but we could smell them long before we got close to them.

"Ugh," Candy said. "I just took her to the groomer yesterday, and now she reeks!"

Daisy and Baby stood panting with bright eyes, tongues extended. Both were happy as pigs in slop. I couldn't help snapping a picture.

#MastiffsInEauDeDeerPoop #BathTime #StinkyButHappy

April may not have had Daisy long, but she had definitely gone over the top when it came to doggie supplies, which came in handy since I merely dropped Baby off with Michael when he needed a bath. Thankfully, he had a dog groomer at his veterinary clinic. However, there was no way I could get him groomed on a Sunday afternoon. Fortunately, Candy was willing to share her many supplies. The least flowery-scented shampoo smelled of apple blossoms. I chose that for Baby.

He gave me a look that indicated his dissatisfaction with my choice, but I ignored him.

"It's your own fault for rolling in deer poop."

Using a large sponge, buckets of water, and a half bottle of shampoo, I finally got to the point where I didn't smell anything except apples no matter how hard I sniffed.

Baby rewarded my hard work by shaking himself and getting me even wetter than I was before.

Once Baby was clean and smelling good, then it was time to focus on me. After a long, hot shower, I was clean and excited. There weren't a lot of opportunities for dressing up in New Bison. High tea at the Carson Law Inn was a new adventure, and I was excited to finally meet Mrs. Law.

I'd Googled her and learned that Carson Law was not only a world-famous milliner, but she was also an animal lover. Every year the inn sponsored a tea to raise money for an animal rescue organization called Pet Refuge. I reserved a table months ago. Well-behaved dogs were welcome, so Baby and I had both been looking forward to this.

I glanced over at Baby as he lay sprawled across my bed. "Well, *I've* been looking forward to attending for months, anyway."

It was nice to have someplace to go where I could get dressed up. Normally, I only got dressed up for church and date nights with Michael. However, Michael's taste didn't always lend itself to high-end restaurants—dinner could range from a nice meal at a winery or a five-star French restaurant to a burger joint or a hot dog cart near the beach. Working at Baby Cakes wasn't a great place for fashion, either. When I first moved to New Bison, I was doggedly determined to continue wearing my beloved fashion just as I had in L.A. After multiple mishaps where outfits that I loved had to be thrown out when they became caked with a cement mixture made from flour and water, I learned to embrace clothes that were more practical but still stylish: Khatie jeans or Fe Noel denim pants, Pyer Moss Sculpt sneakers, and a nice blouse, all protected by a Baby Cakes Bakery apron.

I pulled on the Isabel Sanchis and enjoyed the feel as the soft fabric floated over my body. April was right, it was beautiful. It wasn't as dramatic as some Isabel Sanchis gowns, but it had a vintage feel that I feel confident Mrs. Law would appreciate.

"What do you think?" I asked Baby.

He lifted a fold of flesh over his left eye. He was still angry about the bath.

"Look, I'm sorry about the bath, but there's no way they would let you inside the Carson Law Inn smelling like deer poop." I sat on the side of the bed and scratched his ear. "It'll be really nice, and they even have a special menu just for canines. April and I will have scones and clotted cream and cucumber sandwiches, and you're going to get liver treats, peanut butter biscuits, and . . . cheese."

That last word got his attention. He sat up.

"Plus, because Leroy's mom works at the Carson Law Inn, she made special arrangements with the chef for you to get an extra special treat. So, please, please, please be on your best behavior."

I wasn't above begging my dog to behave well. I gazed into his eyes, and I felt that we had an understanding. "Great. Now, let's go."

Baby jumped off the bed and trotted downstairs like a prize stallion entering the gates of the Kentucky Derby.

If only I didn't have such a feeling of foreboding in the pit of my stomach.

CHAPTER 8

We arrived in the kitchen just as April came upstairs from her lower-level apartment.

"You look spectacular." I pulled out my phone and snapped a few pictures.

She spun around. "You two clean up pretty good, too."

#PetRefugeFundRaiser #CarsonLawInnTea #BabyBathed&SmelingGood #LuvMyBaby

"How was the Easter Egg hunt?" I asked.

"Awesome. The naturally dyed eggs came out great. I had no idea you could dye eggs with table scraps like red onions and cabbage, but they came out amazing. There was a big crowd, and I passed out lots of flyers."

"Think it'll make a difference?"

April shrugged. "I hope so, but only time will tell. Sadly, it usually takes some major catastrophe before people appreciate the police department and want to give us money."

"It isn't like you're asking for much."

We talked about the Easter Egg hunt and the police department, but we were just rehashing conversations we'd had many times.

With Baby in tow, we climbed into my Rivian and made the short drive downtown. The parking lot of the Carson Law Inn was packed, and New Bison's hatted and well-dressed supporters of both two and four legs stood outside.

Inside information from Leroy's mom Fiona, who was a maid at the Carson Law Inn, had provided a hang tag that allowed us to bypass the parking lot for patrons and enter the staff lot in the back. I made a mental note to send a few dozen thumbprint cookies along with my thanks.

There were two lines. One line was for people who had already purchased a seat. Stanchions and a velvet rope blocked one of the inn's massive doors. A podium and a liveried waiter manned the podium. Ticketed guests presented their golden tickets to the maître d' and were escorted inside to their tables. The other door, which was approximately six feet away, featured a similar setup, but the guests were added to a waitlist. A large tent was set up on the side of the property. Anyone willing to wait would be added to a list for a second seating later. For a reduced price, the exterior tent was offered as an option.

April, Baby, and I made our way to the door for ticketed guests.

"Glad you told me to get my ticket in advance," I whispered to April.

"This event is always a big success and a huge fundraiser for the local pet rescue. I've worked security in the past, but I've never attended as an actual guest. As much as I love supporting canine rescues, I never would have dreamed of shelling out that kind of money for a tea." April glanced around at the crowd and picked a piece of imaginary lint from the front of her dress.

"I'm glad you agreed to come with me." I gave her arm a squeeze.

"I'm sorry Michael didn't want to come."

"I know this type of dressy affair isn't his thing, but I thought as a veterinarian, he might come to support the cause." I shrugged.

We inched our way closer to the entrance, and I handed our tickets to the maître d'.

He smiled and crossed our names off the list. "Ms. Montgomery, Ms. Johnson, and this must be Baby." He glanced down at the large mastiff, who was standing by my side.

At the sound of his name, Baby glanced up at the man and gave a low bark.

Like a well-trained butler, the maître d' was unphased. He reached under a shelf, fumbled around for a few moments, and then came out with a large biscuit. He glanced at me for permission, and then with a sweeping gesture and a bow, he presented the dog bone to Baby.

Drool dripped from Baby's jowls as he accepted the biscuit.

With a similar flourish, he presented two menus and was just about to hand them to a waiter standing behind him when a commotion from the line caused us all to turn to look.

"Madison Montgomery."

I didn't need to turn around to recognize Brandy Denton's voice.

Brandy pushed, shoved, and elbowed her way to the front of the line and flashed her fake smile. "When I saw your post, I just had to come and see what entertainment looked like in New Bison."

Brandy Denton looked fabulous in classic Balmain denim jeans that I knew cost more than thirteen hundred dollars, a stunningly beautiful green cutout blouse by Maximilan Davis, and a pair of Jimmy Choos that made my mouth drool worse than Baby's.

"It's a fundraiser, Brandy. I'm surprised to see you here. I would never have guessed you were an animal lover."

"Absolutely. I've even considered getting a pet." She glanced at Baby and frowned. "Something small that I could carry around in my purse, like Paris Hilton . . . I wouldn't want a big horse like that."

"I'll have you know, Baby is a champion English Mastiff,

not a horse." I refused to remember that, just a few short months ago, I'd mistaken him for a pony when we first met. "He's a member of my family, not a pet. And for the record, dogs should be loved, *not* worn like fashion accessories."

"Amen!" someone from the crowd shouted, and polite applause broke out.

Brandy's face grew red, and her gaze narrowed.

I turned to walk away.

"Well, of course I agree one hundred percent." Brandy grinned. "Which is why I'm here. Unfortunately, I didn't get my ticket in advance, but when I saw you, I knew you wouldn't mind if I joined your party."

Allowing Brandy Denton to join my table for tea was the last thing I wanted. I'd been looking forward to this event for months. I had many great memories of tea and scones in various restaurants throughout the United Kingdom. Enjoying the indulgence in a mansion in New Bison would be a new experience, and I didn't want anyone patronizing the experience.

"It'll be a perfect way to show everyone back home that you aren't still angry over Elliott dumping you for me." Brandy whipped out her phone and quickly snapped a picture of me. "I think you're just so brave going out in public, especially in a dress that's a few seasons behind. But, I'm sure no one *here* will even notice."

Darn it. With that picture, Brandy would waste no time uploading it online and telling everyone that my dress wasn't straight off the runways. She'd post that picture and make sure that everyone saw it. I could just see it now, *Oh poor Madison Montgomery! Living in a backwater and wearing last season's dress! #pathetic.*UGH! What a mean, spiteful cat! I glanced at the smile in her eyes and knew she had just outmaneuvered me. Either I let her join my table, or she'd humiliate me online.

Baby growled.

I turned to look at what had captured his attention.

He stared back at me.

I saw the truth in his soft brown eyes. In that moment, I knew the truth. I didn't care what Brandy Denton posted. I didn't care what she or any of the other people I once considered "friends" thought of me. I liked my out-of-season dress. I liked New Bison. I liked my big droopy, drooly English Mastiff and my new life. What I didn't like was Brandy Denton, and I refused to allow her to ruin my day. I was just about to tell her so when there was a murmur in the crowd, and the maître d' snapped to attention.

The crowd erupted in cheers and applause, and I turned to see what caused the change.

A small, redheaded woman in a Veni Infantino dress with a lace bodice, roll neckline, and A-line skirt approached the front. She had a blue pillbox hat with a veil that matched her dress perfectly perched atop her head. She climbed the steps and inclined her head.

The maître d' clicked his heels. "Mrs. Law."

Before entering, the small woman stopped to greet us. "You ladies look lovely. Is that Isabel Sanchis?"

I nodded.

"I love that line. And, if I'm not mistaken, you're wearing one of my hats." She reached out her hand and touched my hat.

"Yes, ma'am." I'd met many dignitaries over the years including royals, diplomats, and several sheiks. Yet, this small milliner made me want to curtsy. I resisted the urge.

She turned and flashed her smile at Brandy. "I've never been a fan of denim, although Balmain is lovely. I was telling my good friend Olivier Rousteing how much I loved his designs."

Brandy gasped. "You know Olivier Rousteing?"

"Oh yes, lovely human being." She smiled and asked the maître d', "Is there a problem?"

He quickly whispered something to Mrs. Law, who turned and gave Brandy a disappointed pout.

"I understand that you had hoped to join your friend inside for tea. I'm terribly sorry, but we have a strict dress code prohibiting blue jeans and requiring women to wear hats for tea. It's an old-fashioned custom, but I'm afraid it's one that we'll need to honor since Claude tells me he's already denied admittance to others." She paused and then flashed a smile. "But, since you're such a good friend of Ms. Montgomery and our sheriff, I feel confident that Claude will be able to find you a seat outside." She smiled, hooked one arm through my arm that wasn't holding Baby's leash and the other through April's arm. "Shall we go in?"

CHAPTER 9

I didn't need to look behind me to know that Brandy Denton was seething. Yet, thanks to Carson Law, I wasn't the source of her ire. However, I knew Brandy well enough to know that she wouldn't let that stop her from blaming me. She may or may not have known who Carson Law was, but she would know enough to Google her. She was also smart enough to know that it wouldn't be in her best interest to attack someone who was well connected within the fashion industry. No. She wouldn't lash out against Mrs. Law. She'd attack me, but I didn't care.

Inside, I assumed Mrs. Law would abandon us and move to the table of honor. However, I was surprised to see that wasn't the way things went. Instead, she invited us to join her.

I looked down at Baby, who was still dragging his biscuit and dripping drool, and was ready to decline, but Mrs. Law reached down, patted his head, and said, "Who's this good boy?"

Baby gazed up into her kind hazel eyes, dropped his biscuit, stood up, and licked her face like a pup cup.

After a moment of shock, I pulled his harness and ordered him off. "Baby, no. Off."

However, my words were ignored as Mrs. Law laughed and muttered baby talk to him. "You're a good boy. What a nice dog."

Eventually, I managed to get enough leverage that I was able to get him back down on all fours.

Carson Law poked out her lip and told Baby, "Your owner doesn't understand, does she? Well, I understand, and I'm going to make sure that you get an extra special treat for being such a good boy." She pulled a handkerchief from her sleeve and wiped the drool and mastiff slobber from her face. Then, she pulled a compact from her purse and adjusted her hat.

"Mrs. Law, I'm so sorry. He didn't mean to—"

"Of course he did, and I loved every minute of it." She laughed. She looked at my shocked face and burst out laughing again. "Don't look so stunned. I love dogs. That's why I host this event every year. Now, let's sit down and get some tea and scones and get better acquainted."

The Carson Law Inn had been a family home that was now converted into an inn, so the majority of the furniture had been removed from the first-floor public rooms. The living room, dining room, and parlor were all packed with tables for dining. The living room was the nicest room and was set up for a presentation with a head table that guests had paid extra to sit at. I was surprised when we bypassed the head table and were escorted to the study, which was a wood-paneled room with bookshelves and a large fireplace, and it was near the back of the house. On the few occasions when I'd dined at the Carson Law, I'd sat in the light-filled sunroom. While I loved the books and bookshelves in the study, I found the room dark and stuffy.

We were directed to what I assumed was a window, but when the maître d' pulled back the curtains, I saw that the drapes were covering a private alcove, which had a huge window that overlooked the garden. There was also a built-in window seat. When the drapes were opened, Mrs. Law surprised us by sitting on the window seat. When she was settled in place, two waiters moved a table laden with the best linen and china in front of her and then pulled up two chairs for April and me. A third waiter brought a large dog bed.

Mrs. Law pointed to a spot near her side. With the dog bed in place, Baby turned around three times and then lay down and began making short work of his biscuit.

"What a cozy spot. I had no idea this was here. These curtains are always closed." April glanced around the room.

"It used to be my special hiding place when I was a child. I used to sneak in here, close the curtains, and read nearly every day." Carson Law smiled fondly. "By special request, the staff keep the alcove closed from the public."

"Thank you so much for allowing us to share this space with you," I said.

"Well, I have a small confession." She smiled sheepishly.

April and I exchanged a glance. What could this woman possibly need to confess to us?

"When I was a small girl, we had a mastiff. My dad called him a bull mastiff. His name was Archibald, and he was my best friend. We were inseparable." She pointed at a picture in a silver frame that was on the mantel.

A waiter hovered nearby, and she leaned close. "Joel, would you be so kind as to bring me that picture?" She pointed.

Joel hurried to the mantel and brought the picture. It was a photograph of a well-dressed redheaded girl of about eight with a large dog similar to Baby. The dog was larger than the girl. She gazed at the picture and then passed it to April and me.

"He looks a lot like Baby," I said.

"Forgive me, but I hate to admit that my goal was to spend more time with your dog." She grinned and reached down and scratched Baby's head. "Although, I'm thrilled for an opportunity to meet Baby's friends."

We spent an enjoyable afternoon drinking tea and eating tea

sandwiches and the most delicious scones with clotted cream and strawberry preserves. Carson Law was well read, humorous, and a great storyteller. She shared stories of life in Paris with some of the most famous fashion designers and artists. We talked about fashion, hats, and English mastiffs for hours. Before we left, Mrs. Law asked Joel to take a picture of all of us, including Baby. After sharing it with our hostess, I uploaded the picture.

#BestTeaEver #CarsonLawHatsRock

I had ignored my phone for nearly three hours during tea. So, uploading the photo was the first opportunity that I had to see that Brandy Denton had tagged me in a post.

#HowTheMightyHaveFallen #OutdatedFashionOutdatedMindset

I expected the jabs about my out-of-season outfit. So, that didn't hurt . . . well, it didn't hurt much. What hurt was the second picture Brandy had posted. A picture of Michael. My Michael. Smiling. And a puckered Brandy Denton holding up a kitten. The caption?

#WhenTheCatsAway #TheMiceWillPlay #EnjoyYourTea #ThisCatIsGoing4TheCream #Meow

CHAPTER 10

"Maddy, what's wrong? You look like you're going to explode?" April said.

I passed my phone to her so she could see and took several deep breaths. My heart was beating so fast, and blood rushed through my head. I could barely hear anything but the pounding as my blood pulsed in my veins.

"Not again. I'm going to kill her," I muttered.

"Maddy!" April yelled to get my attention.

I turned and blinked several times to help focus.

"She's only doing this to get under your skin. It doesn't mean anything. It doesn't mean that he's doing anything wrong."

I don't remember much of the rest of the afternoon. I don't remember leaving the Carson Law Inn or driving home and changing my clothes, but I must have done it since I wasn't wearing my fancy dress and Carson Law hat. I was wearing my Pyer Moss Sculpts, Khaite jeans, and a Baby Cakes T-shirt. My next clear memory was pacing in the Baby Cakes kitchen.

Baby was sitting in a corner staring at me.

"What am I doing here?"

Baby stood up and gave himself a shake.

I took several deep breaths and glanced around at the pristine kitchen in the hopes of catching a clue.

"Right. I need to breathe." I took several deep long breaths. I held them and then released them slowly. When I finished, I did it again and again and again. Eventually, my pulse stopped racing. I glanced around the kitchen.

"Leroy always says baking calms him down. Maybe I should try it." I looked at Baby.

He stared at me, and if I didn't know better, I'd say he had one eyebrow raised. Was that possible? Could dogs raise an eyebrow? Did dogs even have eyebrows?

I bent close and stared. Baby had folds of skin above his eyes, but then he had a lot of folds all over. The jury was out on eyebrows, but he certainly managed to adjust his skin folds into a look of skepticism. The thought that I should ask Michael whether or not Baby had eyebrows crossed my mind, but then I felt my heart rate pick up again. I quickly banished that and all thoughts about Michael Portman to the back of my mind.

It was Sunday, and Baby Cakes was closed. The bakery was quiet and peaceful. After I inherited the bakery, I promoted Leroy to head baker. He'd worked with Great-Aunt Octavia and knew the business. Plus, he at least knew how to bake, which was more than I could claim. He usually prepped for the upcoming busy weekday, but we could never have enough thumbprint cookies. I knew how to make those. But, I didn't feel like making thumbprint cookies.

I pulled out my phone and swiped. Great-Aunt Octavia had left me a recipe box with her favorite recipes. I kept the treasured recipes at home where I knew they would be safe, but I had taken pictures.

"Blondies?" I looked over the recipe. "Brownies without chocolate?" Great-Aunt Octavia's comments read, *Brownies so good they'll make you wanna slap your mama! Ha ha! But, don't try it if you value your teeth.*

I smiled and wished for the one-millionth time that I had gotten to know Great-Aunt Octavia. I think I would have liked her. And, for the one-millionth time, I wondered if she would have liked me. I looked at the directions that looked easy enough. "I bet I can make these."

Baby yawned and slid down into his sphinx pose.

"Everyone's a critic." I glared and then couldn't help but smile. "Still, maybe I'll make a small test batch just to be sure."

I pulled out the ingredients and placed them on the counter. There weren't a lot of them. Just seven ingredients, which was a plus.

I tied on a Baby Cakes apron and measured out my ingredients.

"I need to film a video. Might as well kill two birds with one stone."

I went to the closet and pulled out the ring light I kept for recording Leroy's baking classes. I placed my phone in the holder in the middle of the ring. Before pressing RECORD, I touched up my lipstick.

Two deep breaths and then I started the video. I melted the butter and mixed in the brown sugar, eggs, and vanilla as instructed. Then, I added the dry ingredients and mixed more. *That was easy.* I poured the batter into the glass baking dish and popped it into the oven.

It was so simple and so quick. I wondered if I'd forgotten something. I pressed PAUSE and rechecked the recipe.

Nope. Now, it was just a matter of waiting. The instructions said to bake for forty-five minutes or until the edges were golden brown.

Hmm. I hadn't been baking for a long time, but forty-five minutes seemed like a long time to me. I set a timer and waited.

There's nothing worse than waiting.

To kill time, I snapped photos of me. Photos of Baby. Photos of me and Baby.

#MeAndMyBaby #BakingWithMyBaby #MondaySample Surprise

When the buzzer sounded, I checked the oven. The blondies were golden brown, and the kitchen smelled wonderful. I placed the dish on the counter and took several more pictures.

#GreatAuntOctaviasBlondies #MondayFreeSamples #Baby ApprovedBlondies

I put the dish back in the oven, placed my phone in the ring-light stand, and turned the video back on. Then, I pretended I was taking the dish out of the oven for the first time. I cut a small piece and took a bite. They were warm, gooey, buttery, and delicious. I didn't have to pretend to like them.

"These blondies are buttery and delicious. Swing by Baby Cakes for your free sample." I smiled big and took another bite. "So yummy."

I was about to turn off the video when I was surprised by a knock on the door.

It was Sunday. The bakery was closed. Who could it possibly be?

"Maybe it's Leroy." The upper level of the bakery had a tiny apartment. Leroy sometimes slept there rather than driving nearly forty-five minutes to his equally tiny apartment in a nearby village.

When I got to the front of the bakery, it wasn't Leroy's face staring at me through the door. It was Brandy Denton's.

I scowled at her through the glass. "We're closed."

"I know that, you twit. Open up. We need to talk."

What could we possibly need to talk about? Your attempts to steal the man I love? No way.

I stood with my arms folded and glared at her. "I don't have anything to say to you."

"Good, then open the door and try listening for a change." Brandy huffed.

I fumed. Brandy Denton was the last person that I wanted to talk to.

"Look, are you going to open the door so we can talk face-to-face? Or should I just stand here screaming on the street so everyone in town can hear?" She scowled for two beats and then held up her phone. "Or perhaps you'd prefer me to post everything online for all the world to read?"

I longed to tell Brandy exactly what she could do with her cell phone, but she was starting to attract attention. I didn't recognize most of the people who stopped to gawk, but in a small town, there's never more than one or two degrees of separation from anyone. My first thought was to let her scream her head off. My second was that word of a woman screaming outside of my bakery wouldn't be good for business. My third was that I didn't care what people think. My fourth, fifth, and sixth were more of the same. I was just about to walk away when I got a glimpse of Blue Eyes standing across the street.

Without thinking, I unlocked the door and rushed outside. Focused on my target, I hurried past Brandy Denton and charged into the street.

"Maddy!" Brandy yelled.

Tires screeched to a halt, and a little old lady wearing a bright yellow T-shirt, with a cigarette hanging from one corner of her mouth, stuck her head out the window of a blue pickup truck and screamed. She questioned the legitimacy of my parents' marriage and made some suggestions that were anatomically impossible. Having spent the majority of my life surrounded by sailors, I wasn't shocked. I'd heard a lot worse, but none of those other comments were directed at me. It took a few moments for me to shake it off enough to step back and allow the truck to pass. I stood in the middle of the street in a daze as I gazed after the woman and tried to appreciate the irony of her HONK IF YOU LOVE JESUS bumper sticker.

When she was gone, I remembered Blue Eyes, but he was nowhere to be found.

"Madison, are you okay?" Chris Russell asked.

"Yes. I'm fine. I thought I saw someone . . . What are you doing here?"

"I was shopping. I could ask you the same question, but perhaps we could continue this conversation on the sidewalk." He placed a hand on my elbow and another on my back and guided me back to the safety of the sidewalk in front of Baby Cakes.

"Are you freakin' nuts walking out in traffic like that?" Brandy screeched. "If I knew you had a death wish, I wouldn't have wasted my time coming down here to warn you."

I turned my back to Brandy and started to thank Chris Russell, but after a couple of moments, her words sunk in, and I turned back to face her. "What do you mean, warn me?"

"Oh, you want to talk now?" Brandy glanced at the claws she called nails as though her manicure was the most important thing in the world.

I waited.

After a few moments, she sighed. "Well, after my visit with the delicious Dr. Portman, I just happened to be walking down on the beach. Someone told me you lived back there."

"Wait. Why did you want to know where I lived? It's not like I'd ever invite you over for anything."

She gave me a wide-eyed innocent stare that didn't fool me for one moment. I knew beyond a shadow of a doubt that she had pumped people in the community to find out where I lived. She waved away my comment. "Like I said, I just happened to be walking on the beach when I overheard—"

"And while I'm thinking about it, you can just stay away from Michael."

"What's wrong? Scared of a little competition?" She flipped her hair over her shoulder and grinned.

It took every ounce of strength within me to keep from snatching those extensions out of her head, but with her three-inch nails, I'd have to break all of those tips off or she'd shred my face like a head of lettuce.

"Competition? You're not Michael's type."

Brandy smiled sweetly. "Who said I was talking about me? I've seen what I needed to know. Now, I'm going back to civilization first thing in the morning."

"Good." I turned away, but Brandy wasn't done.

"Your competition is right here under your very nose."

I looked up, and that's when I saw Michael walking toward me.

"What's going on?"

Hanging on his arm was Rihanna.

CHAPTER 11

When they got closer, I realized the beauty queen hanging on his arm wasn't really the famous singer Rihanna, but she looked enough like her to be a younger sibling. She was tall, dark, and slender, with light eyes and clear skin. I hated her at first sight.

I stared at Michael and the goddess for what felt like an hour. Brandy Denton's cackle pulled me out of my stunned stupor.

"Maddy, are you okay?" Michael shed the goddess and grabbed me by the shoulders. "What's wrong?" He glanced at Brandy.

"I'd say she just got the shock of her life." Brandy pulled out her phone and snapped a few pictures. "I'm just thankful I was here to see it."

This was too much. I turned to Brandy. "Drop dead."

Brandy threw her head back and laughed. Then she blew a kiss and spun around on her heels. "Ta-ta." She wiggled her fingers over her shoulder and marched away.

Baby took a few steps toward the Beauty Queen. He gave

her a sniff, and then my big dog stood up on his back legs and licked her face.

The Beauty Queen giggled. "Well, hello, big boy."

"Et tu, Baby?" I mumbled.

That was the last straw. Brandy Denton, Michael, the Blue-Eyed Stranger, the Super Model, and a crowd of onlookers was too much. I shrugged away from Michael, turned, and marched into my bakery.

CHAPTER 12

I didn't bother locking the door. Michael's new friend may have stolen the heart of both my boyfriend and my dog, but I seriously doubted that she was prepared for an eighth of a ton drooling mastiff for long. She'd send him home when he was done worshipping at her feet.

I walked to the back, washed my hands, and cleaned up the mess from the blondies. It wasn't until I saw my phone still in the ring stand that I realized I had forgotten to stop the recording.

The bakery door chimed as it was opened. Footsteps followed.

Baby pranced his happy body back to the kitchen, sat, and stared at me.

"Traitor." I gave him a sideways glance and continued to clean up.

The next footsteps were Michael's, followed by those of the Beauty Queen.

"Maddy, are you okay?" he asked.

Okay? Are you joking?

"Yep." I lied.

Long pause.

"I'd like to introduce you to my new partner."

Partner? That's a lot of progress for one afternoon. Or, how long has this been going on?

Longer pause followed by a heavy sigh.

"Maddy, I'd like to introduce you to Dr. Alliyah Howard. My new partner in the veterinary clinic." He took a deep breath. "Alliyah, this is my . . . this is Madison Montgomery."

Alliyah? Alliyah Howard. Why did that name sound familiar?

I took a deep breath, turned, and plastered a big fake smile on my face. "Dr. Howard, nice to meet you."

The Beauty Queen flashed a smile that would get her a job selling toothpaste with any of the major manufacturers and extended a hand. "I'm pleased to meet you. Michael has told me so much about you."

"Really? He hasn't told me anything about you." I glanced at the outstretched hand. "I'm sorry, I've been baking, and I—" I held up the dish of blondies as a prop. I might have to pretend to be nice to this boyfriend-stealing Siren, but shaking hands as though we were good sports was more than I could handle.

"I wondered what that glorious smell was." She grinned.

The polite thing would have been to offer her a blondie, but I wasn't feeling polite.

"Thank you. This is going to be the sample for tomorrow, or I'd offer you some." I wished I could have left it there, but for some reason, I heard my great-aunt Octavia's voice in my head, and she wasn't pleased. "If you swing by tomorrow, we'll have a lot more, and I'll be glad to give you a few . . . on the house." *Darned good manners.*

We stood by in an awkward silence for several moments.

"I love your dog. Michael said his name is Baby. What an unusual name."

"He belonged to my great-aunt Octavia. She named him after Frank Sinatra, her favorite singer, but I'm sure Michael's already told you that."

"Actually, he didn't tell me." She paused. When I didn't continue she said, "I'm afraid I still don't get the connection between Baby and Frank Sinatra."

"He's a champion show dog. His registered name is *Champion Crooner Ol' Blue Eyes, One for My Baby.* His call name or nickname is Baby."

"Ah . . . I get it now. Well, he's a beautiful dog."

"Thank you."

We stood around in an awkward silence for several minutes until Dr. Howard said, "I think I'll go. I have a lot to do to get ready for work tomorrow. It was nice meeting you."

I mumbled what I hoped sounded like a nice to meet you, but it would have been hard to distinguish.

"Are you sure? I can—" Michael started but was halted by a hand.

"No, I'm good. I'll see you bright and early tomorrow."

The Beauty Queen turned and walked out.

Michael and I stared at each other in tense silence until the chime indicated Dr. Howard was gone.

"What was that about? You were incredibly rude."

"Was I?" I turned my back to him and started wrapping blondies.

"All right, what's wrong?" Michael asked.

"Nothing."

He took a deep breath. "I hate it when you do that."

"What?"

"Lie. Squid, if something's wrong, tell me. Or tell me you don't want to talk about it. But don't tell me nothing's wrong, when clearly something is wrong. Alliyah was—"

That's when I remembered why the name Alliyah Howard was so familiar.

"Why would anything be wrong when my boyfrie—When you waltz into my bakery and tell me that you've just made your *ex-girlfriend* your new partner at your veterinary practice?"

CHAPTER 13

The argument that followed was our first serious disagreement. Michael kept trying to get me to talk, and I wasn't in the mood to talk. Not about Dr. Alliyah Howard anyway. So, instead I got mad about him always calling me Squid, even though I knew he didn't mean anything by it. He tried to explain and apologize, but I said some uncomplimentary things about the Army. It ended with Michael walking out.

I felt like crap after he left. I waffled between running after him and deleting every picture I had of him on my phone. In a small section of my mind, I knew that my problem wasn't with Michael or even Alliyah Howard. My problem was that Dr. Alliyah Howard was drop-dead gorgeous. She was smart and she and Michael had a lot in common. They were both veterinarians. They were both runners who were in great physical shape. Plus, I knew without even asking that she wouldn't have a problem making decisions and wouldn't have one insecure bone in her body. Given the fact that I was already feeling anxious about our relationship, his highly successful, beautiful ex-girlfriend had sent me into a jealous frenzy. Would Michael drop me for Dr. Alliyah Howard the same way that Elliott had dropped me for Brandy Denton? If they were working together side by side every day, it would only be a matter of time until they rekindled their old passions. At least, that's what the green monster in my head kept repeating. I paced around the kitchen for a few moments before I sat down on the floor and balled my eyes out.

Baby came over and tried to comfort me, but I wasn't ready to forgive him, either. He'd licked the goddess's face.

"Don't you dare try to cozy up with me after you licked and drooled all over Michael's new girlfriend. All males are the same. See a pretty face and you get all drooly and lose your mind. Well, you can sleep on the floor tonight and forget about that ham bone I've been saving for you in the freezer."

I don't know for sure if Baby knew what was going on, but he was smart enough to back off and keep his distance.

There was a rap on the closet door. After a few seconds, the door opened, and Candy stuck her head through.

"You mad at the whole world, or just the male population?" Candy slid down on the floor next to me.

"You heard?"

She nodded and passed a box of tissues that she'd brought with her. Then she wrapped a hand around my shoulder and pulled my head onto her shoulder. "You just have a good cry. I ordered a pizza and a half gallon of Coffee Coffee BuzzBuzzBuzz! for you and Cherry Garcia for me. It'll be here in twenty minutes."

For some reason that made me cry even more.

Somewhere between my sobs, I told Candy everything.

The pizza and ice cream were delivered, and we moved from the kitchen floor to one of the small bistro tables in the bakery and ate.

Candy had brought down Daisy and extra-large bones for the mastiffs. Both dogs curled up in a corner and gnawed on their treats.

"He kept saying he couldn't understand why I was upset.

After all, I was the one who had pushed him to get a partner. *Seriously? He's making this my fault?*"

"Men." Candy shook her head.

"Sure, I said he needed help, but I'm one hundred percent certain I never said, 'Go find your supersmart, extremely gorgeous supermodel *ex* and make her your partner so you can spend ten to twelve hours of your day with her.' Of course, I couldn't say that to him."

"Of course you couldn't."

"Have you seen her?" I asked.

Candy nodded. "She's a runner, too. I've seen her jogging around the beach."

"I'll bet she doesn't even sweat like normal people. She probably just glistens."

"Yeah, like one of those vampires in *Twilight*."

It took me a minute to catch the reference, but when I did, I laughed. For some reason, that was the funniest thing I'd ever heard, and I laughed until my side hurt. My phone vibrated, and I looked down and saw Michael's picture.

I glanced at Candy.

"Well? You gonna answer? Or, do you want to make him suffer a little longer?" she asked.

I thought for a split second too long, and the ringing stopped. My heart sank. *Surely, if he really cared, he wouldn't have hung up so quickly*. I shrugged. "Probably for the best. I mean it would never have worked, right?"

Before Candy could answer, Baby and Daisy ran to the back door and began barking.

"I don't think I locked the door," I whispered.

I picked up my phone and was about to dial 9-1-1 when Michael rushed into the bakery followed by Daisy and Baby. I put my phone down. I rose to stand but stopped when Michael held up a hand.

"Wait. Listen, Alliyah and I were over long before I met

you, and there is absolutely nothing between us. But she is a good veterinarian—one of the best. That's the *only* reason I even considered her. She's also a canine ophthalmologist, which would be great for New Bison. The closest canine ophthalmologist is in Chicago. And she's a medical doctor. But I don't want her or my practice or anyone to come between us. That's why I called her and told her that it's not going to work out for her to join my practice. I've been doing fine, and I can scale back. I just—"

He didn't get to finish because I hurled myself into his arms.

We kissed until we were both hot, bothered, and out of breath. When we separated, Candy and Daisy were gone, and Baby was lying in his bed watching us.

He stared hard into my eyes. "So, are we okay?"

I nodded.

"You're sure?"

I backed away. "Almost."

"What? I can't do anything about being an Army veteran, but I will do my best never to call you Squid. I thought you knew I didn't mean it as an insult, but I—"

I kissed him quiet again. "Will you stop talking?"

"If I don't, will you shut me up again?" He grinned.

"I'm sorry for the terrible things I said about the Army. I didn't mean it. I have always had nothing but the highest respect for the men and women who dedicate their lives to protecting our nation, whether it's in the Navy, the Marines, the Air Force, or even the Army."

"Hey!"

I chuckled. "And I don't mind when you call me Squid . . . well, I don't mind much."

"Okay, so are you going to explain why we were fighting?"

"I was . . . jealous. I thought—"

"Madison, what could you possibly be jealous about? Alliyah can't hold a candle to you."

"Right. She's tall, thin, athletic, and supermodel gorgeous. Plus, she's smart. She's a freakin' veterinarian, and now you tell me she's also a doggie ophthalmologist as well as a medical doctor. How am I supposed to compete with someone like that?"

He wrapped his arms around me and pulled me close. "You don't have to compete with her. There's no competition. You are smart, funny, beautiful, and you can bake . . . well, you're getting there."

I swatted his arm and tried to pull away, but he tightened his hold. "Haven't you figured it out yet?"

"What?"

"I'm not letting you go."

He kissed me hard, and I felt as though I was drowning. That's when Baby started to growl. This wasn't just any growl. This was his *Danger-Danger-Will-Robinson* growl. Then, he ran to the front door, bared his teeth, and lunged at the window with his best impersonation of Cujo.

Michael stepped in front of me and shoved me toward the kitchen. "Call the police."

CHAPTER 14

From the kitchen, I quickly dialed 9-1-1. The beauty of a small town is that everyone knows everyone else. The call was short, and I knew the response would be swift. That left me with plenty of time to think. I paced for a few moments before I realized that I didn't hear the sounds of Baby ripping an intruder to shreds. Nor did I hear the sounds of Michael breaking the bones of an intruder.

What am I doing in here? Alone!

Classic horror movie mistake number one: separating the hero from the heroine.

Darn it!

I glanced around at the expensive knife set that Great-Aunt Octavia spent a small fortune on from Japan. Yeah, with my luck, I'd probably end up hurting myself. Instead, I grabbed my handy-dandy cast-iron skillet.

Wielding my weapon like the Admiral's favorite baseball player, Hank Aaron, I rushed back into the bakery, prepared to bash in the head of the first stranger I ran into.

The bakery was empty. No Michael. No Baby. No ominous stranger intent on evil. Well, not one that I could see.

I tentatively looked for any good hiding places where serial killers lurk in horror movies. Nothing.

After a few minutes, I heard a noise and moved into the kitchen with my skillet at the ready.

I hid behind the door, prepared to bash whoever came through.

The door swung open.

I lifted my skillet and was just about to smash like the Incredible Hulk, but I hesitated for a half second before lowering the boom.

In that pause, Michael ducked, grabbed my wrist, and managed to disarm me in one swift, ninja-like maneuver. "You could have cracked my skull with that thing."

"That's the intention."

He grinned. "Okay, at ease. You can stand down."

Sirens blared.

We walked to the front of the bakery. There were eight police cars in front of the building with headlights pointed at the building.

"I didn't know New Bison had eight police cars," I said.

"They don't. Half of those are from surrounding villages. Plus, I think at least one is your buddy."

Something in his voice told me he wasn't talking about April.

He turned and winked. "Trooper Bob."

I groaned.

Baby accompanied Michael to the door. Thanks to April, we were familiar with most of the officers from the New Bison Police. We'd met State Trooper Robert Roberts when April's late husband was murdered and he was called in to investigate.

State Trooper Robert Roberts, or Trooper Bob as he liked to be called, described himself as a "good ol' boy." He was a big bear of a man who came across on first impression as a large version of Barney Fife from the old *Andy Griffith Show*. However, Miss Hannah said he was sharper than a Ginsu knife, which made him just as dangerous. He liked to spout a lot of old-fashioned ideas, but as a single parent with a teenage daughter, he was more progressive in his thinking about women than he would admit openly. He reminded me a lot of the Admiral—tough as a Sherman tank with everyone except his daughter, Holly. Our relationship started out rocky, but once I found his Achilles' heel, things were a lot better. Still, I'd hardly call us buddies.

"All right, Nancy Drew. Where's the sniper?" Trooper Bob scowled.

Michael looked at me. "Sniper?"

I might have exaggerated a bit.

"I didn't say anything about a sniper. I said there was a suspicious character hanging around outside of the bakery."

"I believe your words included the words 'serial killer' intent on murder. The boiled egg sniper was yesterday's crisis." Trooper Bob folded his arms. "You realize there are laws against wasting police time."

"Actually, I'm the one who saw a stranger lurking outside," Michael said. "When I went outside to ask him what was up, he took off running. Baby and I chased him for a few blocks, but he jumped a fence. I didn't want to leave Maddy here alone, so we stopped."

Trooper Bob pulled out a notepad. "Did you get a good look at him?"

Michael was Trooper Bob's veterinarian, so he respected him. Plus, Michael was a man, and in his chauvinistic mind, that carried more weight than the complaints of a mere woman.

Michael was better at estimating height, weight, and build than me. However, based on the description, I'd bet a year's worth of thumbprint cookies that it was Blue Eyes.

I pulled up my phone and swiped through the pictures Leroy sent from his baking class until I found one with Blue Eyes.

"That's him," Michael said.

"Who is he?" Trooper Bob asked.

I shrugged. "I've noticed him hanging around the bakery, but I didn't pay much attention until I saw Leroy's pictures. Now, I see him every time I turn around."

"I don't like this," Michael said. "Why didn't you tell me someone was stalking you?"

"I'm not one hundred percent sure he was stalking me. Besides, we were fighting. Remember?" I grinned.

"Probably just some lovesick sap trying to get thumbprint cookies," Trooper Bob said.

I wasn't sure if I should be insulted that Trooper Bob thought the only thing someone might be interested in were my thumbprint cookies or not. I decided to let it slide.

Michael argued that I needed additional protection.

"Are you joking?" Trooper Bob said. "Her father's a naval admiral, she's dating an ex-Army commando, lives with the town sheriff, and walks around town with a two-hundred-fifty-pound horse who recently ate his way through an SUV when he thought she was in danger. Who in their right mind would come close to her? She's got more protection than the freakin' governor." He turned and walked out. "If you see your blue-eyed stranger again, offer him a plate of cookies."

Michael and I stared outside as Trooper Bob gave the all clear and the police cars pulled away. When the last car left, Michael folded his arms and turned to glare at me.

"What?" I asked as innocently as I could.

"When were you going to tell me about this stalker?"

"What's to tell? It's not like he's approached me or even spoken to me. For all I know, I may not even be the one he's stalking."

"Who else could he be after? Baby?"

"I don't know. Maybe we just happen to both be in the same place at the same time. As much as I hate to admit this, Trooper Bob just might be right. He really hasn't done anything. He hasn't said anything to me, and when I tried to approach him, he ran away—"

"Wait. You approached him?"

"Ahh . . . didn't I mention that?"

"No." He glared at me like a drill sergeant at a new recruit who was late for reveille.

I quickly mentioned seeing Blue Eyes at church. I noticed about halfway through that a vein on the side of Michael's temple was pulsing. He clinched his jaw. When I finished, he stared. "Madison, what were you thinking?"

"I wasn't thinking. I just acted. I mean, we were at church. There were people everywhere. I was in more danger from that usher Sister Sylvia than Blue Eyes. That woman was ready to body-slam me for trying to leave during prayer. Trust me, if Blue Eyes tried anything, she would have wrestled him to the ground and cast the devil out of him."

His lips twitched.

That's when I knew he wasn't really angry with me. I wrapped my arms around his neck and snuggled close. "I'm pretty sure the only person who would wish me harm is running around town in a Maximilian Davis top that is to die for and a pair of Jimmy Choo boots that I would actually kill for."

He wrapped his arms around my waist and pulled me close. "Maddy, I don't know what I'm going to do with you."

"Hmm . . . I have an idea." I whispered a couple of ideas and had the pleasure of hearing him growl before pulling me into a kiss that swept me off my feet. It was a long time before I remembered anything more about blue-eyed strangers, Maximilian Davis tops, or Jimmy Choo boots. At one point, I thought I heard a sound, but Baby trotted to the kitchen to investigate. There were no unexplained noises or cries for help, so I returned all my attention to Michael.

When Michael's phone rang, we both swore. He tried to ignore it, but the caller wouldn't be ignored, and when it rolled over to voicemail, they called again and again and finally sent a text message.

I pulled away. "You better respond, or you won't get any peace. I'm going to get ready for tomorrow."

After a few minutes, he came to the kitchen. "I'm sorry. There's been an emergency and—"

"I know. You have to go."

"Maddy, I'm sorry . . . *really* sorry."

"I know. It's okay. Go."

He stared into my eyes as though trying to read the truth. "Are you sure?"

"I am. I even packed you some treats." I handed him a bag with a blondie and a dozen thumbprint cookies for the road.

He gazed into his bag. "Not exactly the treats that I was hoping for . . ."

I chuckled. "In that case, you better call Dr. Howard and tell her you've changed your mind."

"What?"

"You heard me, GI."

"You want me to have her join my practice? Are you sure?"

"Absolutely. Now, go take care of your four-legged emergency."

"I don't like the idea of leaving you alone for a lot of reasons. Maybe you should have gotten that gun the Admiral wanted to give you. I have one that—"

"I don't need nor do I want a gun. I have plenty of protection." I glanced at Baby, who was sitting by the door, and then I held up my skillet that I'd taken earlier.

"Trooper Bob was right. I've got Baby, and April will be home when I get there. What could possibly happen?"

CHAPTER 15

Monday morning, I was startled when I tried to roll over and couldn't move my arm. I opened my eyes and realized it was because of the English mastiff lying on it and not because I had a stroke that paralyzed one side of my body.

It took a bit of shoving, but I managed to shift Baby enough that I was able to free my arm. Regaining circulation took a bit longer, but I eventually managed it.

Baby continued to sleep while I showered and dressed. He eventually got in his morning stretches, and we went to take care of business.

Our morning routine hadn't changed much in the few months since I moved here, but today my phone rang while I was packing Baby's lunch. I assumed it was Michael and, without looking, answered in my sexiest voice. "Good morning, I missed you."

There was a pause. "Maddy?"

That was definitely *not* Michael.

"Leroy?"

"Hey, I came by the bakery early to get started making shortbread cookies and . . . you'd better come down here."

"Why? What's wrong? Don't tell me the dishwasher flooded. I knew I shouldn't have started that load of dishes before I left last night, but— "

"It's not the dishwasher."

Something in his voice alerted me that whatever had my head baker requesting my presence wasn't your run-of-the-mill mishap.

"What's wrong?"

He paused and then said, "That friend of yours from Los Angeles, Brandy Denton— "

"Brandy Denton is *not* my friend." I sighed. "What's she done now? Don't tell me she's been posting trash about me online again." I put my phone on speaker so I could talk and look through my social media pages to find out what havoc she was unleashing. I paused when I saw the video of us arguing outside of Baby Cakes from yesterday. "Good grief. How did she manage to video us? She must have had someone else recording us. There's no way she could have done it herself. I'll bet it was that assistant of hers. What's her name? Jamie? Jordan? Jessica. That's it. Jessica Barlow. She's got our entire argument. And it's trending. That dirty little conniving troublemaker. When I get my hands on her, I'm going to kill her."

"Too late."

"What? What do you mean?"

"That's what I've been trying to tell you. When I came into the bakery this morning, I found her. She's dead."

CHAPTER 16

I'm not proud of the fact that when Leroy told me that Brandy Denton's body was found in Baby Cakes Bakery, my first thought was, *Not again.* Brandy wasn't the first or even the second body to turn up there. Dead bodies were definitely not good for business.

I drove to Baby Cakes in record time. There was a platoon of police cars in front and behind the bakery, but I managed to squeeze into the spot next to the dumpster. I remembered Baby's harness that declared his status as a service dog and snapped it in place and then got out. I walked over behind Candy Hurston's coffee shop and let Baby hike his leg on her dumpster since I felt confident that Trooper Bob would have a cow if I let him relieve himself at the crime scene. I stepped over the crime scene tape and held it down for Baby to climb over and entered through the back door.

A policeman I didn't recognize guarded the back door and stopped me from entering. When I explained who I was, he pulled out his radio and told Trooper Bob I was here. After a few squawks and a lot of static, he must have gotten the green light to let me through.

I swallowed the comments that bubbled up when he tried to give me directions around my own bakery and went to the demonstration area.

Inside, there were a ton of people dusting, taking photos, and making a mess of my spotlessly clean bakery.

Trooper Bob and April were talking in a corner. It wasn't until I walked into the main bakery area that I saw Brandy. We had a trolley with wheels that was close to six feet tall. The trolley was made of metal and allowed us to cart large amounts of baked goods from the kitchen to the main bakery area. The killer had removed all the racks. The trolley was capable of holding fifteen trays of thumbprint cookies, pastries, cakes, and pies—or one dead social media influencer.

CHAPTER 17

"What's that mangy mutt doing at my crime scene?" Trooper Bob yelled.

I looked around at one of the policemen who was standing nearby, snickering. "I don't know. I'm guessing he snuck in with the rest of your team."

Trooper Bob didn't have much of a sense of humor, but neither did I when it came to people insulting my dog.

Someone else snickered, and Trooper Bob cut him a look that stopped the snicker.

Trooper Bob released a heavy sigh and motioned for me to come toward him.

One glance at that mobile trolley and my feet were glued in place.

"Hey, are you coming?" Trooper Bob yelled.

I shook my head and stared.

"You drove all the way out here, barged in on my crime scene, and now you're not coming? What's wrong, Nancy Drew? Real-life murder too much for you?" Trooper Bob smiled.

I struggled to move and walk over to the counter, but my

legs felt like cement. I stared at Brandy Denton, scrunched up and shoved inside that trolley, and I felt bile rise in my throat.

Trooper Bob laughed.

April hurried around the counter to me. She grabbed me by the shoulders and gave me a shake. "Maddy, are you okay? You look a little green."

"Don't even think about contaminating my crime scene!" Trooper Bob shouted. "Get her and that dirty mutt out of here."

Trooper Bob and I were in agreement on one point: I needed out.

It took a good pull from April and all of my strength to get my feet unstuck, but I managed. I suspect the extra push came from redirecting all of my anger for Trooper Bob into my legs.

Propelled by April, I headed toward the door, but I stopped when I got to the policeman who snickered at the state trooper's first insult directed at Baby. "He wants you to leave."

The policeman scowled. Molten lava flowed up his exposed neck and up into his face. He looked as though he wanted to comment, but I intercepted a sharp look from April, and a growl from Baby froze the words on his lips. Laughter rang through the building.

Outside, I leaned against the car and took several deep breaths.

"Are you going to puke?"

I shook my head, but it was a bad idea. April, Baby, and all of New Bison spun like a merry-go-round. I closed my eyes and swallowed hard. Two seconds before my stomach reached my mouth, April put a plastic bag to my mouth.

When I was empty and exhausted, she opened the car door and shoved me down on the passenger seat. I heard the lid of the dumpster close and knew she had disposed of my shame. "I'm sorry," I said.

"For what? Being human?"

She opened the glove compartment and pulled out the pack of wet wipes I kept for drool removal and a bottle of water that I kept in the car for Baby.

I wiped my face and took a swig of warm water and swished it around to clean my mouth.

"That was Brandy," I said. "What was she doing in Baby Cakes?"

"We were hoping maybe you might know."

Something in April's voice alerted me that something was wrong. Really wrong. "Me? Why would I know?"

April avoided the question and turned away so she wouldn't need to make eye contact.

"What's going on?" I asked.

April glanced around. "Maddy, you're my friend and my landlord. I'm not going to be able to work this case." She held up a hand to stop me from interrupting. "We don't have much time before Trooper Bob will be out here. It won't be as bad as the last time when C.J. was murdered. I won't be suspended or put on desk duty, but I won't be the lead investigator. I'm going to argue to be allowed to stay on the case, so I can stay close to things, but Trooper Bob is going to come after you."

"Me? Why me?"

"Because you were the only one in New Bison who really knew Brandy Denton. She stole your fiancé. And she was trying to ruin things between you and Michael. As far as he knows, you're the only one with a motive."

"But I didn't kill her."

"I know you didn't, but it looks bad. I mean, you argued with her just a few hours before she was murdered in your bakery. If I didn't know you would never kill anyone, I might think you did it, too. Plus that video went viral."

It took a few moments for her words to sink in. "Viral? Which one?"

April pulled out her phone and swiped until she found what she was looking for. She held up her phone for me to watch the same video I saw earlier. I closed my eyes and leaned back on the headrest. "Wouldn't you know that would go viral."

"Maddy, this is serious. I think you need to call Chris Russell. You're going to need a lawyer."

CHAPTER 18

Chris Russell picked up after a few rings. "Madison, you keep the strangest hours." He sounded groggy, but I didn't have time for sarcastic comments.

"Listen, I'm at Baby Cakes, and I need an attorney. Brandy Denton's been murdered, and April thinks Trooper Bob is going to arrest me."

I heard rustling that sounded as though he had moved from lying down to sitting upright.

"Brandy Denton? How? When did this happen?" He fired questions at me like a military assault rifle.

"I don't know the answers to any of those questions. I just know that Leroy called and . . . OMG! Leroy. Where is he?"

April used her hands to indicate I should settle down. "He's fine." Her hands twisted together in a strange form of sign language that I didn't understand. After a few seconds, I realized she was simulating knitting. That's when I realized he was down the street with Tyler Lawrence.

"Madison!" Chris Russell yelled.

I pulled the phone away and rubbed my ear for a few seconds. "I'm here. At Baby Cakes."

"I'll be right there. And do not say one word to Trooper Bob or April until I get there."

I glanced at April. "I have no intention of talking to Trooper Bob, but April—"

"Madison, I need you to listen to me. I know you think April is your friend, and I'm sure she is, under normal circumstances. These circumstances are *not* normal. You must never forget that first and foremost she is a sworn officer. It's her duty to upload the law. Unlike me, she could be *compelled* to divulge anything that you tell her. Some of your innocent conversations could ultimately be used against you. As your attorney, anything you say to me is protected. Now, I need you to promise me that you will refuse to speak to either April or Trooper Bob or anyone without me. Can you do that, please?"

I didn't believe for one minute that April would say or do anything to hurt me, but I gave him my word. When I hung up, an awkward silence hung in the air like a foul stench.

"Maddy, it's okay. He's right."

I stared at my friend. "What?"

"I'm your friend, but he's right. You shouldn't say anything to me that you wouldn't want to be repeated in a court of law. I would never deliberately do anything to hurt you, but if I were subpoenaed, I'd have to tell the truth."

"I wouldn't want you to lie."

"I know. I also know you didn't kill Brandy Denton, and I'll do what I can to stay on the case so I can find the real killer. In the meantime, you listen to your lawyer." April hugged me and then turned and walked back inside.

I sat in the passenger seat of the car and stared at the door after April left.

Baby placed his massive head in my lap and drooled on my leg.

I scratched his ear. "This is a big mess. I don't know how we're going to get out of this one, boy. April's right. No one in

New Bison knew Brandy Denton. No one hated her like me. I have no idea how she got into Baby Cakes or why she was there. This may be the last straw."

Chris Russell pulled into the alley behind Baby Cakes in his fancy McLaren Spider. Whenever I saw the car, I wondered how he could afford it. Business in New Bison must be good. In L.A., I didn't blink whenever I saw a Bugatti, a Bentley, or a Lamborghini. I wasn't into cars. Shoes, purses, and clothes were my thing. I appreciated a nice car, but I didn't gasp and hyperventilate when I saw one. Not like Elliott, my ex. He was the one who dreamed of cruising around the Pacific Coast Highway in a fancy sports car. Personally, I found convertibles caused havoc with my hair, and I preferred to sit enclosed from the elements and bugs. In my previous circles, a McLaren Spider wouldn't have garnered more than a casual glance. In New Bison, that car stood out like . . . like a cheap pair of shoes in a sea of Jimmy Choos.

Chris Russell approached the car. "Madison, are you okay?"

I started and must have made Baby nervous because he turned and growled.

Baby lunged.

Chris Russell squealed, turned, and tried to climb on top of my car.

Baby opened his jaws, prepared to take a bite out of my lawyer's rear. At the last minute, Michael leaped between Baby and the lawyer.

"Baby, no!" Michael ordered.

Drool dripped from Baby's mouth. He never took his gaze from Russell, but he stopped trying to eat him alive.

Michael grabbed his collar and guided Baby to the back of the SUV. Once he had Baby confined inside, he closed the back hatch.

Chris Russell, red-faced and angry, panted. "That dog is a

menace. I'm not sure what's happened to him. He never did that when Octavia had him."

That hurt. Was I a bad dog mom? "I'm sorry. It's my fault. I wasn't expecting you to arrive so quickly. You startled him."

Chris Russell straightened his clothes and adjusted his face. "I am well aware of the terms of Octavia's will, but if that dog is deemed a danger to the public, then we can get a judge to remove that stipulation from the will."

"What do you mean?" I asked.

"If he bites someone or is deemed a danger to the public, then you can't be expected to keep a dangerous animal. I think we can challenge that stipulation, and I feel confident—"

"Baby's not dangerous," Michael said.

"And I don't want to challenge the will." My lips quivered, and I was two seconds away from crumbling into a simpering, blubbering mess. The idea of losing Baby on top of possibly going to jail for a murder I didn't commit was too much.

"As Baby's veterinarian, I won't let that happen." Michael folded his arms and adopted the stance. Legs apart. Body straight and rigid. Brow furled. Soldiers ready for battle worked themselves into a mental state that went along with *the stance.* Michael stared, and every muscle in his body flexed. Chris Russell would need to go through Michael to get Baby.

Chris Russell's eyes flashed for an instant, but as quickly as the flash started, it was gone. "Well, of course. Of course. I only meant . . . well, I'm sure he was merely startled . . ."

Michael must have noticed the momentary spark because he didn't stand down.

The air crackled with tension.

The back door opened. "Trooper Bob is ready for you," April said.

"I'll just go inside and . . . wait," Chris Russell said.

April hesitated a moment and glanced from Michael to me. After a brief moment, she turned and followed Russell inside.

Then and only then did Michael move from battle station to condition-three all clear. His shoulders went down a half inch. He unfolded his arms. And his brow smoothed out.

I whimpered.

Michael wrapped his arms around me and held me tight. "Hey, Squid. Sailors don't cry."

"Then it's a good thing I'm not a sailor."

"You know I'll never let anyone take Baby from you. You know that, right?" He pulled away and gazed into my eyes.

I sniffed and nodded.

He pulled me close and kissed me.

"Geez!" Trooper Bob yelled from the back door. "I'm trying to conduct an investigation here. Do you mind?"

Michael mumbled an expletive just loud enough for Trooper Bob to hear. Then, he escorted me toward the door.

At the door, Trooper Bob held up a hand. "Where do you think you're going? This is a murder investigation, not some afternoon soiree."

I felt a volcano of anger bubble up inside Michael. Before he unleashed it, I placed a hand on his chest. "It's okay. I'll be fine. Mr. Russell's here." *And April.* "Could you take Baby back with you?"

"Are you sure?" he asked.

"Yeah. I'm sure." I reached up and kissed him again and whispered, "Sailors don't cry, but I think you better call the Admiral."

CHAPTER 19

I wasn't sure that calling in the Admiral on Trooper Bob was a good idea, but relations between us were a lot better, and he would want to know. Besides, there was something bracing about knowing that my formidable father would unleash a tsunami of trouble if I were arrested.

"What are you grinning about?" Trooper Bob asked when we were inside the bakery kitchen.

"Nothing."

Trooper Bob mumbled something that sounded like "airhead," but I ignored him.

I avoided looking at the bakery and kept my back to that area.

"The body's been moved," April whispered.

I didn't care. I would never be able to look at that mobile trolley again.

I sat in one of the folding chairs in the demonstration overflow area and waited.

Chris Russell sat next to me.

Trooper Bob stood, so he towered over me. "All right, let's hear it."

"What?" I asked.

"Your statement. What happened?" Trooper Bob asked.

"I have no idea. When did she die?"

Trooper Bob frowned. He waited. The silence was overpowering, but I resisted the urge to fill it.

After what felt like an hour, Chris Russell broke the silence. "Trooper Bob, I suggest you ask your questions or let Madison go home."

He moved what I can only assume was a wad of tobacco to the back of his cheek. "Why don't you start by telling me what you did yesterday, and I'll tell you when to stop." He grinned, and a drop of brown spit spilled from his mouth.

I closed my eyes and took a deep breath. Then, I opened my eyes and recounted my movements from the time I woke up and sat outside on the bluffs with Candy to the tea at the Carson Law Inn. I deliberately went into an excruciating amount of detail simply because I knew it would annoy Trooper Bob to hear about my dress, shoes, hat, and the outfits worn by everyone else, including April and Brandy Denton. However, that's where I made my first mistake.

"Brandy Denton was at this tea?" Trooper Bob asked.

"Yes. Well, technically she wasn't because she didn't get to come inside. She was dressed nicely, and those Jimmy Choo boots were amazing, but there's a certain dress code when attending a high tea. Her outfit didn't meet the dress code. So, she wasn't allowed to go inside, even though she tried to pretend like we were besties or something. But, Mrs. Law was there, and she saw right through her. Anyway, it was—"

"Wait, so Brandy Denton was angry about not getting to go inside for tea?" Trooper Bob asked.

"I doubt it. I mean, she was ticked off because she didn't get her way, but I seriously doubt that Brandy Denton had ever been to a *real* tea. She just wanted to goad me."

"So, you and Brandy Denton weren't . . . *besties*?"

"Of course not."

"Madison . . ." Chris Russell sounded the warning bell, but I'd warmed up to my subject now, and there was no stopping me.

"Well, we weren't besties. Everyone with a phone and access to social media knows it. She stole my fiancé, Elliott. That was why I was so eager to move to New Bison in the first place. I needed to get away until some of the attention died down. So, when Chris Russell told me that Great-Aunt Octavia died and left me this bakery, her house, and Baby . . . well, everything worked out."

"You must have been upset about Brandy Denton ruining your wedding and stealing your fiancé," Trooper Bob said. "She humiliated you."

"Well, I was upset at first. Who wouldn't be? She pretended to be my friend. She was always hanging around with Elliott and me, but I had no idea that she was sneaking around behind my back with my fiancé. Elliott and I had been together for years, through college and medical school, and then just when we were about to seal the deal, in swoops Brandy and—"

"Maddy," Chris Russell said. "Trooper Bob doesn't need all of the details."

"Sure, I do." Trooper Bob grinned. "Go on. Get it off your chest."

"Well, I was upset at first, but it turned out for the best. She saved me from making a huge mistake. I didn't love Elliott. If it hadn't been for Brandy Denton, I might have married the two-timing louse. Instead, I came here, and I met Michael." Thinking about Michael made me smile.

"So, the picture of Brandy Denton with your new boyfriend, Michael Portman, had to have made you angry." Trooper Bob watched my face with the same intensity as Sister Sylvia whenever she was passing the offering plate at church.

"Of course it made me angry. She only posted that picture to get under my skin. She was just being malicious. You could tell that by her post, 'When the cat's away, the mouse will play.' That was a deliberate reference intended to make me angry. She had no intention of—"

"Maddy!" Chris Russell yelled. "Just answer the question. No need to volunteer additional information."

Maybe I hadn't completely shed my habit of oversharing when I was nervous. I clamped my mouth closed and waited for the next question.

Trooper Bob seemed like he wanted to spit, and if looks could kill, Chris Russell would have been writhing on the ground.

"Trooper Bob, please don't spit inside," I said. "I mean, this is a bakery, and the . . ." I glanced around at all of the police and forensics team and swallowed the rest of the sentence. I would be lucky if the health department didn't shut me down on principle alone.

April walked to the pantry closet and pulled out a small pail. She handed it to the state trooper.

Trooper Bob glared at the pail as though it were a snake. Instead of using the pail, he walked outside, took care of his business, and walked back inside.

"So, you read the post Brandy Denton put up on social media?" Trooper Bob asked.

I glanced at Chris Russell, who nodded. "Yes. I saw it."

"Did it make you angry?"

"Yes. I was angry. Who wouldn't be? But, I certainly wasn't mad enough to kill her simply because she managed to find Michael at a pet adoption and got a picture with him." I folded my arms.

"Then what happened?"

"I came back to Baby Cakes and made blondies."

He glanced up from his notepad. "Blondies? What's that?"

"It's like a brownie, only instead of white sugar, you use brown sugar. It tastes buttery and reminded me of butterscotch. I found one of Great-Aunt Octavia's recipes, and I decided to give it a try. I made a batch. They came out really good. Leroy said baking always helped him calm down and relax. He said it would ease my mind. I didn't really believe him, but by the time I'd finished, I wasn't angry anymore. I didn't feel like making enough to sell. So, I planned to cut what I had into tiny pieces and give them away as samples. I— "

"Yeah, right. But, while you were at the bakery, Brandy Denton showed up, and the two of you got into another argument. Is that when you decided to kill her?"

"I did not kill Brandy Denton. She came to the bakery, and I told her we were closed. I wasn't even going to unlock the door, but then I saw the blue-eyed stranger and— "

"Wait. What blue-eyed stranger?" Trooper Bob asked.

"You know, the one I showed you the picture of. The one Michael and Baby chased down the street last night. The one who's been hanging around the bakery. Anyway, I opened the door to try to talk to him. I wanted to know who he was and why he was stalking me."

Trooper Bob mumbled something that sounded like, *Dumber than a box of rocks*.

I chose to ignore him. "Anyway, I didn't catch him because Brandy accosted me, and that's when we got into a . . . disagreement."

"Is that when you threatened to kill her?"

"I never threatened her."

"You deny telling her to 'drop dead'?" Trooper Bob watched me like a hawk.

I didn't need a mirror to know that I was blushing.

"I might have said it, but I wasn't threatening her."

"Do you tell all of your friends to drop dead?" Trooper Bob asked.

I wondered who overheard me and ratted me out to the state police. Darn it.

"Madison, I don't think you should answer any more questions," Chris Russell said. He turned to Trooper Bob. "Is my client under arrest?"

"Not yet, but she needs to stay in the area."

Chris Russell escorted me outside to my car. "Maddy, you're in big trouble. I hope you realize how much."

Thanks, Captain Obvious.

"I didn't kill Brandy Denton."

"Maybe not, but death row is full of men and women who all claim they're innocent. Trooper Bob has a lot of circumstantial evidence, but convictions have been made on less. Whatever you do, watch your step."

CHAPTER 20

Chris Russell's words rang through my mind for the entire drive home. *Death row is full of men and women who all claim they're innocent*. Holy freakin' Jimmy Choos. Death row. He said death row. The words sent a shiver through my body.

At home, I wasn't surprised to see Michael's car. I wasn't even surprised to see Leroy's or Tyler Lawrence's trucks. They were my friends. There was another car I didn't recognize, though. Who could be visiting this early in the morning?

Once I got out of the car and went into the house through the garage, Baby greeted me by standing on his hind legs, wrapping his paws around my neck, and giving my face a lick.

"Hey, do you mind?" Michael growled.

Baby glanced at him and got back down on all fours.

"Thank you." Michael moved Baby out of the way and then pulled me into his arms.

For a few moments, I stood there. His warmth and support enveloped me like a warm, cozy blanket. The wall I'd built around my emotions that kept me from collapsing like a rag doll in front of Trooper Bob slipped down. I wanted nothing more than to put my head on Michael's shoulder and sob. But, once I opened the floodgates and allowed the tears to flow, there would be no stopping them. So, I pushed myself away. I summoned the Admiral's voice as he barked orders to new Seaman recruits: "*Man up, Seaman!*" I took a deep breath.

Michael dropped his arms and stared. "Are we okay?"

I leaned up and gave him a quick kiss, careful not to linger. "Yes. We're good, but if I stop and think, I'll collapse like one of those inflatable Christmas decorations when it's out of air."

Michael nodded. "Okay, Sailor. Then, you better get to work."

I tilted my head to the side and stared. "There's no way Trooper Bob is going to let us open Baby Cakes today, and it's too late to do anything here."

When Great-Aunt Octavia originally started Baby Cakes, she'd converted a detached garage out front to be used as a roadside stand. When Baby Cakes was closed for renovations after a fire, I'd been able to notify customers that we were utilizing the original facilities. But, it was too late for that.

"I'm not talking about baking." Michael fought a grin.

My brain was still pretty fuzzy, and for the life of me, I had no idea what he was talking about. Eventually, he took pity on me.

"Your Baker Street Irregulars are in the dining room, ready for their assignments. So, come along Sherlock. It's time to get busy figuring out who killed Brandy Denton."

CHAPTER 21

I took several deep breaths and started walking toward the dining room, but right before I went in, Michael stopped me. "You may want to brace yourself first."

Brace myself? I stared and waited.

"You have a visitor."

"I noticed a strange car in the driveway. Who is it?"

"Alliyah . . . Dr. Howard. She heard about the murder and said she wanted to help. She's filling in for the medical examiner while he's out having his appendix removed, so I thought it might be helpful to have her around, but I can tell her to leave if—"

I held up my hand to halt him. "It's okay. I'm going to need all of the help I can get."

He stared at me for a few moments and then kissed me hard.

Hannah Portman stood at the doorway. "Hey! We need to get this party started before Barney Fife arrests Maddy."

"Yes, ma'am," we said.

Michael and I headed into the dining room, but Hannah wasn't done being bossy.

"Candy and her mom said they'd take Baby and Daisy for a long walk on the beach so we could meet in peace." She turned her gaze to Michael. "You better take his harness or he'll drag them straight into Lake Michigan."

"Yes, ma'am." Michael's lips twitched. The only indication that he'd battled a smile was the twinkle in his eyes when he looked at me.

The Baker Street Irregulars was the name Great-Aunt Octavia used for her close-knit group of friends: Tyler Lawrence, Leroy, Miss Hannah, and April. After April won the election as the New Bison's sheriff, the group began meeting regularly. April was a former beauty pageant contestant who'd fled a husband who saw her as a commodity he could trade in a business deal. Her skill in winning pageants served her well when it came to the election for sheriff. She won the election and learned the job, but she lacked confidence when it came to her knowledge and expertise in solving complex crimes. Confidence was something that my great-aunt had in abundance. She was a big mystery fan and loved reading and solving mysteries, which was one of the things we had in common. Although, there wasn't a lot of crime to keep the little gray cells stimulated in New Bison, Michigan. Most of the crime that happened in this sleepy little resort town on the shores of Lake Michigan was straightforward. For the occasional challenge, the group met here and put their heads together.

The dining room table was laden with food. One of the perks of owning a bakery was the abundance of baked goods. Leroy baked to relieve stress. Hannah had been baking since she was a small girl. As her dementia progressed, she was slowing down a bit but was still able to bake. We knew she would eventually have to stop, but baking was something she enjoyed. It was second nature and didn't require a recipe or a great deal of thought. It was as though her body knew what to do from years of practice. Michael referred to it as muscle memory.

When she was at home, Michael tried to keep an eye on her, and Leroy and I took turns watching out at Baby Cakes.

I sat down and filled my plate, but I knew better than to eat without waiting for Hannah to say grace.

I bowed my head, closed my eyes, and squinted at Dr. Alliyah Howard.

It was early, but her makeup was perfect. Her clothes were a couple of seasons old but were expensive by New Bison standards.

"Amen," Hannah said and turned to me. "Now, what can you tell us?"

I took a moment to swallow before responding. I quickly filled everyone in on the little bits of information that I knew. When I finished, Hannah stared at me in disbelief. "That's it?"

"Trooper Bob is a bit tight-lipped, but I suspect his key point is that I was one of the few people in New Bison who knew Brandy Denton."

"True. You knew her, and she stole your ex-fiancé," Tyler said. He looked up at me from his iPad where he had been taking notes. "Sorry."

"Maddy had a motive, and you claim to have been home alone with only Baby to alibi you, so technically you had the opportunity to kill her," Leroy said.

I stared at him. "Claimed?"

"I mean, I believe you, but without a person to corroborate . . ." Leroy's voice trailed off.

"Right." I shoved a croissant into my mouth and tried not to take any of this personally.

Alliyah frowned and glanced at me. "There's also the fact that she was found in your bakery."

"That doesn't mean anything," Tyler said. "Not with the tunnels."

"Tunnels?"

A light went on behind Tyler's eyes. "Most people aren't

aware of the underground tunnels that are in this area. Ever since we found the tunnel between Maddy's bakery and Candy's coffee shop, I've been scouring the town records."

"Fascinating." Alliyah leaned close. "What have you found?"

Dr. Howard had hit upon Tyler's newest favorite topic. Leroy groaned and rolled his eyes.

"We don't have a lot of definite proof, but the proximity to Lake Michigan has led many to believe the tunnels were probably created by smugglers."

"Smugglers? Like pirates?" Dr. Howard asked.

"Many of the caves and tunnels in this area were likely created eons ago. Native Americans were undoubtedly aware of them, but there's a theory that many were expanded during slavery by abolitionists to assist in hiding slaves who fled the South and were making their way to Canada. However, there are also indications that the caves and tunnels closest to Lake Michigan were used by bootleggers during Prohibition to hide and transport illegal liquor from Canada to Detroit and Chicago. We know for a fact that the notorious Purple Gang, which was originally called the Sugar House Gang, trafficked bootlegged liquor from Canada into Michigan using Lake Huron. Some even believe Al Capone may have used these tunnels and caves," Tyler said with enthusiasm.

Leroy's phone rang. Initially, I thought it was a ploy to avoid another lecture on the tunnels until he mumbled, "It's my mom."

In spite of the side-eye he got from Hannah, he stood up and slipped out of the room and into the kitchen.

"Wow, that's fascinating," Dr. Howard said. She gazed at Tyler as though he'd just given her the keys to eternal life.

"Isn't it? I've been researching old maps, and I've found—"

"Yeah, that's all great," Hannah said, "but we're not here to talk about tunnels and Al Capone. We're here to help Maddy."

From the moment Tyler started spending more and more

time with Candy, he'd been fascinated by the tunnel that linked Baby Cakes Bakery with Higher Grounds. He rarely missed an opportunity to share the knowledge he'd gained. Hannah, like the other Baker Street Irregulars, had heard him wax on and on about Al Capone many times before. I could understand his excitement at finding a new listener, but I still felt bad for him.

"Is it possible that's how Brandy got into the bakery?" I asked Tyler.

"It's possible. It looks as though the tunnels just lead between those two buildings, but there could be a secret wall." Tyler's eyes lit up.

"How would she know about the tunnels?" Hannah asked. "She was new to town."

I shrugged. "I have no idea, but I've been racking my brain to figure out how she got in the bakery. I know I locked the door when I left."

"That's a good question, and since Tyler is obsessed with the tunnels, then I think it would be a good idea if he looked into it," Hannah said.

I gave him my best damsel-in-distress look. "It could be important. Would you mind?"

"Absolutely." Tyler smiled.

"Okay, what other areas do you want us to investigate?" Hannah asked.

Leroy came back and sat down with a smile on his face and a light in his eyes. "I just heard some great news."

"I could use some great news right about now," I said.

"As you all know, my mom works at the Carson Law Inn. She just called and said—"

"Isn't your mom in England visiting her mother?" Hannah asked.

"She is, but I sent her a text after I found the body, so she wouldn't worry if she heard someone was murdered at Baby Cakes," Leroy said.

"That's nice, but what could she know about the murder? She was in England long before Brandy came to town," Hannah said.

"True, but she reached out to some of her coworkers at the Carson Law Inn, and you'll never guess what she found out." Leroy gazed around the room, but none of us had any guesses. After a few beats, he continued. "She heard from Louise Hamilton, one of the maids, that Brandy Denton got in a big argument with someone who was staying at the Carson Law."

"Really?" I said. "Well, Brandy could be a real shrew when she wanted to be. Don't tell me, the sheets at the Carson Law weren't Charlotte Thomas?"

"Who is Charlotte Thomas?" Tyler asked.

"She's a famous designer of bedding and linen. She makes the most luxurious sheets."

"Never heard of them," Hannah said. "What's so special about Charlotte Thomas sheets?"

"They're handmade, so it takes three months to get them. They're made with Merino wool, backed by silk Jacquard, and added to a thousand-thread-count Egyptian cotton. Oh, and they have twenty-two-karat gold woven into them."

"Gold?" Tyler said. "You're making that up."

I shook my head.

"What's a pair of those cost?" Leroy asked.

"Around twenty-four hundred," I said.

Tyler took a sip of juice and nearly choked. He coughed while Leroy gave him several loud smacks on the back. When he could speak, he asked, "Dollars?"

I nodded.

"What's the point?" Hannah asked.

I shrugged. "They're luxurious."

"They darned well better be for that price," Hannah said. "What's anyone need twenty-two-karat gold sheets for?"

"I've heard they're very comfortable," Dr. Howard said.

Hannah shook her head. "Loads of nonsense if you ask me."

"I'd be afraid to drool on anything that expensive," Leroy said.

I swiped my phone and found the website and held up my phone. My friends were awed by the expensive sheets, but Dr. Howard wrote down the address. After a few moments, the intrigue of expensive bedding ended. "So, if it wasn't about the sheets, what was Brandy's problem with the Carson Law Inn?" I asked.

"She wasn't arguing with the staff," Leroy said. "As far as I know, she wasn't even staying there. She was staying at one of those new hotels that looked out over the beach. According to Louise Hamilton, Brandy Denton found out someone she knew was staying at the Carson Law. That's who she fought with."

There was a gleam in Leroy's eyes when he leaned close and said, "Apparently, she ran into an ex of both of yours. Elliott."

CHAPTER 22

"Elliott? Elliott Lawson?" I forced the words out of my mouth.

"Mom had Louise check the guest list, and there's a Dr. Elliott Lawson registered at the Carson Law Inn in room two thirty-four."

This was not computing. *Elliott. Here in New Bison. Why? Does it matter? No. It doesn't.* I shook my head like Baby. "Maybe he wanted to get back together with her."

Leroy was shaking his head before the words were out of my mouth.

"Why not?" I asked.

"Because he wasn't alone," Leroy said.

"What?" My brain was really not working well. "Who?"

"Louise didn't know a lot about the woman who was sharing his room, but she says there was definitely a woman there." Leroy smiled.

"That's strange. I wonder why he came to New Bison with another woman?" I said.

Tyler stared at his plate as though he'd never seen one before. However, it was clear that his mind was elsewhere.

I waved my hands in front of his face to get his attention. "Earth to Tyler!"

"Sorry. I was just thinking of something Candy mentioned. She said there was a woman who dressed like Maddy and Brandy who came into the coffee shop." He stopped abruptly, and a deep red crept up his neck.

"What do you mean, she dressed like me?" I asked.

Tyler slumped in his seat and avoided eye contact. After a few moments, he swallowed hard. "She could tell that the woman's clothes were expensive. Plus, she wore a lot of makeup. Not that you wear a lot of makeup . . . well, not anymore, but when you first arrived, you wore quite a bit . . . Maybe it wasn't a lot. It was just the false eyelashes and the long nails and . . . Not that you didn't look great. You looked beautiful. You still look beautiful . . . I just meant—"

I held up a hand to stop him. "Tyler, it's okay."

"Open mouth and insert foot," Leroy muttered.

He gave me a sheepish glance. "Sorry."

"It's okay. Just tell us what Candy said. The person wore expensive clothes and a lot more makeup than most people in New Bison?" I asked.

Tyler nodded. "She could tell she wasn't from here by looking at her, but when she opened her mouth and spoke, Candy knew she wasn't from here. She had an accent."

"Did she know what type of accent? Was it Spanish? French? German?" I thought I had a good idea of who was here in New Bison with Elliott, but I didn't want to jump to conclusions.

"She said it sounded European, but she couldn't swear to it." Tyler looked hopeful. "Does that help?"

"Actually, it does." I smiled.

"You look like a cat in a field of catnip," Hannah said.

"If it's who I think it is, then our job may have just gotten a lot easier."

"Are you gonna tell us who it is? Or are you just going to sit there grinning like a Cheshire cat?"

"Galina Forkin. Her parents were famous dancers in the Bolshoi Ballet who moved to the United States when she was in grade school."

"Fine, but what does she have to do with Brandy Denton?" Leroy asked.

"Brandy and Galina's rivalry was bigger than anything that went on between Brandy and me." I swiped my phone until I found Galina's Instagram. I held it out for everyone to see.

Hannah frowned. "They're hugging as though they're best friends."

"Ah, you didn't read the comments." I turned the phone around and found several of the snarkiest comments and read them out loud.

Pea green isn't Brandy's color, but I love that she doesn't let that stop her from wearing it. #PukeIsn'tAGoodColorOnYou #JealousOrJustMotionSick? #FriendsDontLetFriendsWearPuke Green.

"Ouch!"

I scrolled until I found another good example. "Here's one from Brandy's page from last January."

Do they celebrate Halloween in Russia in January? Or is Galina Forkin just having a really bad hair day? #ScareCrowHair #DontLickTheLightSocket #EinsteinWasNotAFashionRoleModel.

"That's just mean," Hannah said.

"Especially while pretending to be friends. That's cold." Leroy rubbed his arms as if attempting to warm himself.

"Why are you smiling?" Dr. Howard asked.

"Because Galina is a big-city girl. There's only one thing that could drag her out of L.A. Don't you see?" I glanced around at all of the blank faces.

"Nope." Everyone shook their heads and waited.

"Galina would only leave L.A. to come to a small town like New Bison for a *really good reason.*"

"Like what?" Dr. Howard asked.

"Like if she had an opportunity to rub Brandy's nose in the fact that she was now with Elliott. I mean, Elliott's last two girlfriends are here in one place. Of course, she doesn't hate me as much as she hates Brandy, but still . . . it would be a major slam dunk if she could get a picture with the three of us together."

Hannah shivered. "She sounds vicious."

"Plus, if Galina is with Elliott, that makes things even more interesting."

"Okaaay," Tyler said. "Why?"

"That means Trooper Bob has someone other than me who might have wanted Brandy Denton dead."

CHAPTER 23

"Good point."

I didn't realize April had come in until she spoke. She looked exhausted and collapsed onto the nearest chair.

Hannah poured her a cup of coffee, and Leroy filled a plate with pastries and slid it across to her. Food was definitely his love language.

"You look like death warmed over," Hannah said.

"Thanks." April sipped her coffee.

I was bouncing in my seat. "Did you hear everything? There are at least two other people in New Bison who knew Brandy Denton and might have wanted her dead. Three if you count Brandy's assistant."

"What assistant?" April asked.

I explained my theory that Brandy must have brought her personal assistant along with her to make sure she captured the video of us arguing.

"Who is this assistant?" April asked.

"Her name's Jessica Barlow. She's mean, ambitious, and would sell her soul to have Brandy's following. She'd love to knock Brandy off her pedestal."

"Why work for her if she hated her?" Tyler asked.

"Jessica is a Southern Belle who moved to L.A. to become famous. But making it in L.A. isn't easy, especially if you didn't grow up there. The ones at the top all went to the same schools. They belong to the same clubs. It's hard for an outsider to break through the ranks. Jessica needed someone to make the introductions. I suspect she took a job working for Brandy so she could get invited to the right parties. Meet the right people. You know, get her foot in the door."

"Okay, but then why would she want her dead? It sounds like she needed Brandy," April said.

That took me a few moments. "Maybe she didn't need her anymore."

"I can ask one of the guys to check the beachfront hotels to see if there's anyone named Jessica Barlow staying there," April said.

"Did you hear the other part of our conversation? About Galina and Elliott?"

"I heard."

"Could you check them out?" I asked.

"I'll make sure that Trooper Bob knows about Galina and Elliott before they have a chance to leave town. I'm not allowed to work the case. Apparently, I'm too close to the primary suspect." April gave me a pointed look.

"Don't tell me they've suspended you again?" Hannah asked.

"No, but I've been told in no uncertain terms that I am to stay as far away from this murder as possible." April sighed.

"Who told you that?" Tyler said. "You're an elected official. When I joined the town council, I started looking up rules and ordinances. Did you know that you don't *technically* report to the town council? As an elected official, you report directly to the citizens who elected you."

"True, but New Bison's weird. Technically, the sheriff should be over the entire county and not just a small town the size of New Bison. Plus, the police department is usually separate from the sheriff's department. However, my predecessor, Sheriff Harper, was a man with a lot of power. He had the two offices combined into one, which is why I have authority over the New Bison Police Department."

"Such as it is," Hannah mumbled.

April grinned. "It's only ten people, but they're good people. They love this town, and they work hard." She paused for several beats. "Anyway, when I defeated Harper and became the sheriff, I learned that part of the agreement he'd made for the police department meant that he would take direction from the mayor."

"But the mayor's dead," I said. "Geez. Not only is the mayor dead, but the interim mayor's dead, too."

"Right," Tyler said. "We don't even have enough people for a quorum, so the governor is going to take over until we can get an election set up. We're moving as quickly as possible, but there are rules about the length of time that candidates have to file applications and the length of time that public notices have to be posted. It's a lot."

April nodded. "In the meantime, the governor's sending two people to help get everything organized, and I've been assigned to robbery detail."

"Robbery?" I said. "In New Bison? I didn't know New Bison had a robbery detail."

"We don't," April said.

"Then what? How?" I couldn't find the words to express my frustration. April shouldn't be removed from doing her job simply because of me. This sounded like a made-up job to get her out of the way.

"There have been some art thefts in Chicago, and they think the stolen merchandise is following the I-94 corridor."

"What's that?" I asked.

"Interstate 94 is the east-west freeway that connects the Great Lakes with the Great Plains. Law enforcement sees a lot of drugs and illegal activities with criminals moving between Detroit and Chicago," April explained.

"Just like the Sugar House Gang," Tyler said. He sat up in his seat, prepared to launch into another discussion about smuggling and tunnels.

Hannah held up a hand to halt his enthusiasm. "Hold up. We're not going down that path again. Besides, that was mostly on the water."

Tyler deflated like a balloon.

"Usually, it's drugs I worry about, not art, but I guess it's all part of the job," April said. "It'll be my first time working with the FBI, but I wish I was going to be helping Maddy." She sipped her coffee.

Dr. Howard knocked over a glass of water, and everyone scrambled to clean up the spill.

"I'm sorry. I didn't mean to . . . all of this is just so fascinating," Dr. Howard said. "Murder and art theft? But what's the FBI's involvement?"

"I don't know much yet. I just got assigned to the project about . . . an hour ago." April paused. "There have been several high-profile art heists from private collections. Local law enforcement got a tip that maybe the thieves were transporting the stolen goods using the interstate to get the goods farther away from the center of activity. Authorities at all of the ports in Chicago are on the lookout for the stolen objects, but no one around here would be looking for them. So, they're pulling in more local law enforcement in small towns up and down the interstate to help." She shrugged.

"How terribly exciting. What's—"

"Yeah, that's all interesting, but we're not here to talk about lost art," Hannah said. "We're here to help keep Maddy out of jail." She turned to me. "Now, who else might have wanted to kill Brandy Denton?"

"We have Jessica Barlow, Galina Forkin, and Elliott Lawson."

"And?" Hannah asked.

"Isn't that enough? I'm really liking them as suspects. Galina hated Brandy, and I think twenty years behind bars would do Elliott a world of good. Nothing would give me more pleasure than to have him arrested for Brandy's murder."

Silence covered the room like a wet blanket.

I looked around the room as my friends avoided making eye contact. Eventually, Hannah leaned forward. "Look, we ain't got time to pussyfoot around your feelings. If these are the only suspects, we're in trouble. Galina and Elliott are just going to alibi each other, and we don't even know for sure that this Jessica Barlow person is here. Am I right?" Hannah looked at April.

April nodded.

"Right. So, we'll investigate them, but we're going to need to come up with someone else, besides you, who hated her enough to kill her."

Hannah spoke the truth, but it didn't make it easier to hear.

"Now, let's figure out who else might have done it," Hannah said.

"Couldn't it have been some deranged lunatic who was traveling through town on I-94?" Dr. Howard said. "He got hungry and stopped to eat in New Bison. He spots Brandy Denton and is filled with passion, but she scoffs at his approach. Enraged, he kills her." She smiled as though she'd just figured out who D. B. Cooper was and where the rest of the money was buried.

There was a long silence.

"He kills Brandy Denton and hides her body in Baby Cakes Bakery?" Leroy said.

"Oh . . . I guess he would need to be a local to know about the tunnel," Dr. Howard said.

Something she said lit a spark in my brain. "Maybe not."

Hannah stared at me. "Don't tell me you're buying into that deranged stranger nonsense. You're too smart for that."

"Well, not exactly, but Dr. Howard made me think of something."

"Please call me Alliyah," she said.

"Alliyah." I gave her a big smile, hoping that it would make up for Hannah's rudeness. "I was thinking about the blue-eyed stranger that I've seen hanging around Baby Cakes."

"Blue-eyed stranger?" Alliyah asked.

I pulled up the photo on my phone and explained that I'd seen him all over town, but when I approached him, he took off.

Hannah was last to look at the photo. She glanced at the photo and said, "That's no stranger. That's Oliver Freemont."

We all turned to stare at Hannah.

"Who's Oliver Freemont?" I asked, but one look into Hannah's eyes and I knew she wouldn't be able to tell me.

"I have no idea. Now, who are you?" Hannah asked.

CHAPTER 24

Hannah's memory lapses came and went in this early stage. When she was tired or stressed, she frequently experienced memory lapses. Eating properly and resting often helped, and we'd been amazed that after a brief rest, she would usually be almost back to normal. I knew Michael was worried. Her memory lapses were occurring more frequently, and she wasn't snapping out of them as quickly as she once had. Still, we found that even when resting didn't resolve the issue, it at least helped.

April got Hannah comfortable in one of the guest bedrooms. Leroy and Tyler went to the kitchen to get refills and remove some of the platters, leaving Alliyah and me at the table alone.

"Does that happen often?" she asked.

"Mostly when she's tired." She knew what Hannah's diagnosis was, and she was a doctor. She undoubtedly knew more about her condition than me. While Hannah's diagnosis wasn't a secret, I didn't like talking about it with her.

"It's not easy living with someone with dementia. That was just one of the reasons Michael and I broke up."

"What? Why would that matter?"

"Don't get me wrong, I like Hannah, but . . . That's not entirely accurate." She chuckled. "The truth is, I tried to like her. It's hard to like someone who doesn't like you. No matter what I did, she just never liked me. I have no idea why." She shrugged. "I guess it's just one of those things old people get in their heads."

Maybe they resent being called "old people."

"Anyway, I was as nice as could be, but nothing I did mattered. I tried to stick it out with Michael. It was just a matter of time before he'd have to put her into a nursing home. I told him that, but he just didn't want to face the facts." Another shrug.

Of course he doesn't want to put his grandmother in a nursing home. She helped raise him.

"I'm sure Michael will do what's best for her when that time comes, but family is important to him."

"Yes, but as a doctor—well, a veterinarian—he has to know there's no hope. She's just going to get worse and worse until eventually she can't remember him at all. He can't put his life on hold to care for someone who won't even remember his name in a few months or years."

Something snapped, and I felt a rage build up inside, and I unleashed it. "First, Michael *is* a doctor. A veterinarian is a doctor—"

"I know, I was—"

"Second, Miss Hannah is a wonderful woman who helped to raise him when his mother died and his father was deployed. He loves her. It doesn't matter if she remembers his name or not. *He* remembers. He remembers all the sacrifices she made to take care of him. He—"

"I didn't mean—"

"I'm not finished." I held up a hand. "I think it's wonderful that Michael is willing to put his family above his career. And if you can't see how special that makes him, then you're blind as well as heartless."

There was a moment's pause and then applause.

I turned, and that's when I saw Michael, Leroy, and Tyler standing at the door to the dining room.

Michael walked over and kissed me. "And that is why I love this woman."

"I didn't know you were standing there," I said. "How much of that did you hear?"

"Enough."

It isn't easy to make a Black woman blush, but Dr. Howard was blushing. "I think you misunderstood my point. I wasn't—"

"No. I didn't misunderstand. I understood you perfectly. Now, understand me. I think it will be best if you left my home."

After a bit of fumbling, Dr. Howard gathered her things together. She stood up and rushed to the door. At the dining room door, she turned and said, "I'm sorry."

"Well, you told her," Leroy said as the front door closed. He and Tyler high-fived before sitting down.

April entered and glanced around. "What just happened?"

"The Queen of Snobbery made some disparaging remarks about Miss Hannah," Tyler said.

Leroy snapped his fingers. "And Maddy told her about herself and then tossed her royal snootiness out on the street."

I buried my face in my hands.

Michael squatted down beside my seat. "What's wrong, Squid?"

"Other than the fact that I just insulted the doctor filling in for the medical examiner while he's out, the person who might just decide to get even by saying she found my fingerprints all over Brandy Denton's liver, so obviously I must have murdered her, I also insulted your new business partner. Now, she won't work with you, and I'll never get to see you again."

Michael pulled my hands away from my face. "Alliyah Howard *is* a snob. She's selfish, materialistic, and vain. That's why I broke up with her. We don't want the same things out of life."

Materialistic, selfish, and vain. Those were the same words that Elliott used to describe me after he dumped me at the altar.

"She's all of those things, but she's also a good doctor. She takes her oath seriously. She won't manufacture evidence that isn't there. Besides, I may just be a veterinarian and not a 'real doctor,' but I'm pretty sure you can't get fingerprints off a liver, even if your fingerprints did somehow manage to get on Brandy Denton's," he joked.

"You know what I mean."

"I do. I also know Alliyah. She's all about business and the Benjamins. Partnering with me is good business. She can walk into a practice that's already established. She can piggyback off my name and reputation without having to go through all of the years and the money it takes to build up her own client base. I'm sure she'll still want to partner with me—that is, if you're okay with it."

I flung my arms around his neck in response.

CHAPTER 25

"Now, that's settled," Michael said, "what did I miss?"

It took a few minutes to fill him in.

"Leroy is going to have his mom check if the woman with Elliott is Galina," I said. "Tyler's going to look into the tunnels to see if there's some way to get into Baby Cakes from outside. April is going to get one of the cops to see if Jessica Barlow is in town."

"What do you want me to do?" Michael asked.

"I have several tasks for you. First, I was hoping you might be able to use your connections with Trooper Bob to find out what's going on with him," I said.

"My connections? Are you joking? I nearly throttled him today. There's no way he's going to let me close to this investigation."

"But what happened to the kitten?"

"What?"

"The kitten Brandy adopted? You know, the one in the picture she snapped with you to make me jealous. What happened to it?" I asked.

He blinked. "I have no idea. I suppose it's in her hotel room."

"When you show up at Brandy's hotel, you can mention it to Trooper Bob. Then, when he gives you the kitten, you can do a little surveillance."

Michael sighed. "Fine, what else?"

"Miss Hannah mentioned the name Oliver Freemont. Do you think you could find out who he is and why he's here?"

"I'll do my best. What's the last thing?"

"Did you call the Admiral?"

Michael nodded. "He wasn't happy, but he said he'll be here by five. He's commandeering a seat on a Clipper."

"What's a Clipper?" Leroy asked.

"A C-40 Clipper. It's a transport plane for VIPs in the Navy and the Air Force. Imagine a 737 with all of the luxuries," Michael said.

"Good. Then, the last thing I need you to do is to keep my dad from taking out Trooper Bob."

"What will you be doing?"

I squirmed but I knew it was coming. "I'm going to talk to Elliott."

Michael revved up to object, but I held up a hand to stop him.

"Look, I need to talk to him alone. I can't explain it, but it's something that I need to do, and I need you to trust me. I'm over him. I just need to talk to him. That's all."

Michael reached over and squeezed my hand. "I do trust you, but it could be dangerous. He could be the killer."

"I'll only talk to him when there are other people around. I'll be careful. I promise." I smiled. "I'll even bring Baby."

CHAPTER 26

Assignments were doled out, and we talked a little longer. Eventually, we needed to get busy with our investigations and disbanded.

Before I forgot, I uploaded a picture I found on my phone of the bakery and notified our patrons that the store was closed due to a tragic accident, but the original location would be open for business on Tuesday.

#YouCantKeepAGoodBakerDown #BabyCakesDownButNotOut #FreeBlondieWithEveryPurchase

When Miss Hannah woke up, she didn't remember Michael's name. However, she thought he looked nice and agreed to let him take her home. I almost missed the hurt that flashed across his face. It came and went so quickly. Instead of forcing names and memories, he tried to accept her wherever she was. Today, she remembered his dad and mentioned that he looked like him. He smiled and told her that he heard that a lot.

When they left, I had a nearly uncontrollable desire to track down Alliyah Howard and beat her. Miss Hannah's mental state may not have been Dr. Howard's fault, but her callous disregard for all that Michael was losing made me want to square up.

Instead, I went upstairs and went through my closet. If I was going to see my ex-fiancé, I certainly was not going dressed in jeans, tennis shoes, and a Baby Cakes Bakery T-shirt. I didn't love Elliott, and I certainly didn't want him back. However, I did want him to regret his decision, and that was going to require an entirely different uniform.

Choosing an outfit that accentuated my finer points without seeming as though I was trying to impress wasn't easy. By the time I finished, my bed was covered in discards. Eventually, I realized that my outfit not only needed to make Elliott regret dumping me but also make Galina jealous. I landed on a blue mesh Coperni asymmetrical minidress, which used ruching to create a figure-flattering style that hugged my hips. The back panel was cut out below my shoulder blades and had a crisscross neckline. I was curvy and more endowed up top, whereas Galina had the slim, flatter body of a ballerina.

I took extra care with my makeup and hair and slipped on a pair of Amina Muaddi Gilda crystal-embellished shoes that matched my dress perfectly. I took a final glance in the mirror.

I admired the image I saw reflected back. "Not bad."

Baby sat up on the bed and stared at me.

"What do you think? Does this outfit say, '*You were a fool to walk out on me, but I've moved on, so eat dirt, loser?*'"

Woof!

I chuckled. "Thanks for the vote of confidence. Well, we better get this over with before my courage fails. Come on, boy."

Baby hopped down off the bed and followed me to the door and out of the room.

* * *

At the Carson Law Inn, I put Baby's harness on, looked him in the eyes, and had a serious conversation with him.

"Look, I know you were just here yesterday." *Was it only yesterday that we were enjoying a pleasant afternoon with Carson Law, and Brandy Denton was alive and as mean as ever?*

"Today, I need you to be on your best behavior. Okay?"

Baby tilted his head to the side and gave me a look that said, *I have no idea what you mean.*

We walked into the front door of the Carson Law Inn. I bypassed the maître d' and walked around the corner to the reception area. Standing at the counter was a man wearing sunglasses and a baseball cap. He kept the brim of the hat pulled down so it hid the upper part of his face, but I'd recognize those curly frosted locks anywhere.

I took a deep breath and sauntered up to the counter. "Elliott. I heard you were here."

At the mention of his name, he turned around. He slid his sunglasses down, tilted his head down, and stared. "Madison? Madison Montgomery, is that you?"

I could tell by the gleam in his eyes that my outfit was a success. *The jerk.* I pushed all thoughts of hatred and vengeance to the back of my head, plastered a smile on my face, and strolled to the reception desk.

He reached out as though to pull me into an embrace, but Baby growled.

"I don't think Baby likes you very much. Perhaps we should skip the hugs."

Elliott backed off and stared. "That's some guard dog."

"This is Baby. He's usually very friendly. I don't know why he doesn't care for you, though," I said as innocently as I could without choking on the lies.

Elliott turned his attention back to me. He looked me up

and down, giving me the same look he'd once given a sports car he wanted to buy. He grinned in approval. "But, with a body like that, you need a killer dog to fight off the men."

I swallowed several responses that would indicate which bridges I would like to toss him from and forced another smile. "I heard about Brandy, and I had to come and express my condolences."

That froze the smile on his lips. "Condolences?"

I gasped. "Oh no. I assumed you knew. News travels fast in a small town, so I thought you knew. Brandy was murdered last night."

He fumbled with his sunglasses, room keys, and car keys. *My, my. All thumbs now, aren't we?*

His gaze darted around the lobby. An older couple was waiting to check out, so Elliott stepped aside to allow them to move ahead of him. "Maybe we should move someplace a little more private to talk." He extended his arm to guide me toward a set of chairs near the window, but Baby growled again, and he retracted his arm.

"Baby!" I reached down as though reprimanding Baby, but when my lips were close to his ear I whispered, "Good boy. Remind me to give you a treat later."

I followed Elliott to the chairs and sat.

When we were both seated, Elliott crossed his leg over his knee and leaned back in a casual pose. "Now, what were you saying?"

"I was extending condolences. I know you and Brandy were close. I just wanted you to know that I don't harbor any ill feelings toward either of you. I mean, the heart has a mind of its own. You certainly can't control who you fall in love with."

"Look, Madison. I wanted to apologize for . . . you know, leaving you at the altar like that. I certainly didn't mean to humiliate you."

Oh yes, you did.

"Pish posh." I waved away his apology like a troublesome gnat. "You and Brandy were made for each other. Besides, it turns out you did me a favor. If you hadn't left, I wouldn't have come here and fallen in love with Michael." My cheeks hurt from forcing them into an unnatural expression when all I really wanted was to punch Elliott in the throat.

"How did you know I was here?" Elliott asked.

"I knew if Brandy was here, you couldn't be far away. I mean, a love like the two of you had was wonderful." I batted my eyelashes and fanned my face like a contestant in a beauty pageant trying to dry their tears.

Elliott rummaged around in his pockets until he found a handkerchief and then passed it across to me. "Actually, Brandy and I . . . we broke up."

"*No.* When? That must have been horrible for you." I paused and then gave him a shy smile. "Is that why you followed her here?"

"What? I didn't—"

"You can tell me. You heard Brandy was here, and you followed her all the way to New Bison to win her back." I clutched my heart. "That is the most romantic thing I've ever heard."

"No. It wasn't like that. I didn't follow her. I wasn't—"

"Elliott, what is taking so long? I'm ready to leave." Galina marched over to Elliott.

Galina Forkin was thin. I'd seen a picture of her as a young child. At one point, everything about her had been thin. That was until she discovered what nature hadn't given her, she could get for a price. Her lips were thin, but thanks to the marvels of modern medicine, she'd filled them to rival Mick Jagger's. Her blond hair had been thin, but she had a weave that was impossible to distinguish from her own. Her body was thin, too, but I'd heard a rumor that she wore extra padding to help provide curves.

Galina stopped and stared. "Madison."

I stood and stretched, allowing Galina to get the full effect, and then we leaned forward and air-kissed. "Galina. I had no idea you'd come to New Bison, too. It's like old home week."

"Madison. You look . . . Is that a Coperni?"

"Yes." I turned and struck a pose, knowing the mesh fabric wasn't hiding anything. All of my curves were entirely natural.

The look on Galina's face was worth every bit of effort.

"Are you here to offer your condolences, too?" I asked.

"Condolences?"

"For Brandy. I knew Elliott must be devastated."

"Elliott broke up with Brandy weeks ago." Galina reached up and planted a kiss on Elliott's cheek and then hooked her arm possessively through his.

"NO. Really?" I feigned surprise.

"I suppose it takes quite a while for news to make its way to a backwater like this." Galina glanced down her nose.

Backwater? How dare she. I wanted to wipe that smug, superior look off her face, but before I could think up a scathing retort, the doors to the Carson Law Inn were flung open, and in marched the naval brigade in the form of Admiral Jefferson Augustus Montgomery.

"Madison. What on earth is going on?"

"Dad. What are you doing here?"

"Me? What am I doing here? Michael called and said you were in trouble."

"Well, I know you were coming to town, but what are you doing *here?*" I leaned forward and whispered. "At the Carson Law Inn?"

The Admiral turned around as Michael walked in.

Michael stared at my dress but quickly turned and noticed Elliott and Galina. He may not have been a math major, but he quickly added up the situation. He walked over, kissed me, and placed a possessive arm around my waist.

Baby stood up and wagged his tail but otherwise contained himself.

"Elliott, this is Dr. Michael Portman." I turned to Michael, "Michael, this is Elliott Lawson and Galina Forkin."

Galina said, "It's Doctor—"

Michael extended a hand. "Sorry, Dr. Forkin."

The blood rushed up Galina's neck and all the way up to her hairline. "No . . . I'm not the doctor. Elliott is a doctor. It's Dr. Elliott Lawson."

I smiled. "Did I forget to include that? What was I thinking?"

Elliott and Michael shook hands. Michael was taller, broader, and much more handsome than Elliott. Galina definitely noticed.

"You both know my dad."

In his midfifties, the Admiral was still in excellent shape. He was six feet tall, and had dark eyes. His hair was short, with only the slightest sprinkling of gray. Thirty years in the military meant his posture was straight as a board. Dressed in his khaki service uniform, he reflected power and authority.

Elliott extended his hand. "Admiral."

The Admiral glanced at the hand as if it were a grenade, then did a quarter turn and glared at me. "Madison, explain what is going on and why is he here?"

I opened my mouth, but before any words came out, the rest of the platoon arrived. Trooper Bob wasn't as tall as the Admiral, and when the two stood side by side, the state trooper looked even more slovenly than usual.

"What's all this?" Trooper Bob asked.

He knew Michael, so I quickly introduced Elliott, Galina, and the Admiral.

Trooper Bob scowled at me and looked as though he were about to explode when Galina saved the day.

"Elliott, I'm ready to go home. Let's get out of here." Galina tugged on Elliott's arm.

"Hold it right there," Trooper Bob said. "Nobody's going anywhere until I get to the bottom of this mess." He turned to me and pointed a fat finger. "Start explaining!"

CHAPTER 27

We amassed a crowd of curious onlookers, and the manager must have gotten nervous and called for reinforcements.

"Ladies and gentlemen, should we move this into my office where we can be more comfortable?" Carson Law smiled broadly, but there was steel behind that smile that indicated she wasn't asking a question.

In a vintage, white V-neck, A-line dress covered in large, bright yellow flowers, Carson Law looked as though she'd just stepped off the front porch at Tara from *Gone with the Wind*. She turned to the Admiral and flashed a bright smile, placing a gloved hand on his arm. "This handsome man has to be Madison's father, the Admiral."

I was stunned when the Admiral did something I'd never seen him do before. He stuttered. "Ye—ah, yes . . . ah. . . . Yes, ma'am. I'm Admiral Jefferson Augustus Montgomery, but please call me Jeff."

On the arm of my father, Carson Law led the group around a corner and down a short corridor like the Pied Piper.

I stood staring at the back of the group.

"What's wrong?" Michael asked.

"What just happened? 'Call me Jeff'? Who was that man, and what did he do with my father?"

"Come on, we don't want to miss any of this." Michael led me along with the group.

Carson Law's office was a large room that had probably been a parlor for the family's private use in days gone by. Now, there was a small desk in a corner and a drafting table. There was also a sofa and several comfortable chairs.

Mrs. Law must have requested tea because before we were all seated, there was a soft tap on the door, and two waiters entered pushing carts loaded with tea, scones, and buttery pound cake.

Joel, one of the waiters who served us yesterday, brought in the dog bed Baby had used yesterday.

"You can place that bed right here next to me, Joel," Mrs. Law said. "Thank you."

Joel did as instructed, but before leaving, he passed Mrs. Law a tray with a large bone. "This is the largest bone the chef could find."

"Perfect." She smiled.

Baby knew that bone was for him and could barely contain his excitement. His back end wagged like a flag in the wind, and his jowls dripped drool like spaghetti.

"Baby, sit," she ordered.

It took every muscle in his body to sit and remain sitting. After a couple of false starts, he forced his butt to remain down long enough to earn his reward.

Carson Law glanced at me, and I nodded. Only then did she hand over the bone.

Baby grasped what appeared to be a large ham bone in his jaws, turned around three times in his bed, and then laid down and started working on his treat.

Carson Law looked fondly at Baby for a few moments before taking her tea. "Please help yourselves. I always find that conversations go a lot better with tea."

Regardless of what happens in my life, I'm sure I will never forget that tea. The Admiral kept stealing glances at Carson Law while sipping his tea and eating scones. However, more disconcerting was the image of Trooper Bob trying to discretely dispose of the wad of tobacco in his mouth while holding a delicate china cup and balancing a plate on his knee.

Galina looked stunned as though she was having tea with royalty.

"Now, Madison, perhaps you can tell us what's going on?" Carson Law asked.

I'd have rather walked on hot coals, but I'd had a few moments to think while the tea was being distributed, so I launched into my cover story. "Certainly. When I heard of the tragic murder of Brandy Denton, I immediately came to offer my condolences to Elliott."

"Why?" Trooper Bob asked. "Didn't he dump you?"

Galina snickered.

"Actually, Elliott did us a favor. If it hadn't been for him, we might never have found each other." Michael gazed into my eyes, and my insides melted.

"Isn't that romantic?" Mrs. Law asked.

Trooper Bob wasn't a romantic. "Right. So, you came to *thank* him for dumping you."

"It all seems like such a long time ago. Anyway, Elliott and Brandy Denton were much more suited for each other than Elliott and me." I smiled.

"So, you came here to offer your condolences," Trooper Bob said.

"Yes. I—"

"She's lying," Galina said. "Elliott dumped Brandy, just like he dumped her." She pointed at me. "She knew it. She had to know it. It was all over social media."

"That's true. I did know that they broke up, but when I found out Elliott was here in New Bison, I assumed he must have wanted to get back together with her. I mean, why else would he come here?"

"Good point." Trooper Bob turned his attention to Elliott. "Why *are* you here, Mr. Lawson?"

"It's Dr. Lawson," Galina corrected him.

"Excuse me. Dr. Lawson."

Elliott was never good at thinking on his feet. He glanced around the room like a scared, trapped rabbit. "Well, actually, coming here was Galina's idea."

"*It was not!*" Galina screeched. "You're the one who said I could score one over both Madison and Brandy if I got them both in a picture. You're the one who wanted to humiliate Madison *and* Brandy." Galina hopped up and paced from the sofa to the window. The angrier she got, the more pronounced her accent became. "This is all your fault."

"Why me?" I asked softly. "Why did you want to humiliate me?"

Elliott squirmed in his seat.

"Because you weren't crushed," Galina said. "He thought you'd be devastated after the way he treated you, but you weren't. Instead of rolling over and playing dead, you were strong. You left. You moved away and got your bakery and your dog and your handsome veterinarian boyfriend. Elliott didn't want a strong wife. He wanted a trophy he could pull out to show his friends for dinner parties and then shove back into the closet later. He said you would never be able to make a decision without him and would come crawling back to him like some—"

"Galina, shut up!" Elliott shouted.

"Excuse me," I said. I stood up and hurried out of that room as quickly as I could.

I ran outside and got in my car and drove far away from the Carson Law Inn.

CHAPTER 28

There were two things that had the power to calm me down whenever I was upset: the ocean and driving. When I was a small child and something upset me, the Admiral took me to the ocean. He used to say the ocean was in my blood. There was something about sitting on the beach or atop a naval destroyer and looking out on the waves that always brought me peace, no matter how angry the waves were. The second thing that brought me calmness was driving. When I got my license and was able to hit the road, I found it relaxing. Not the bumper-to-bumper gridiron of L.A. at rush hour, but the open roads, especially around the coasts. From the comfort of my car, I could crank up the music, roll down the windows, and fly along the interstate. Inside my car, I could scream or cry and no one would be the wiser. If you talked to yourself, anyone you passed would simply think you were singing or talking on your Bluetooth.

Michigan wasn't close to the ocean, but driving down Interstate 94 still provided a great outlet for screaming while careening seventy miles per hour through eight lanes of traffic. Interstate 94 bypassed all of the small towns in Southwest Michigan and provided a fast, straight path from one major city to another. Before the interstate was completed, the route from Michigan to Illinois and beyond was a meandering two-lane road called Red Arrow Highway. Red Arrow was a winding road that followed the Lake Michigan coastline and curved through small towns and villages with streetlights and stop signs that required drivers to slow down for pedestrians, school buses, and the occasional pet. Old-fashioned signs and merchandise pulled from windows and placed on the sidewalk enticed travelers to stop and patronize the local businesses. One weekend, April and I spent a lovely day stopping at antique stores, art galleries, and mom-and-pop diners that were dotted along the highway.

On autopilot, I drove east on I-94 to St. Joseph, Michigan. It wasn't far from New Bison, so I used the twenty-mile drive to scream and cry. This wasn't my first scream-fest, so Baby barely registered the difference. He popped his head up from the back seat, but whether by instinct or experience, he merely looked on. The first time he'd been in the car during one of my screaming, crying fits, he barked and howled to the point that I ended up pulling over to reassure him that I wasn't being attacked by some invisible lunatic and didn't need saving. Focusing on him got my mind off myself and my own troubles. One glance in the rearview mirror showed me that Baby was concerned but not distressed.

By the time I arrived in St. Joseph, I was all cried out and hoarse. I pulled off the interstate and followed the signs to Silver Beach, a small beach where I could sit on the sands and look out over Lake Michigan toward Chicago. It wasn't the Pacific, but in a pinch, it worked just fine.

My phone rang nonstop. Michael's, my dad's, and even April's faces popped up periodically. I didn't want anyone to worry, so I sent a message that I was fine and would respond soon, and eventually the calls stopped.

I have no idea how long Baby and I sat on the beach. It was early April and still cool, so there weren't many people enjoying the frigid water or the cold breeze coming off the lake. It took quite some time before the wind cooled my mood to the point where I could feel anything other than anger. Sitting on the beach, looking across the lake soothed my soul. I shivered. My mesh dress was beautiful but completely unsuitable for April in Michigan.

I glanced at Baby, who was lying on the sand with his head in my lap. "Are you ready to go home?"

Baby lifted his head and yawned and then gave himself a shake.

"I take that as a yes." I scratched his ear. "It will be good to go home. Michael, the Admiral, and April will be there. We can look at Lake Michigan from the bluffs behind our house if we want, right?"

Baby barked.

I snapped a picture of him standing on the sand against a backdrop of the lake and St. Joe's lighthouse.

#DetoursOftenLeadToBetterPlaces #NotThePathIThoughtI Wanted #SoMuchBetter #Grateful #WaterIsInMyBlood #LoveMy Baby

I turned around and found myself face-to-face with the Blue-Eyed Stranger.

CHAPTER 29

"Stop right there or my dog will rip your throat out," I said.

Baby bound around me and leaped in the air.

The Blue-Eyed Stranger was thin, and Baby had at least a hundred pounds on the man. Blue Eyes fell to the ground under Baby's weight. He lay flat on his back with two hundred pounds of dog on his chest.

I pulled out my phone and prepared to dial 9-1-1. That's when I heard laughter.

"Baby, stop," Blue Eyes said, chuckling. "That tickles."

Instead of ripping out the man's throat, Baby was licking every inch of his face and neck.

"Ow. You've packed on some weight since the last time I saw you." The two wrestled on the ground for a few moments, and then the man flipped over and was able to extract himself from the mastiff, who was drooling with his chest down and butt in the air, indicating that he wanted to play.

The Blue-Eyed Stranger smiled and then reached into his pocket.

I pressed SEND on my phone and heard the 9-1-1 operator say, "What's your emergency?"

Blue Eyes pulled a rubber ball from his jacket pocket. "Is this what you want?" He held up the ball, which sent Baby into a drooling frenzy.

Woof!

Blue Eyes tossed the ball out toward the water.

Baby galloped off after the ball.

"9-1-1 What's your emergency?"

"Wrong number. Sorry." I hung up the phone and looked over this strange man.

Up close, I was able to see that he was older than I had originally thought. He was probably in his mid- to late forties. He was about five feet seven and had vibrant blue eyes, long dark hair that he wore pulled back into a ponytail, and a goatee. Obviously, he knew Baby, and Baby knew him.

"Why have you been stalking me?"

"I'm not stalking you, Maddy. I'm following you. Not stalking. There's a difference." He wrestled the ball out of Baby's mouth and hurled it again. "Stalking sounds bad, like I want to harm you. I don't want to harm you."

"Really?"

"Let me introduce myself. My name's—"

"Oliver Freemont."

That froze the smile off his face. "You know who I am."

"No. I know your name, but I don't know who you are or why you've been *following* me." I used air quotes to emphasize following.

He had flung the ball several times. This time when he brought it back, Baby dropped the ball and sat down, panting.

I glanced around and saw a water fountain nearby. "I need to get some water for Baby."

While I didn't have a bowl, this wasn't our first excursion. I held the lever, and Baby stood on his hind legs, leaned forward, and lapped up the water. When he was full, he ambled over to the trash receptacle, hiked his leg, and relieved himself.

There was a park bench near the water fountain. I sat.

"Okay, Oliver Freemont. You know my name. Clearly, you know my dog. But I have no idea who you are. So, why don't you tell me who you are and why you've been following me?" I folded my arms across my chest and waited.

"I was a friend of your great-aunt Octavia's. She sent me to find you."

"Alrighty. Well, it's been nice meeting you. You can tell Great-Aunt Octavia that you found me. Mission accomplished. Now, I'm leaving. Give my regards to Mother Teresa and Joan of Arc. Let's go, Baby." I stood and started walking toward my car.

"Maddy, I'm not crazy."

"I never said you were. Baby, get in the car." I held open the back door while Baby climbed inside. Then, I got behind the wheel and started the motor.

"Before she died, she gave me a package for you!" he yelled through my window.

That made me stop. Great-Aunt Octavia had left a lot of things for me, mostly messages and notes. She made videos in which she alluded to some big secret she'd uncovered. I'd watched and rewatched all of the videos in the hopes that I could gain a clue as to what it was. But she never said. Great-Aunt Octavia had become paranoid. She believed one of her friends, someone in her inner circle, was spying on her. She claimed she had a "spy in the camp," but never mentioned who the spy was. In fact, I'm not sure she even knew who it was. If there was anyone spying on her. But, this made sense. If she thought there was someone she couldn't trust in her close-knit group of friends, and she wanted to get a package to me, then maybe she would give it to someone else. Someone no one would suspect. I rolled down the window. "Great-Aunt Octavia's been dead for months. Why are you just coming to give me the package now?"

"I've been out of the country. I didn't even know she'd died until a couple of weeks ago. Octavia was an amazing woman and a good friend." Oliver Freemont took a deep breath. "Look, could we start this over?" He extended his hand, indicating he wanted me to get out and go back to the bench. He held up both hands. "Five minutes?"

Should I get out of the car and listen to what he has to say? Just because he knew Great-Aunt Octavia doesn't mean he isn't a serial killer. But, he might have the missing piece of the puzzle. Maybe she told him who she suspected was spying on her. Or, he might just be a crazy person who stopped by the bakery for Chocolate Soul Cake. But, Baby liked him. I turned off the engine, grabbed my Taser from my glovebox, and got out of the car. I opened the door and let Baby out and walked to the seat and sat. "Okay, you have five minutes. Make one move toward me and I'll zap you like a bug zapper."

He grinned and held up both hands to show he wasn't going to try anything that would get him zapped.

"Miss Octavia was a wonderful woman. She used to bake these shortbread cookies that she dipped in chocolate." He closed his eyes and moaned. "They were amazing. Everything she baked was amazing."

"You don't have much time. I suggest you get to the point."

"Right. So, I'm an artist—a painter. I used to come to New Bison every summer to hang out and paint. I didn't have a lot of money, so I'd sleep on the beach. I'd leave early before anyone had time to call the police to report a vagrant, but one morning I overslept, and she found me. I had a fever. This was before the pandemic when everyone learned to be frightened of sick people who had fevers and were coughing. Octavia dragged me up the stairs and put me in one of her guest rooms. She nursed me and shoved so much homemade chicken soup down my throat that I still have trouble eating chicken." He smiled at the memory but then hurried on. "Anyway, when my fever broke and I was well enough to leave, she loaded me down with bread, cookies, cakes, and sandwiches. After that, things started to change for me. I sold some artwork and some important people started to notice. I credit that change to Miss Octavia. She was my guardian angel. Anyway, I started getting work all over. I traveled the world. We stayed in touch. I sent postcards to her from Greece, Paris, and Switzerland. One day, I got a package. There was a letter telling me that she'd discovered some 'funny business' in New Bison and it had her worried."

"Did she say what it was?"

He shook his head. "She only said she'd crossed the wrong folks, but she wasn't worried. She had Baby, and if it was her time, then the Good Lord would take her home. But she was worried. She left her property to her great-niece, and she— "

I smiled. "It's okay. She didn't think I had the sense God gave a turnip?"

He chuckled. "No. She said you were smart—book smart. But these people were dangerous. She said something about a 'spy in the camp.' She didn't want to leave the package lying around where anyone could get it. So, she sent it to me. If anything happened to her, she wanted me to see that you got the package."

"Where is it?" I asked.

He hesitated for several beats. "Look, I firmly believe that Miss Octavia saved my life. She was a lovely woman, but . . . but all this talk about a 'spy in the camp' sounded a bit . . . well . . ."

"A bit cuckoo for Coco Puffs?"

"Yeah. Anyway, I thought I'd come and check things out for myself. Check you out. It was hard to get a chance to talk to you alone. I mean, I wasn't sure who the spy was. Everyone in New Bison knew Miss Octavia. They all loved her. Or they loved her baking." He laughed. "Seriously, I just couldn't imagine anyone deliberately doing anything to hurt her. I was worried. I talked to her lawyer, Chris Russell."

"Worried about what?"

He avoided eye contact but eventually continued. "I wondered if she might be suffering from some type of paranoia or dementia. Like Miss Hannah."

"What did he say?"

"He never got a chance to respond. Anyway, there were some unusual things going on."

"Unusual how?"

"People hanging out on the beach who shouldn't have been there and strange lights at night. That real estate developer, Bradley Something-Or-Other, was always trying to get her to sell. It's a nice piece of property, but the amount of money he was offering her was outrageous. You could have bought a jet. No way property in New Bison was worth that. That's what made her suspicious. Most people—myself included—would have taken the money and ran, but not Miss Octavia. Anyway, I didn't believe it at first, but then I saw that woman who was murdered down on the beach."

"Brandy Denton? What was she doing on the beach by my house?"

"It looked to me like she was taking pictures."

"That sounds like Brandy." *She was probably planning some snarky posts designed to humiliate me.*

"Well, I respected Miss Octavia, so I didn't want to discount her fears by announcing the package and handing it over in the middle of a crowd. She wouldn't have wanted that. She went to a lot of trouble to keep it secret, so I wanted to honor that. But, like I said, you're never alone. So, when I saw you fly out of the Carson Law Inn like a bat out of hell, I decided to follow you. It's one of the few times that you've been alone."

"Okay, I'm alone. Now what?"

"I put the package in a safe place. It's near your house. I just need to go get it, and then I'll bring it to you. Would that be okay?"

Baby lay sprawled at my feet, and I didn't feel the clamoring anxiety inside my head. Great-Aunt Octavia thought someone that she was close to wanted to do her harm. I found that hard to believe, but I knew one person who was beyond reproach.

"Fine. I'll meet you, on one condition."

"What's that?"

"I'm bringing my dad with me."

Oliver Freemont agreed to my terms, and we parted ways. The drive home was short and uneventful. No screams. No tears. No hysterics. I had a lot to think about. Driving wasn't just great for having a meltdown, but it was also good for thinking. I drove and thought through everything I'd heard. Baby slept.

Oliver Freemont hadn't believed that Great-Aunt Octavia had been in danger, but he'd made me think. What about Miss Hannah? She loved my great-aunt like a sister, but she did have dementia. There were times when she didn't know who anyone was. *Could someone have used her illness to get information they could use against Great-Aunt Octavia?* The idea made my stomach hurt. When she was in her right mind, she would never have said or done anything that would hurt her friend. However, she wasn't always in her right mind. I tucked that idea away in the back of my mind, because if Miss Hannah was the spy who betrayed my great-aunt's secrets, then she could also be betraying me.

CHAPTER 30

"Ugggh!" I let out a bloodcurdling scream.

Baby must have thought I was done screaming because this last one pulled him upright. He glanced around for the assailant. When he didn't see anyone except me, he gave himself a shake.

"Good idea." I shook myself, too. Then, I pulled off the interstate and followed winding, curving Red Arrow Highway past seven antique shops, a car dealership, and two restaurants until I came to my street.

I pulled into my driveway and sat. Michael, April, and Leroy were there. I spent a few moments fixing my makeup before raising the garage door and pulling inside.

Michael came to check on me.

"You okay?" he asked.

I didn't trust myself to respond, so I walked into his arms. I let him envelop me and snuggled into his chest. He didn't say anything for a long time. Eventually, he cleared his throat.

"I'm sorry about what happened to you. You deserve a lot better and—"

"Wait. What are you talking about?" I looked up into his face.

"I'm talking about Elliott and the things Galina said. I know you loved him and—"

"I didn't love Elliott."

He paused. "Maddy, it's okay. I know you two were together for years, and we have only been together a few months. You don't have to—"

"I don't have to what? Tell the truth?"

"No . . . the truth is good." He shook his head. "But I'm confused."

"I was upset about the things Galina said, but not because I was in love with Elliott."

"You're not in love with Elliott now, but—"

"I was never in love with Elliott. I was in love with the idea of being married to a doctor." I gazed in his eyes and looked for a spark of anger . . . disappoint . . . repulsion. Anything that would tell me how he felt that I was so shallow that I would marry someone simply because of their profession.

"All right, but you must have loved him once."

I thought about it for a few moments. "I think I convinced myself that I loved him. Honestly, I don't know that I'd ever really been in love before. I thought that I was, but it wasn't until . . ."

"Until what?" he asked.

Deep breath. "It wasn't until I fell in love with you that I realized whatever I felt for Elliott, it wasn't love."

Michael stared at me for what felt like years.

"Aren't you going to say anything? I mean, it's okay if you aren't in love with me. Well, I'm disappointed because I love you, but if you don't love me, especially now that you see how shallow I am. But, I—"

"Shut up, Squid." Michael pulled me to him and kissed me hard.

I have no idea how long we kissed, but the overhead lights in the garage went out. Baby howled, and my dad flung open the garage door and flipped on the lights.

"Dad!"

"What the . . . ?" He scowled.

Michael raised his hands. That's when I noticed the Admiral was pointing a gun at us.

"Dad! We were just—"

He turned around, went back into the kitchen, and slammed the door.

After a few beats, Michael and I both burst out laughing.

"We can finish this conversation later." He grinned. "For now, we better get inside before the Admiral declares war."

When Michael, Baby, and I entered, everyone was sitting at the island eating pizza. It wasn't until I smelled the pizza that I realized how hungry I was.

Leroy asked, "What took so long?"

April elbowed him in the ribs. "Have some pizza."

I quickly washed my hands and grabbed a slice of pizza from the box.

Michael pulled Baby's food from the cabinet and shoveled several large scoops into his bowl. Then, he opened one of the tubs of adder that I kept on hand to mix in with the dry food. Baby had been a champion show dog. Now that he was retired, he earned his keep through stud fees. Great-Aunt Octavia made sure he ate a good-quality premium dog food that contained a slew of vitamins, nutrients, and minerals. She also left me a recipe for a stew with vegetables and protein. It was good for him, and he loved it.

It wasn't until Michael put Baby's dog bowl down that I saw his right hand was bandaged.

"What happened to your hand?" I asked.

Michael shoved his hands in his pockets. "Nothing. It's fine."

"Don't tell me Rocky Balboa didn't tell you what happened after you stormed out of the Carson Law Inn today?" the Admiral said, his eyes gleaming.

"Sir, I don't think we need to go into that," Michael said.

"Why not?" Leroy asked.

"Yeah, I want to hear," April said. "It's bound to be more exciting than my day sitting around talking to FBI art experts and looking at pictures of fancy paintings."

I glanced from my boyfriend to my dad and back. Clearly Michael didn't want to discuss it, so I turned to my father. "What happened?"

The Admiral made a production of chewing, swallowing, and wiping his lips while Michael squirmed. "So, after you marched out of the room, all hell broke loose."

"Sir, I really don't think—"

"Atten-tion!" the Admiral barked.

Michael assumed the position. Heels together. Toes at a forty-five-degree angle. Arms at his side. Straight back. Chin up. Chest out. Shoulders back. Hands curved into fists, with his thumbs following the seam of his pants. He stared straight ahead.

After a few seconds, the Admiral said, "Pah-raid rest!"

Michael moved his left leg out twelve inches. Moved his hands behind his back. Even though he was facing me and I couldn't see behind him, I knew his palms were facing out. His fingers were extended, and his thumbs were interlocked.

I sighed. "Dad, come on, really?"

"That's cool," Leroy said.

After a few moments, the Admiral relented. "Fall out."

Michael took a step back with his right foot and relaxed. Well, he relaxed about as much as a soldier who's just been drilled can relax.

"As I was saying, after you left, Lover Boy over there grabs

Elliott by his collar and drags him to his feet. Then, he gave him a punch in the gut followed by one to the face. One-two. Muhammad Ali couldn't have done it better." The Admiral chuckled. "You could hear the bones in his nose crush. Blood was everywhere."

"Yuck." I dropped my pizza, but the Admiral wasn't done.

"I didn't know the Army could throw a punch like that. I hate to admit it, but it was impressive. That fool Elliott dropped like a sack of flour."

"That's not impressive," Michael said. "I let my temper get the best of me. In the Army, we're taught to control ourselves. I shouldn't have hit him."

The Admiral looked at Michael with respect and admiration. "The punch was good, and that weasel deserved it. However, the truly impressive thing was what happened next."

"What happened?" I asked.

"Trooper Bob called for an ambulance, and while we waited for the EMTs, Dr. Portman here administered medical care."

"Another reason I shouldn't have hit him," Michael said. "I'm a doctor, even if I'm just an animal doctor."

I flung myself into Michael's arms.

"Let's not get that started again," the Admiral said. "I'm not finished with my story."

"You are a compassionate human being and a doctor," I said, glancing up at Michael. I took a step away and turned to face my father. "Okay, finish telling your story."

"That Russian woman—"

"Galina," I said.

"Whatever. She was having hysterics. Mrs. Law actually had to slap her." He shook his head. "Fine woman."

"Galina?" I knew who he was talking about but wanted to see his response.

"God no. I'm talking about Mrs. Law. That woman has a

head on her shoulders. Kept calm. Did what needed to be done. Fine woman." The Admiral smiled for a few moments.

April and I exchanged a glance, but neither of us said anything.

"At least if Trooper Bob arrests you," Michael said, "I'll be in the cell right next to you, charged with assault."

CHAPTER 31

"That Yogi Bear buffoon isn't going to arrest either one of you," the Admiral said. He smacked the island with his hand. "Not while I'm alive. We'll get you a good lawyer."

As if on cue, my phone rang. One glance at the screen made me wonder if my house was bugged or if this was just cyberspace spying and anticipating my needs. It was Chris Russell.

Our conversation was short. My part consisted of listening and making periodic grunts of agreement. When I hung up, there were four humans and one canine staring at me.

"Well?" April asked.

"Wrong number," I joked, but no one laughed. "He wants me to come to his office tomorrow so we can come up with a game plan."

"Game plan?" Leroy said. "What does that mean?"

"No idea. I guess I'll find out tomorrow."

"I've never heard of this Chris Russell," the Admiral said. "How do you know if he's a good lawyer?"

"I don't. He was Great-Aunt Octavia's lawyer. I inherited him with the house and the bakery."

"That's not good enough. You can't just trust your future to anyone. Murder is too serious. We have to make sure you have the best. Have you talked to any of his previous clients? Has he ever tried a murder case?"

"No . . . I don't know."

"Maddy, this isn't the time to be indecisive. You can't just float along wherever the current takes you. Not this time. Now, we need to look into his background. I'm going to make some calls. I know some folks who can not only tell us what he ate for breakfast, they can tell us what color underwear he's wearing. You just leave that to me."

Part of me wanted to sit back and let the Admiral take care of everything. It was a comfortable position that I knew well. It's what he'd done all my life. He was good at making decisions and taking care of problems. After all, that's what the government paid him to do. I didn't look at my friends. They would expect me to adult, but adulting was hard.

Baby walked over and put his head in my lap. He looked up at me with his big soulful eyes, and I knew that he would be disappointed in me.

"Admiral, you're right. I do need a good attorney. I'm not sure if Chris Russell is the best choice or not, but I'll meet with him tomorrow and see what he has to say. He did a good job advising Great-Aunt Octavia, and so far he's done okay with me." I could see the Admiral revving up for another attack, but I held up a hand to stop him. "I'm not ruling out a different attorney with more trial experience—Perry Mason and Matlock would be my first and second choices. But, since I can't have either one of them, I'm going to keep an open mind and make an informed decision. We'll talk to him tomorrow and decide."

The Admiral was used to advancing. Retreat wasn't in his nature. Surrender was an absolutely foreign concept. "I've been checking around. I've got a friend who's a judge in Chicago. He's not licensed to practice law anymore, but he's going to call with the name of the best criminal defense lawyer in the country." He paused for a few moments. "Mrs. Law was also going to provide the name of an attorney. She's going to call me later with the name and telephone number."

"Really? That was really nice of her. Did you give her your number or is she going to call here?" I asked.

"Of course I gave her my number. It might be good to talk to her. I mean, she is from here, and she seems to have a good head on her shoulders. She's a businesswoman. We could ask what she knows about Chris Russell." The Admiral didn't crack a smile, but I saw a spark in his eyes that I hadn't seen for . . . ever.

"That would be great. Maybe you could tackle that. Preferably sooner rather than later."

"Trooper Bob isn't going to arrest you," April said. "Well, not yet. I can't say for sure."

"How do you know?"

"Did he say something?"

"Spill it."

We pelted April with questions until she held up a hand to halt the barrage. "Look, I don't know much more than you do. I do know that he ordered Elliott and Galina not to leave town."

"Elliott couldn't leave anyway," Leroy said. "Isn't he in the hospital?"

April poked him in the ribs again.

"Sorry."

"That must mean Trooper Bob's at least considering the possibility that someone other than me could have killed Brandy Denton, right?" I glanced around.

April nodded, but it wasn't as enthusiastic of a nod as I would have liked.

"Leroy, were you able to talk to that maid, Louise?" I asked.

"Um, yeah. She talked to Trooper Bob."

"I would have loved to have been a fly on the wall for that. I don't suppose Louise overheard what Elliott and Brandy were arguing about?"

Leroy flushed and looked away. He started fidgeting and drumming his fingers on the counter, a sure sign that he was hiding something. I glanced at April, who was the first person to mention Leroy's tells, signs that he was nervous, bluffing, or lying.

"Did she hear why they were arguing?" I asked.

"No . . . Not exactly." Leroy looked like a rabbit in a trap. He squirmed for several beats and then shot a nervous glance at the Admiral.

"*Je ne pense pas que nous devrions discuter de cela devant la police.*" The Admiral tilted his head in April's direction.

What? How can he suggest we not discuss things in front of the police?

April stood up. "I may not speak French, but I'm pretty sure I understand."

"April, wait. You're my friend. I don't—"

"No, he's right. I'm a sworn officer of the law. If this case goes to trial, and I pray it doesn't, I could be forced to testify." April took me by the shoulders.

"But you're my friend."

"I am your friend, but you need to be smart. Besides, I have homework." She smiled.

"Homework?"

She reached down and lifted a bag that was by her feet. She pulled out a large binder. "Art. I need to familiarize myself with this stuff."

She excused herself and went downstairs.

I glared at the Admiral. "That was rude."

"Listen, I'm sure she wouldn't deliberately say or do anything to hurt you, but she could be *forced* to testify. We just need to make sure we cover our flank." The Admiral reached out a hand, but I wasn't ready to forgive him. Not yet, anyway. I stepped out of reach, folded my arms across my chest, and brooded.

After that, the conversation was stilted and awkward with large blocks of silence. I didn't want to believe that April or any of my friends could have had anything to do with Great-Aunt Octavia's spy, but now that the Admiral opened the door, it was impossible to close it.

"I should go," Leroy said, flushed and miserable. "I have a lot of baking to do to get ready for tomorrow." He stood up and headed outside.

"Where were you all this time?" Michael asked.

I shoved a slice of pizza in my mouth and mumbled something about needing to think. I could tell that Michael wasn't fooled. He knew me well enough to know when I was hiding something. He also knew me well enough that he didn't bring it up.

Baby stood up and stretched. Then, he walked to the back door.

I started to get up but was halted when the Admiral announced he was going to take Baby outside, and the two left.

Michael stared at the door. "That's an unusual pairing."

"Baby loves almost everyone, but I honestly never thought I'd see the day when the Admiral would accept a pet, especially not a giant of a beast like Baby, but I suspect it has something to do with the instinct that Baby wants to protect me."

Michael looked at me. "You okay?"

Before I could respond, he got a call. He glanced at the phone and then stepped outside to talk.

That was different. If it was an emergency, why was he being so secretive?

My brain went into overdrive. I hated this. It was bad enough that Great-Aunt Octavia thought she had a spy in her inner circle, but now . . . I was questioning them, too.

After a few minutes, my cell phone vibrated. It was a text message from Michael.

Have to go. Call u later

Hmm. This seems suspicious.

K

What could be so important and so secret that he couldn't talk about it? My brain went into overload and went down a black hole of death. *Tilt. Tilt. Tilt. There's no way. No way. There is absolutely no way Michael can be the spy in the camp Great-Aunt Octavia was worried about.*

CHAPTER 32

My heart raced, and my brain fogged over like tule fog rolling down onto the I-5 in the San Joaquin Valley. I walked in circles, flapping my arms like a bird trying to fly while hyperventilating.

The Admiral and Baby came back into the kitchen. One look at me and the Admiral went into action.

"Maddy, stop. Calm down. Breathe." He shook me by the shoulders.

His eyes were granite and bore into mine. Not blinking. Not looking away.

Whether by some form of hypnotism or the sheer force of his will, I gasped and sucked in air. My lungs remembered how to work, and I could feel myself calming down. Air . . . it's everywhere all the time, why didn't I notice before?

"Thanks, Dad."

He went to the cabinet, filled a glass with water, and handed it to me. "You okay?"

I sipped my water and nodded. "Yes, I just . . . had a moment. I'm fine now."

His raised brow told me he didn't believe me, but he didn't want another episode, so he let it go. For now.

After all of the excitement, Baby refused to leave my side. He sat at my feet and stared at me as though he was waiting to see if I were about to fall apart again.

The Admiral looked at the squeaky-clean kitchen. "That's a sight I never thought I'd see. When you were at home, I couldn't get you to pick up your shoes. Now, here you are, cleaning. If only Mrs. Nowak could see you now." He chuckled.

"How is Mrs. Nowak?"

"She's talking about retiring. She says without you to pick up after, she doesn't have anything to do, and she feels like she's stealing my money. She'll never believe it when I tell her you're actually cleaning. Maybe I need to send her a picture."

"She probably still wouldn't believe it. When I think back to the state my bedroom used to be, I can't believe it either. I used to have clothes everywhere." I shook my head. "Michael says it's because this is my house."

"Speaking of Michael . . . is everything okay with you two?"

"I don't know. One minute, I'm ecstatic. I know beyond a shadow of a doubt that he loves me as much as I love him . . . then, the next minute . . ."

"The next minute?"

"The next minute he's rushing off to some emergency without kissing me goodbye, and I wonder if he loves me at all. Or, is he just like Elliott, who obviously hated my guts." I sobbed.

The Admiral opened his arms, and I rushed in and cried on his shoulder like a four-year-old. I sat on his knee and wept until I didn't have any more tears.

"Princess, I don't know Michael well, but I've worked with a lot of young men in my career. I consider myself a fairly good judge of character. For what it's worth, I think he cares about you. I also think you two need to talk. Tell him how you feel."

"What if he doesn't feel the same way?"

"Then it's better to know the truth."

"I don't want to know the truth if it's bad. Because if he doesn't love me, then I can't stay here, and I want to stay here. I love it here. I love my house, my friends, and my bakery." I glanced over at Baby, who was staring up at me like I was the center of his universe. "I especially love this big drooly mastiff."

"Michael seems like a good man."

I pulled away and glanced up at my father. "You're only saying that because he was in the military."

"No, I'm saying that because I've had a chance to talk to him, and his head is screwed on straight. In spite of the fact that he was in the *Army*, I do like him. It takes a special type of person to put their lives on the line for their country, and he did that. I especially like the way he treats you. He opens doors and always behaves the way a gentleman should. He also defended your honor and punched Elliott's lights out. He's a man of honor and I do like him."

"You never liked Elliott, did you?"

"Elliott was weak. Not weak physically. He was fit enough. He was weak mentally. He isn't the type of man that will defend a lady's honor. He wouldn't take a bullet for you. He's the type who would use you as a shield and cower behind you." He shook his head. "No, I wasn't a fan, but then I wasn't the one marrying him. So, it wasn't important whether I liked him or not. What does your heart tell you?"

"Pshaw. My heart is the problem. With Elliott it was easy. He was a good catch. He was handsome. He was going to be a doctor, and I thought we made a great couple. It was . . . logical. When it comes to Michael, logic flies right out the window. My heart has a mind of its own, and it refuses to listen to me."

"That's the thing about love. It's seldom logical. I don't think I ever told you this, but when I first met your mom, she was engaged to someone else."

"What?"

"She was engaged to a guy she'd known her entire life. Childhood sweethearts. He was nice. He came from a good family. His grandfather was a prominent minister. His father was a mortician, and he sold insurance. They had the market on the afterlife for all families in their small community. Marrying him would have been the logical . . . safe thing to do. But, when I saw her, I knew." He gazed into space as though he were reliving that moment again.

"Did she feel the same?"

He chuckled. "I think she felt it, but she was in denial. Her family wanted her to marry this other guy . . . Davis Theodore Witherspoon the fourth. Her mother wasn't as adamant as her father, but she wanted her to marry someone local. Someone that she knew, knew their family's background."

"She didn't want Mom to marry you?"

"They didn't know me. I didn't grow up in their small town. I came for basic training. I met your mom at a party, and now here I was trying to take their little girl."

"But you were in the Navy. You were . . . respectable."

"Well, I wasn't always the respectable man you see before you." He tugged on his ear. "Plus, not all seaman recruits behaved honorably where beautiful women were concerned. But, it wasn't just that. I wanted to see the world. My dream was to make the Navy my career. Your grandfather served in Vietnam, and he knew the dangers and the toll it can take on the family."

"Wait. I never knew Grandad served in Vietnam. He and Grandma both died when I was young, but I remember him carrying me on his back."

"Your grandad didn't talk about it. War can be brutal. He didn't like the fact that I could drag their daughter and grandchildren all over the world—that is, if I survived." He hung his head and took a deep breath. "I can't fault your grandparents or any of them for that. We tried to stay apart, but . . . that didn't work, either. We were both even more miserable when we were apart. Eventually, she came to the base and said she was sick and tired of being miserable, and if I was, too, then we should just stop wasting time and get married."

"Wait. Mom proposed to you?"

He chuckled. "She did. Of course, I fixed it up later. I got down on one knee and did the thing right, but your mom knew what she wanted and, well . . . thankfully, what she wanted was me."

I couldn't remember the last time the Admiral and I had talked like this. He wasn't ordering me around like a new recruit just out of boot camp. Talking about Mom always made him sad, so he rarely did. This was nice. I hated to ruin the moment. "Dad, how well did you know Great-Aunt Octavia?"

"Not well. She was one of the only members of your mom's family who thought your mom shouldn't marry Davis Witherspoon the fourth. She said he would bore her to death, so I suppose I owe her. Your mom loved her. She used to talk about spending time with her *favorite* aunt. That was a joke between her and Octavia because she was your mom's only aunt. When your mom was small, they used to bake thumbprint cookies and have tea parties. She used to say your great-aunt Octavia made the best pound cake on the planet. She loved pound cake and Chocolate—"

"Soul Cake." I finished his sentence. "It's pretty good."

"I know. I got to taste some of your prize-winning cake the last time I was here."

"Did Mom ever mention anything about Great-Aunt Octavia being . . . a little . . . off?" The look on his face told me I would need to explain. I used my finger to make circles at the side of my head to indicate the universal sign for crazy.

"Not that she ever mentioned. She always spoke very highly

of Octavia and her intelligence. However, it's been twenty-five years since your mom passed, and a lot can happen in that time. Why do you ask?"

Making decisions wasn't my strong suit. However, right then, I made a decision. I told my dad everything. I told him about the messages Great-Aunt Octavia had left for me. I told him about "the spy in the camp" and all that I'd learned over the months that I'd been in New Bison. The Admiral sat silent and still and listened. When I was done, I was exhausted, but I also felt as though I'd just lost twenty pounds.

While I talked, the Admiral pulled out a cigar. He knew I didn't like them, so he never smoked them in the house. He merely chomped on the end. I'd seen him mangle many cigars over the years as he pondered some of the biggest problems facing the free world. When I finished, he sat silently. When he spoke, he got to the heart of the matter.

"Is that what has you worried? Are you afraid Michael might be the spy?"

"No . . . yes . . . maybe. I don't think he would do it willingly, but maybe he or Miss Hannah did it unwittingly." I explained the thought that had crossed my mind earlier, that Miss Hannah's dementia might have led to her betraying Octavia's secrets.

He rubbed the back of his neck. "I'm no expert on mental health. You'd need to talk to a professional about that. It sounds like Michael, Leroy, and Octavia, when she was alive, all kept a close watch on Hannah. I don't think she would be in danger of betraying any secrets with everyone watching her like you all do."

"That's true. Dad, I want to get to the bottom of this. I want to know the truth. I want to find out if there really was a *spy* in Great-Aunt Octavia's camp. I don't like not being able to trust my friends. April, Leroy, Tyson, Miss Hannah, and Michael are all my friends. I want to be able to share things with them. I don't like keeping secrets. I feel like Great-Aunt Octavia's secret and possibly her death are at the heart of this. And I'm determined to get to the root of the problem."

The Admiral leaned forward. "Okay, then that's what we're going to do. We're going to figure out what secret led to Octavia's death, and if there is a spy, then we're going to find them."

CHAPTER 33

"Sounds great," I said, "but how do we do that?"

"Get me a list of names, and I'll get some intel."

"What kind of intel? I mean, these are just normal people in New Bison, Michigan, not international terrorists."

He smiled. "You'd be surprised what kind of intel I can get, but financial records would be important. I'd bet my pension that money is at the root of all of this. You said that real estate developer was pressuring her for this property."

I nodded. "Bradley Ellison. She didn't want to sell. Somehow, I think the former mayor, Paul Rivers, was involved. His wife, Candy, said he wanted her to use her influence to convince her mom and Great-Aunt Octavia to sell."

The Admiral glanced out of the window at the waves crashing across the lake. "It's a beautiful view, but certainly not worth killing for." He tilted his head to the side. "You think Octavia's death is somehow tied to Brandy Denton's death?"

I took a few moments to think. "Wait here. I'll be right back." I hopped up and ran upstairs. When I returned, I had a box.

I put the box on the table. "It's like these style boxes my shopper sends."

The Admiral rolled his eyes.

I opened it and pulled out a pair of black leggings, a floral print blouse, a skirt, a dress, a denim jacket, a beautiful scarf, and a pair of beautiful sandals. I held each item up. "See, this one box has about fifteen different looks. I can wear the blouse with the slacks or the skirt. Or, I can wear the jacket with the slacks or the skirt or the dress. Plus, I can dress each outfit up or down with the scarf." I demonstrated by holding up each item. "Everything goes together, even though it doesn't all match."

"Okay, but I'm still lost. What does any of that have to do with Octavia's or Brandy Denton's murders?"

"They're all separate items, just like each outfit in the box. Even though they're all separate, they also go together to create different looks. The murders are separate, but somehow, they're also linked."

The Admiral shook his head. "Clothes."

"I have to go with what I know. I know clothes." I shrugged.

"You realize if you're right and Brandy Denton's death is somehow tied to Octavia's and all of the other murders that have happened in this town, that we will have to rule out Galina and Elliott as suspects. There's no way either of them could have been involved in those murders."

"Maybe, and maybe not. It's—"

"Maddy, you've got to be logical."

"Please . . . just listen."

He took a deep breath and nodded.

"Just because they didn't do the actual murders, doesn't mean that everything isn't connected. Something's been bothering me, and I just figured out what it is."

His eyebrows asked the question.

"When I saw Brandy on Sunday night, she said she needed to talk to me. She said that she found out something."

"Okay, what?"

"I don't know. We got into an argument, and then the next day, she was dead. But, she said she'd been walking on the beach."

"So?"

I shrugged. "I don't know. Nothing, I guess . . ."

"Maddy. Don't waffle. Trust your instincts."

"That's what Michael says." I wasn't sure Michael and the Admiral saying similar things was good or bad. I shook my head like Baby and took a moment to collect my thoughts. "I think there's something strange going on in New Bison. I feel like there's some puppet master behind the scenes pulling the strings. I don't think he does all of the dirty work. I think he manipulates people and makes them do all the bad things."

"How?"

"I don't know, but the puppet master didn't kill Garrett Kelley or Paul Rivers. He got someone else to do it. Just like Moriarty in the Sherlock Holmes mysteries."

"What?"

"Professor Moriarty. He was Sherlock Holmes's greatest foe. He was this criminal genius who ran all these criminal activities, but he wasn't the one who did the actual bad deeds. He was just the brains behind it all." I stared at my dad.

"How do we know the person who killed Garrett Kelley and Paul Rivers didn't kill Octavia?"

I paused. "Because he said he didn't."

"You can't trust the word of a murderer."

"I know, but why lie? I mean, if you're going to admit to murdering two people, why not three? Why lie about her?"

"Good point. So, you think this puppet master wanted Brandy Denton dead and manipulated Galina or Elliott to kill her?"

"Or someone else."

"Why?"

"I don't know. Maybe we'll find out when we go meet with Oliver Freemont." I glanced at my phone and noted the time.

The Admiral got his gun, and I took the boxes with my recent purchases back upstairs. When I returned, I saw the Admiral scratching Baby's ears and talking baby talk while my dog drooled like a fountain. I stood back and watched the two interact and then quietly pulled out my phone and snapped a picture.

#NavyApprovedMastiff #BabyApprovedAdmiral #TwoTough SeaDogs

I hated the rickety stairs that led down from the bluffs to the beach, but short of getting in the car and driving five miles out of the way and then taking a boat back, there was no other way to get down to the beach from here.

Baby had no qualms about the stairs and bounded down like a five-pound Chihuahua. I followed next, a lot more tentatively. It helped if I didn't look down, but I kept a firm grip on the handrail, closed my eyes, and took a step of faith. It turned out to be thirty-seven steps until I felt the squish of sand underfoot and knew that I was safely on the ground.

The Admiral must have been following closely because moments after I touched the ground, he was right beside me.

Lake Michigan was vast and beautiful. I took a moment to breathe in the smell of wet sand, water, and fish. Baby ran over to examine a pile of debris that had washed up on the beach.

I turned to look at my dad but was greeted instead by a frown. The Admiral whipped his gun out of his holster and pushed me behind him.

"Stay here."

He focused on Baby and what I had thought was a pile of debris. After glancing around, he tramped toward them, his gun at the ready.

I stood still for a few moments before I remembered the classic horror movie mistake number one: *Never split up.* I took off my shoes and hurried to catch up to my dad. Clutching the back of his shirt, I trailed behind him as close as I could and forced myself not to climb on his back like I did when I was small.

The Admiral walked with the stealth of a cat. He barely turned his head, but without watching his face, I sensed his eyes darting from side to side. "I don't like this. Out in the open." He stopped suddenly, and I bumped into his back.

"What?"

He pointed to the ground. Footprints.

Sherlock Holmes could have looked at those prints in the sand and known the height, weight, and education level of the people who left them. I am not Sherlock Holmes. It looked like messy sand to me, with the imprint of a large mastiff over the top. I glanced at Baby, who was uncharacteristically quiet.

Baby laid down next to the pile and rested his head on it.

The fact that Baby wasn't agitated had a calming effect on me. I released the death grip I had on my dad's shirt and inched closer to Baby. Experience told me that Baby wouldn't be lying still if he sensed danger.

I looked closely. What I originally believed to have been a pile of clothes wasn't. I gasped.

Staring up at the sky were the blue eyes of Oliver Freemont. The eyes were vacant, but then they turned and looked into mine. A hand reached up and grabbed my ankle, and I screamed.

Baby barked.

The Admiral knelt down and felt for a pulse. "Madison. Stop screaming and call 9-1-1."

My hands were shaking so much, I dropped my phone. I gave up trying to get my fingers to work and pressed the side button on my iPhone five times.

"Nine-One-One. What's your emergency?"

"We need an ambulance. He's hurt. A man's been hurt. I thought he was dead. He's just lying on the beach. His eyes . . . oh God . . . his eyes were just gone, like no one was there, but then he looked at me and clutched—"

"Ma'am. Calm down. You need an ambulance, right?"

"Didn't I say that? Yes. He needs an ambulance. He's dying. I thought he was dead already, but—"

"What are his injuries? Is he conscious and able to talk?"

"Yes. No. I don't know. I mean, he's conscious because he grabbed my ankle, but he's not really talking. Is he talking, Dad?"

"He was." The Admiral leaned down and put his ear close to Oliver Freemont's mouth. "He's dead."

"Is there someone else with you who could answer questions?" the dispatcher asked.

I handed my phone to the Admiral. He was apparently calm enough to answer almost all of her questions while I walked around in a circle.

At first, Baby followed me, but after a while of walking and going nowhere, he sat down and watched me circling.

Sirens blared over the blood rushing through my veins that pounded inside my head. The sirens drowned out the sea sounds of waves and seagulls, but it couldn't drown out the question: *Who killed Oliver Freemont?*

CHAPTER 34

I sat in my kitchen with a blanket wrapped around my shoulders and holding a steaming cup of coffee in my hands. Still, I couldn't get warm.

One of the best parts about the sheriff living in my basement was that law enforcement was literally only a scream away. When I screamed, she came running and was on the scene in seconds. Trooper Bob, a squadron of police cars, and the ambulance took what felt like an hour to arrive, but was actually much sooner.

I don't remember climbing the stairs, but I must have because I was no longer on the beach staring into the lifeless, super-blue eyes of the man who claimed to have been Great-Aunt Octavia's friend. The man I was supposed to meet. The man who was supposed to have the package from Great-Aunt Octavia that was going to provide all of the answers. I shivered.

Outside, I heard raised voices.

"I don't care who you are and what your orders are. My girlfriend is in there, and I'm going in. If you want to stop me, you're going to need to shoot me."

Hearing Michael's voice jarred me out of my stupor. I shoved off the blanket, set down the coffee, and rushed outside.

Michael was nose to nose with a state policeman who I didn't recognize.

"Michael." I hurled myself into his arms.

"Hey, Squid. You okay?" Michael whispered.

"He's dead. Someone killed him. He's dead. He was on the beach. His eyes were staring up at the sky, but he's dead." The words tumbled out of my mouth, and I couldn't have stopped them if I tried. "I was supposed to meet him, but the Admiral came with me. I don't know who killed him. He must have been waiting down on the beach."

"Madison!"

I turned my head and saw Chris Russell standing behind Michael.

"As your attorney, I feel bound to caution you," Russell said.

Trooper Bob spat a large wad of tobacco and mumbled something that sounded like "*mucking mowyers.*"

"Perhaps we should move this party inside," April said.

My kitchen is large, but with Trooper Bob, April, the Admiral, Michael, me, Alliyah Howard, Chris Russell, an EMT, at least two cops, and Baby, it was packed.

Trooper Bob glared at Michael. "Can we cull this crowd down to only essentials?"

"This is my house," I said, "and I want Michael, my dad, and April."

"Fine. Then can someone remove this horse?" He pointed at Baby.

One of the two cops reached toward Baby's collar but was rewarded with a deep growl. Baby bared his teeth, and drool dripped from his canines.

The cop pulled his hand back and reached for the holster by his side.

"Don't even think about it," Michael said.

"Baby lives here," I said. "He's essential." I reached over and put my arms around his neck.

Baby kept eye contact with the policeman and continued to growl.

Trooper Bob flung his hands in the air. "Maybe we need to move down to the station. That's *my* house."

"Are you arresting my client?" Chris Russell said from the back door.

"Good grief! Please save me from lawyers." Trooper Bob asked the heavens. "I'm trying to get a statement. I have not decided to arrest anyone . . . *yet*."

Dr. Howard flashed a light in my eyes and took my pulse.

"Excuse me, but why is a veterinarian taking my pulse?" I asked.

"I'm also a medical doctor and filling in for the medical examiner, who's out with a medical emergency." Dr. Howard smiled.

"You're a busy woman," I said.

"Fortunately, there isn't usually much for the medical examiner to do in New Bison." Dr. Howard strapped the blood pressure cuff on my arm. Either I'd gained weight or she pulled that cuff tighter than usual as she took a reading. When she was done, she took the cuff off and packed it away. "Your blood pressure is slightly elevated, but given the situation, I think that's to be expected." She turned to Michael. "After she gives her statement, I recommend bed rest."

Michael nodded.

Trooper Bob pointed at Dr. Howard and the two EMTs. "Great. So, you and you two can be the first to go."

Part of me objected to Trooper Bob giving orders on who could stay and who could go in my house, but I glanced at the Admiral and decided to let it drop. One thing I learned from living with a Navy admiral was that you need to pick your battles. You won't win every one, but you need to stay focused on the goal—winning the war. So, I swallowed my objections.

With Dr. Howard and the EMTs gone, the room felt slightly less claustrophobic. Trooper Bob must have felt it too because he gave a nod, and the cop who had contemplated removing Baby left the room. He glanced over his shoulder at Baby, who had never lost eye contact. The cop patted his holster, and Baby growled. Males.

Trooper Bob focused his attention on April. "This isn't your case."

"No, but it is my home. I live here. I was one of the first people on scene," April said. "Plus, I recognize the dead man."

"You knew Oliver Freemont from when he used to come here to paint and when he was friends with Great-Aunt Octavia?" I asked, but April was shaking her head.

"No. I recognized him from the files."

"Files?" Trooper Bob said. "What files?"

"He was listed as a possible person of interest in my art theft and smuggling case."

CHAPTER 35

"Art theft?" Trooper Bob scowled. "Are you saying this Oliver Freemont character was a wanted criminal?"

"He was a person of interest," April said. "He was an artist. He had ties to some people who . . . well, let's just say their hands aren't exactly squeaky clean."

Trooper Bob fumed. "What does that mean? Does he have a record?"

"Not exactly."

"Then what makes him a person of interest?" I asked.

"Several years ago, he was questioned about some forged paintings that had been sold in Europe. He—"

"Forgeries?" Trooper Bob said. "How does that tie into this murder?"

"I don't know that it does. I'm just saying that he was a person of interest in my case. I don't know that he is involved in Brandy Denton's murder. Maybe he was involved. Maybe Brandy Denton was involved. Or maybe she stumbled across something she shouldn't have. I don't know. All I know is that Oliver Freemont is . . . was a person of interest. That means I'm interested in his murder. In fact, the task force will probably want to be involved."

Trooper Bob rubbed his head. "Ugh. The last thing I need is a lot of stuffed-shirt feds walking around, taking over my murder."

"Maybe if April is allowed to stay she can be the federal representative and no one else will need to get involved," I said.

Trooper Bob was backed into a corner. "Fine, but you are only involved as an investigator for Freemont, not Brandy Denton."

"Of course . . . as long as the two cases aren't connected." April turned her back to Trooper Bob and winked at me.

"Now that you've worked that out, can we get on with this?" the Admiral asked.

"What were you doing on the beach with an art forger?" Trooper Bob asked.

"I didn't know he was a forger," I said. "I just met him today."

"I thought you were dating the vet there. Don't tell me you met a strange man just a few hours ago and then agreed to a secret rendezvous on the beach behind your house?" Trooper Bob's lip curled into a snarl.

The Admiral jumped out of his seat. "How dare you."

"That's uncalled for." Michael glared and faced off against the state trooper.

April stepped between the two soldiers and Trooper Bob. "Gentlemen, please."

I took several deep breaths to calm my nerves. I couldn't let Trooper Bob goad me into sharing more than I wanted. "Maybe I should tell you what happened."

Michael and the Admiral were still angry, but they both sat back down, although the glares continued.

I shared the story that Oliver Freemont had told me about how Great-Aunt Octavia had once saved his life. Then, I mentioned that he had been out of the country and didn't realize she had died. "He wanted to give me a gift, so I agreed to meet him."

"What kind of gift?" Trooper Bob asked.

"Was it a painting?" April asked.

"I have no idea. He didn't say, but I told him that my dad would be coming to the beach with me."

"Yeah, yeah," Trooper Bob said. "Who else knew you were going to meet Oliver Freemont tonight? Who'd you tell?" He glanced at Michael.

Michael shook his head. A pulse on the side of his head was pounding, and I knew he was struggling to contain himself. I just wasn't sure if he was angrier with Trooper Bob for implying something improper or with me for not telling him.

After a few moments, Trooper Bob turned his gaze to April, who also shook her head. "If I'd known Madison was going to meet Freemont, I would have went with her."

"You had to have told someone else," Trooper Bob said.

"Why?" I asked.

"If you didn't tell anyone, then who did this?" Trooper Bob pulled up his cell phone. After a few swipes, he held it up for me to see.

On the screen was a picture of me standing over Oliver Freemont's body on the beach. I gasped. Not only was it a picture of me at a murder scene, it was trending and already had over ten thousand views.

CHAPTER 36

"If I find out this was some sick attempt to get publicity for your bakery, I'll toss you in jail so fast it'll make your head swim," Trooper Bob said.

"Are you serious? Why would I want that kind of publicity? *If* I'd killed or planned to kill Oliver Freemont, would I really want someone there to see me?"

Trooper Bob grumbled for a few moments. "Then, who took the picture? And how did they know when and where you'd be?"

"Madison has a good point," Chris Russell said. He looked at me as though he'd never seen me before.

I swallowed the urge to respond, *I'm capable of walking and chewing gum at the same time, too.* I forced myself not to stick my tongue out at him by focusing on the photo. "The photographer posted the picture anonymously, so I have no idea who did it. As far as the *why*? I can only assume the reason was to cast suspicion on me."

"How do you do that? How do you post an anonymous picture? I thought the point of social media was being social.

You tag your friends, and isn't there some type of . . . signature or account needed to post that stuff online? At least, that's what my teenage daughter tells me."

"I suppose the original point of social media was networking and interacting with friends and family, but that was before. Now, it's morphed into something different. People use social media for all types of reasons. Some use it to engage with friends. Others use it for marketing. Then there are internet trolls."

"Trolls? What's that?" Trooper Bob asked.

"Trolls deliberately try to stir up trouble. They intentionally post derogatory posts."

"Why?" the Admiral asked.

"They post inflammatory comments or responses to cause trouble and get people arguing. They vent, verbally abuse, belittle, and spew hatred."

"What's the point of that?" Trooper Bob asked.

"Suppose you support one political party, and you want to make people believe that your opponent is a horrible person. Well, you start a rumor that your opponent did something awful like . . . robbed a bank. Then, people might believe it and will either not vote for your opponent or argue with people who defend the other person," I said.

April turned to stare at Chris Russell. "Isn't that illegal? I mean, they're lying."

"There are definitely laws about libel, but I think Madison's point is that these . . . trolls are posting anonymously. Right?" Chris Russell glanced at me for confirmation.

I nodded.

"But how do they do that?" the Admiral asked.

"There are several ways to post anonymously," I said. "The easiest way is to create a bogus or burner account. Or there are apps that'll let you post anonymously. People will always find a way to wreak havoc."

"Again, what's the point?" Trooper Bob said. "Why you? You honestly want us to believe this anonymous person followed you to the beach and just happened to be in the right place at the right time to get a picture of you standing over the body of Oliver Freemont and then posted it online? Even if I believed all this horse pucky about a 'troll' intent on stirring up trouble, why you?" He gave me a snide look.

I ignored him and continued to study the post. "There's something familiar about the photo."

"It should be familiar. You were there. Weren't you?"

I rolled my eyes and continued to avoid taking the bait that Trooper Bob was dangling in front of me. "Not just because I was there. There's something familiar about the photographer's . . . style." If another photo hadn't popped up and caught my eye, I might not have made the connection. "I got it."

"You know who posted that?" Trooper Bob asked.

"Yes, I do." I swiped a few times until I found the site I was looking for and then held the phone out for everyone to see.

Trooper Bob pushed his way closest to me. "That doesn't make sense. That's Brandy Denton's site. Unless you're telling me she got up from the dead and is following you around taking pictures and posting them on social media, I— "

"Not Brandy Denton. Jessica Barlow, Brandy's P.A."

CHAPTER 37

"What's a P.A.?" Trooper Bob said.

"Who's Jessica Barlow?"

"Why is this the first time we're hearing about her?"

I held up my hands to stop the tidal wave of questions rushing over me. "Wait. One at a time." I took a deep breath. "First, a P.A. is a personal assistant. Jessica Barlow was Brandy's personal assistant." I deliberately skipped the last question since I had told April but not Trooper Bob.

One look at Trooper Bob and I saw the question welling up inside of him.

"Even when Brandy was alive, she didn't take all of her own photos," I said. "When an influencer really becomes popular, you're inundated with emails and direct messages from people who want you to promote their page, products, whatever. Brandy had a lot of followers. So, she hired a personal assistant."

"How do you know this photo was taken by Jessica Barlow?" April asked.

"Jessica wasn't just a social media influencer. She's an artist." I swiped through her personal website and showed them her photos. "Most people who take a photo of a pair of shoes are just trying to capture the shoes. Not Jessica. She is always playing with light and shadows to make the photos more edgy, like an art film or a Hitchcock movie."

"How did someone like her end up working for Brandy Denton?" the Admiral asked.

I explained that Jessica was a Southern Belle who wanted to make it in L.A. as a social media influencer but didn't have the right connections. She became Brandy's P.A. so she could meet the right people.

"I'm not buying it," Trooper Bob said. "This woman followed you around just waiting for the right moment to capture you in a compromising position—for what?"

"Great question. Maybe we should ask her." I turned to April.

April coughed and cast a sideways glance at Trooper Bob. "Maddy mentioned this Jessica Barlow person, so I asked Officer Norris to look into whether she was here."

Trooper Bob scowled, but he swallowed whatever snide remark was on the tip of his tongue. "And?"

April pulled out a notepad and flipped through several pages until she found what she wanted. "There's a Jessica Barlow registered at the Beachcomber Hotel. She and Brandy Denton both checked in on the same day."

"Well, isn't that interesting," I said. "So, she was here when Brandy was murdered. She was also here when Oliver Freemont was killed."

Trooper Bob was already shaking his head before I opened my mouth.

"Before you ask, the answer is *no*. You may *not* come with me when I question her. *I'll* question her, and I don't need any help from Nancy Drew."

Boy, do I hate the Nancy Drew references.

"Fine. But—"

"Yeah, no buts. Now, give my deputy your statement, and we'll be on our way." Trooper Bob folded his arms across his chest and glared. He was done, and nothing I said would change his mind.

Chris Russell stepped forward. "Actually, I'd like to talk to my client in private first."

Molten lava rose up Trooper Bob's core. It flooded his neck and spread from his neck to his head. One look at Trooper Bob and I had a fairly good idea of what Mount Vesuvius must have looked like before it erupted. If he didn't watch his blood pressure, he was going to have a stroke.

I rose and turned to lead Chris Russell toward the living room when I was stopped.

"Forget it," Trooper Bob said. "I've got to get out of here. When you've had time to coach your client on what to say and what *not* to say, I'll be waiting outside." Trooper Bob marched outside and slammed the door to the garage in the face of his deputy, who only managed to avoid needing a nose job because he had to move around Baby.

After Trooper Bob and the deputy fled the scene, April gave me a quick hug and then hurried outside. That left the Admiral, Michael, Chris Russell, me, and Baby. The barometric pressure in the room went down, and I was able to breathe.

"I would prefer to talk to my client alone," Chris Russell said.

Michael and the Admiral both gave the lawyer a dirty look that must have convinced him that he would have an easier time convincing them to dress up like Ballerina Barbie and run down the street covered in glitter than getting them to leave my side.

Chris Russell held up his hands in surrender and then turned to me. "Madison, tell me what happened."

I told him about meeting Oliver Freemont at the beach and agreeing to meet him with the Admiral later.

"Did he say what this . . . package was that Octavia sent him?"

I shook my head.

"He must have given you some indication. Was it an envelope? A box?"

"No. He just said that she wanted me to have it if anything happened to her."

Chris Russell paced from one end of the kitchen to the other. A couple of times, he got too close to Baby's tail and got a growl.

"I'll take him to my room," I said. But Michael stopped me.

"Let me." He grabbed Baby by the collar and coaxed him out of the room.

When they were gone, Chris Russell wiped the back of his neck. "I don't like this."

"Why? I didn't kill him. I was here with my dad the entire time."

"That's right," the Admiral said. "Madison never left my sight. I'll swear to that in a court of law."

"That's hardly helpful. You're her father. You're hardly a reliable witness. Besides, for all the police know, you're more likely to have aided her in killing someone who you might have deemed a threat to your daughter."

"Are you calling me a liar?"

The words were slow and soft—too soft. Chris Russell had pushed the Admiral's button by questioning his integrity and veracity. The air crackled with electricity.

"No. I'm just saying what a jury would say. Of course I *know* you would never do anything unethical like that, but I also believe that Madison didn't kill Brandy Denton or Oliver Freemont." He smiled, but it was too late. The die was cast, and the Admiral had a memory like an elephant. He wouldn't forget. Nor would he forgive.

"Good." The Admiral wasn't a talker, but whenever he was curt, that was never a good sign.

"I'm just trying to help Madison. It doesn't look good. Oliver Freemont was a forger. He— "

"Alleged," I said.

"What?" Chris Russell's head snapped around, and his brow furled.

"April said he was *suspected* of forgery, but he hadn't been convicted of forgery. So, he was an *alleged* forger."

"Semantics. Law enforcement has to be careful about what they say to prevent lawsuits, but we know that where there's smoke there's fire. You know what they say, if you lay down with dogs, you wake up with fleas." Russell gave me the *you poor naïve fool* look, and I could feel the blood rushing up my neck.

"Interesting analogy," Michael said as he came back in the room. "But I resent the comparison."

"My point is simply that Oliver Freemont wasn't trustworthy. For all we know, he might have wanted to lure Maddy to the beach so he could harm her. Criminals— " He saw me start to object and quickly held up a hand to prevent me. "*Alleged* criminals can't be trusted."

The look he gave me made me flush. *I'm the one who had trusted Elliott and been dumped at the altar. Obviously, I wasn't a good judge of his character. I misjudged Elliott's feelings for me. Maybe I'm wrong about Oliver Freemont, too. If I was wrong about them, who else have I misjudged?*

I cast a glance at Michael.

CHAPTER 38

"Earth to Maddy." Chris Russell waved his hand in front of my face.

"Sorry, but I suddenly feel lightheaded. I really think I need to lie down." I batted my eyelashes and forced a smile.

Chris Russell looked at me the same way the Grinch looked at Cindy-Lou Who. Although instead of giving me a cup of water and patting me on the head, he patted my hand. *Ick.*

"That's okay, why don't you leave everything to me? I'll talk to Trooper Bob. As your legal representative, I'll take care of everything. You just go rest. This has been a trying day." Chris Russell smiled and walked out of the house, leaving the Admiral, Michael, and me alone.

"What the heck was that?" the Admiral asked.

"I call it my 'Damsel in Distress' performance. Nine times out of ten, it can get me a warning instead of a speeding ticket."

"That was . . . scary." Michael's lips twitched and he struggled to keep them under control, but he failed. He burst out laughing, and after a few seconds, the Admiral joined in.

"Well, now that he's gone, maybe we can get down to business," I said.

That sobered the men up.

"What business?" Michael asked.

"We need to figure out how we're going to get to Jessica Barlow."

The Admiral frowned. "What do you mean?"

I sighed. "We need to question her. We need to find out who she was following—me or Oliver Freemont? What or who else did she see? Who killed Oliver Freemont?"

"Won't that state trooper be doing all of that? Questioning her?" the Admiral asked.

"I'm sure he will, but he doesn't know Jessica. She's a shrewd one. Plus, he believes I did it. So, how deep do you think he'll really dig?"

"Good point."

I glanced at my dad. He was staring a hole into the counter, a sure sign that something was bothering him.

"What's wrong?" I asked.

He looked up and quickly glanced at Michael before hurriedly adding, "Nothing. I'm fine."

That look wasn't wasted on Michael. "Why don't I leave you two to talk? I'm going home. Call me if you need anything."

I nodded.

Michael left me and the Admiral sitting in silence at the island.

"Are you going to tell me what's bothering you?" I asked.

He paused a few moments and then released a heavy sigh. "Nothing's bothering me. It's just . . . I don't know if I'm doing the right thing."

"About?"

"Oliver Freemont."

I frowned. "What about him?"

"Remember when you were talking to the 9-1-1 dispatcher?

She wanted to know if he could talk, so I put my ear to his mouth?"

"Vaguely. Yeah."

"Well, he did."

"What did he say?"

" 'Galina. Find Galina.' "

"Galina? I had no idea Oliver Freemont knew Galina. I mean, can it be the same one? Of course it's the same one. How many Galinas could there be in New Bison, Michigan?"

"Not many. New Bison isn't exactly a cultural mecca." He scratched his temple.

"Why didn't you tell Trooper Bob or Chris Russell? Maybe Galina killed him. Maybe she killed Brandy Denton. Trooper Bob can go arrest her, and this nightmare will be over."

"Do you really believe that? You've known Galina a long time. Do you honestly believe she killed Brandy Denton and this Oliver Freemont?"

I shook my head.

"Right now, I'm having a hard time trying to figure out who I can trust. I don't know the good guys from the bad guys. I don't know these people. I don't know who to trust. You're the only person that I trust one hundred percent. So, I wanted the chance to talk to you before I shared anything."

I paused and took a few moments to think. "Honestly, Dad, I don't know what I believe anymore. I was certain that Oliver Freemont was telling the truth when he talked about how Great-Aunt Octavia saved his life and how much he cared about her, but as Chris Russell pointed out, my track record isn't very good in determining who's trustworthy and who isn't. After my wedding debacle with Elliott, I'm not doing well in that department, am I?" I was tempted to add Michael's name to that list of fails, but I stopped myself. My heart wasn't ready to believe that he'd let me down, too.

"Madison, stop doubting yourself. You're a good judge of

character. People are not perfect. Even good people don't always behave in a way that makes them proud."

Something in his voice made me realize that we weren't talking about Galina and Oliver Freemont anymore. "Dad, I— "

He held up a hand to stop me. "Maddy, I've tried to be a good person. A good husband to your mother. A good soldier. A good leader. A good father. But I've made mistakes, especially when it comes to you. I haven't always been a good father. I gave you money, clothes, shoes, and— "

"And I appreciate that, too."

He grinned but quickly got serious again. "I should have given you more. I should have given you more of my attention. My time. I hope you know that, despite my fails, I love you more than . . ." He swallowed hard and pinched the bridge of his nose.

I threw my arms around his neck. After a few moments, I said, "I always knew you loved me, but I hoped that I could make you proud so that you would like me."

"Oh honey, I love you, and I like you. I love the woman you have grown into. You are smart, funny, independent, and kind. You're beautiful inside and out, and I'm so incredibly proud of you."

We hugged for several moments. Then, I pulled away and wiped my eyes. "Now what do we do?"

"You're the expert here. I'm just an old Navy sea dog. You're the one with all of the experience solving murders. You tell me. Do I tell Trooper Bob or Chris Russell what Freemont said before he died? Or . . . oh wait." The Admiral rummaged in his pocket and pulled out a small piece of paper. He held it up. "I found this clutched in Freemont's hand."

"You know, you're not supposed to remove anything from a crime scene." I grinned as I took the paper and stared at it.

"It wasn't a crime scene when I took it. He was still alive."

"Is that your story?"

"And I'm sticking to it." He glanced over my shoulder. "What is it?"

I unfolded the paper and smoothed it out. "I don't know, but if I had to guess, I'd say it's some kind of map."

"A map to what? Buried treasure?" the Admiral asked.

"Maybe not a treasure, but if we're lucky, Oliver Freemont may have left us a map to Great-Aunt Octavia's secret package. Maybe once and for all we can find out who the spy was in her camp."

CHAPTER 39

We stared at that paper for what felt like hours, but it was more like thirty minutes. We looked at it from every angle possible. The problem was, if it was a map, then Oliver Freemont hadn't left us any reference points. There was nothing that looked like directions. The only indication that the paper could possibly contain a map were some wavy lines that we took to be water—Lake Michigan.

~~~~~~~

L10, R5, R5

X

But, after staring at the paper until we were cross-eyed, neither the Admiral nor I had any idea what or how to decipher it.

"Maybe it isn't a map," I said.

"You're just tired." The Admiral stretched. "I'm tired, too. Let's sleep on it, and maybe something will come to us in the morning."

* * *
~~~~~~~

I lay in bed thinking, but no matter how hard I thought about it, I couldn't figure out what clue Oliver Freemont had left us. What were the numbers, and where could we even start to figure it out?

"Ugh." I rolled over for the tenth or maybe the fiftieth time. I stopped counting.

Baby must have been frustrated by my restlessness because he stood up and turned around so his back was to me. He was snoring within minutes.

"Traitor."

The only indication that he heard me was a pause in the snores before they started up again.

I took out my phone and snapped a picture of the map and then put the paper in the drawer by my nightstand. Just as I was about to put my phone down for the night, I got a text message from Trooper Bob. They were finished with the crime scene, and Baby Cakes Bakery was cleared to reopen for business.

That was great news, but I wasn't sure what condition the bakery was in. It would need to be thoroughly cleaned before we could reopen. We certainly couldn't serve from here. I seriously doubted if Trooper Bob was finished, and I didn't think he would take kindly to cars blocking the driveway while they collected evidence. Besides, if I'd learned anything in my six months living in a small town, it's that the news of Oliver Freemont's murder would have traveled fast. Everyone would be stopping by to gawk and ask questions. Not that I had any answers to give. I could send a post that Baby Cakes would be closed tomorrow, but . . . that would cut into revenue. That's not what responsible adults do. Is it? I waffled over what the right thing to do was and finally decided that responsible adults don't toss and turn all night trying to make up their minds. No, a responsible adult would get up and do something. What? I could clean the bakery. That way, we could still open as usual. I pulled out my phone and posted a quick note that Baby Cakes would be open for business as usual.

#BabyCakesIsBackInBusiness #ComeEarly2GetUrPastryFix #IfUSnoozeULose #Open4Business

I got up and pulled on a pair of jeans and a T-shirt and slipped my feet into my Pyer Moss Sculpts. Having a plan made me feel giddy. I smacked Baby on the butt. "Come on, boy."

Baby lifted his head and looked over his shoulder at me. He looked as though he thought I was joking. He put his head back down and continued to snore.

"Hey, I'm serious. We need to go clean the bakery. Come on."

Baby didn't move.

"Fine. I'll make sure you have a big treat."

His head came up, but he didn't make one move toward getting down.

"Please?" I wrapped my arms around him. "You know I couldn't possibly feel safe without my big boy there to protect me." I batted my eyelashes and begged.

To my great surprise, it worked.

Baby yawned and stretched. Then, he slowly climbed down from the bed, shook himself, and waited.

"Humph. I guess all males like flattery and saving damsels in distress." I grabbed my purse and opened the door. Baby and I headed toward the kitchen.

Just before turning the corner, I heard voices and halted. One of the voices was the Admiral, but who was he talking to at one in the morning?

I strained to hear. The other voice was too deep to be April's. While I struggled to hear, Baby yawned, walked around me, and went into the kitchen.

"Come back here," I whispered.

Baby ignored me.

I listened for screams or the sound of flesh being ripped from its bones. When it didn't come, I peeked my head around the corner. Michael and the Admiral were seated at the island drinking coffee. With a gun on the counter between them.

"What are you two doing up at this time of the morning? And is there more coffee?"

Michael got up and handed me his mug and then went to my single-cup coffee maker and made himself another mug.

I sipped the coffee to hide a smile. *God, I love that man.*

The Admiral got up and pulled out his wallet and then handed Michael five dollars.

"What's that about?" I asked.

"G.I. bet me five dollars that your caffeine detector would sense coffee and you'd be down wanting a cup." The Admiral shook his head.

"Yeah, and the Admiral swore once you were asleep, not even a Super Hornet landing on the deck of an aircraft carrier would be able to wake you up." Michael pocketed the bill.

"May I ask where you think you're going?" the Admiral asked.

"What makes you think I'm going anywhere?" I said. "Maybe I just came down for the coffee?"

"You wouldn't need your purse to get a cup of coffee," Michael said.

"Maybe I came to investigate the voices I heard. What are you two doing here at this time of the morning, anyway?" They say the best defense is a good offense. With any luck, they wouldn't notice that I didn't answer the question.

Michael took the five-dollar bill out of his pocket and handed it back to the Admiral.

"What?" I asked.

"Nothing. The Admiral bet me five dollars that you would go on the offensive rather than answering a direct question." Michael sipped his coffee.

"Fine." I huffed. "I couldn't sleep. So, I thought I'd go to Baby Cakes and clean so we would be ready for business."

"Sneaking out to clean at one o'clock in the morning? I

never thought I would see the day." The Admiral slid the five-dollar bill back to Michael.

I turned to Michael. "How did you know I'd go clean?"

He held up his phone. "You posted a message making all of the pastry-eating folks of New Bison aware that Baby Cakes would be open for business as usual. No way you'd risk folks showing up to a bakery that wasn't pristine."

"You still haven't answered my question. What are you two doing?"

"I was invited," the Admiral said. 'I'm sitting at my daughter's house, enjoying a cup of coffee and trying to talk some sense into this G.I."

"I'm just listening to sea tales from a misguided sailor and enjoying a cup of coffee." Michael smiled.

"At one in the morning?"

Both men sipped their coffees.

"If this is all so innocent, then why are you both packing heat, and why is there a Glock on my island?"

They glanced at each other and shrugged.

"Just two soldiers comparing guns?" the Admiral said.

I folded my arms across my chest and waited. Neither man was good with silence. It was just a matter of time until one of them caved.

The Admiral folded first. "I guess we both had the same idea. There's a killer out there. He or she killed Brandy Denton and Oliver Freemont, and that last one was just a little too close to home for comfort."

"So, you two are my protectors?"

"I'm your father. That's been my job for over twenty years."

"I'm new to the party," Michael said, "but . . . I'd like to apply for the job." He got up and wrapped his arms around me.

What does that mean? Is he implying that he wants a longer-term commitment?

We kissed until the Admiral broke things up. "All right, that's enough of that."

"You two are incredibly sweet," I said, "and I'm lucky to have both of you in my life, but I'm just going down to the bakery to do some cleaning. I doubt seriously if a killer is lurking around at one in the morning just waiting for me to leave the house. I think you two are just overkill. Besides, I have Baby." I glanced over at my English mastiff, who was curled up in his dog bed with his massive head resting on a Lambchop stuffed animal.

I pulled out my phone and snapped a photo.

#AMastiffAndHisToy #BigDogsNeedLuv2 #Never2Old4Toys #BabyAndLambChop4Ever

"I have all the faith in the world that Baby is a fierce protector," the Admiral said, "but I've got five dollars that says an old Navy sea dog can still whip a retired G.I."

Michael grinned. "You see? I have to protect not only you but the reputation of the Army."

"Fine, but if you two are coming, then don't think you're going to get out of helping to clean. Miss Hannah says, 'Many hands make light work.' "

We all piled into my Rivian, and I drove to Baby Cakes. I pulled up into my space behind the bakery, but something was wrong. The lights were on. Would the police leave the lights on? Someone was inside the bakery. My hands went cold, and my heart skipped a beat.

CHAPTER 40

Baby's hackles were raised, and a rumble started in his belly. He stared at the back door. His eyes held the same intensity I'd seen in Navy SEALs prepared to engage an enemy target.

The Admiral was the first one out of the vehicle. He had his gun out and racked the slide to chamber a round in one swift movement.

I reached for my door but was stopped when Michael reached over. "Madison. Wait here. If we're not out in five minutes, call 9-1-1. Please, let us handle this."

"Are you kidding? I'm not staying here by myself while every male that I love goes running head-first into danger. No way. Classic horror movie blunder number one: Never separate. Absolutely not. No way. Nope. Not doing it."

"You're not going to be alone."

I frowned at Michael, but he had turned to Baby.

He grabbed both sides of Baby's head and forced the mastiff to make eye contact. "Listen to me. Not this time. You need to stay here and protect Maddy. Do you understand me? Let me handle this." He waited. Michael and Baby gazed into each other's eyes. Through that look, some type of canine-to-human communication happened. After a few moments, Baby dropped his gaze, and the rumbling stopped.

Michael scratched Baby's ear. "I'm trusting you. If you let anything happen to my girl, I just might make a slip that'll end your days as a champion stud dog."

Baby gave a yelp.

Michael chuckled and then got out of the car. He glanced at the Admiral, and the two of them went inside.

I glanced at my phone to see the time. Ten seconds later, I glanced at my phone again. I waited fifteen seconds before glancing at the phone again. I tapped my fingers on the steering wheel and tried not to imagine what was happening inside.

Thirty seconds later, Michael opened the back door and beckoned for me to come inside.

I stumbled getting out of the car and nearly fell, but Michael was there to catch me.

I flung my arms around his neck and held on as tightly as I could.

"It's okay."

I pulled away. "You listen to me. I don't care if you are some super-tough ex-Army commando. If you ever leave me like that again, Baby won't be the only one in jeopardy of losing his ability to reproduce." I hugged him tighter and felt his chuckle before I could hear it.

When I pulled away, he saluted. "Yes, ma'am."

Inside, the Admiral was standing over Leroy, who was sitting with his head pushed down between his legs. There was a large bowl and what looked to be a dozen raw eggs on the floor.

"What happened?" I asked.

Leroy lifted his head. "I saw your post that Baby Cakes was going to be open tomorrow . . . I mean, later today. So, I thought I'd better come and make sure everything was clean and ready to go. I also figured I should bake some thumbprint cookies and get some croissants ready, but when I turned around, these two were pointing guns at me."

The Admiral walked over to the counter and reached for a roll of paper towels, but Baby was already cleaning up the majority of the mess.

"I've never been so scared in my entire life," Leroy said. "I dropped the eggs and nearly passed out."

Leroy's face looked green.

"Head down," Michael ordered.

Leroy dropped his head back down.

"I guess we all must have had the same idea," I said, rolling up my sleeves. I glanced around the kitchen and started giving orders. "Dad, there's a mop in the closet. When Baby's done, you're on K.P." I turned to Michael. "You and I will clean the glass cases and get everything ready. Leroy, make some coffee, and when you're feeling up to it, get a batch of thumbprint cookies in the oven." I glanced at my troops.

Dad and Michael snapped to attention and saluted.

There was a knock from the closet.

The Admiral jumped and reached for his gun, but I held out a hand to stop him.

I opened the door, and Candy Rivers came in carrying a carafe of coffee and a stack of Styrofoam cups.

"It's like Grand Central Station in here," the Admiral muttered.

"I saw the lights, and then I read Maddy's post," Candy said. "I knew you'd need coffee." She placed the carafe on the counter. "Since I'm up, can I help?"

Many hands really did make for light work. In just under two hours, Baby Cakes was sparkling clean, with a few dozen thumbprint cookies and a large batch of blondies ready for sale. It was still hard for me to look at the trolley without thinking of Brandy Denton, but it was great for storage. Besides, I was confident she hadn't actually been killed in the trolley, but that the killer had used it to help transport her inside the bakery.

At four, we locked up and went home. I wasn't tired, but if I got into bed I wouldn't get out again, so I took a shower instead. The steam was great for relaxing my muscles and clearing my thoughts. *What is going on? Who killed Brandy Denton and Oliver Freemont? What's the connection between Galina Forkin and Oliver Freemont? And why has Jessica Barlow been following me? Or has she? Holy cow. I assumed that Jessica had been following me, but what if she had been following Oliver Freemont?* "Does it matter?" *I shouldn't ask myself questions that I didn't know the answer to.*

The only way to figure out what the connection was between Galina and Oliver was to go to the source. Oliver was dead, so I was going to need to talk to Galina.

I got out of the shower and dressed. Normally, dressing for work was fairly easy, but then I wasn't going to talk to a fashionista with a svelte dancer's body. I stared at myself in the mirror and realized that owning a bakery meant I had a lot more curves than when I first moved to New Bison. "Maybe I should be running with Michael instead of Alliyah Howard."

Baby lifted his head, yawned, and then lay back down on the bed.

I pulled out a loose-fitting floral dress that looked great and hid a lot of my lower half, but it had a scoop neck that emphasized my neck and other attributes. I spun around and looked from all angles and decided it would be comfortable for work and still stylish for meeting my ex's current attachment.

I pulled my hair up into a high bun and put on a pair of large hoop earrings. It wasn't in the same category as yesterday's attire, but I wasn't the same woman I was yesterday. Yesterday, I wanted Elliott to see what he missed. Today, I dressed for comfort and pride. I wasn't a rival for Elliott's affection. Today, I wanted Galina to see that just because I wasn't living in L.A., I was still fashionable.

I pulled out a pair of black low-top Converse sneakers for work. I wouldn't care if I dropped an entire bag of flour on the sneakers. They could always go in the washer. I packed a pair of sandals that looked amazing with my dress for meeting with Galina. The sandals would not hold up to caked-on flour or eggs.

"Come on, Baby. Let's go."

His eyes were opened, so I knew he heard me, but he didn't move.

I walked over and jiggled his jowls. "I'm not the only one who's packed on extra weight. We're going to need to cut back on your snacks, too."

He didn't bother lifting his head at that. Although, he opened his eyes.

"Pretending to be asleep doesn't mean you won't have to cut back," I teased. "Let's go."

I went to the door, and this time he climbed down from the bed. After a couple of stretches, he followed me downstairs.

Baby Cakes was packed, and we were busy from the moment we opened. All of our hard work cleaning and baking didn't go unnoticed, although I think some of the traffic came from rubberneckers who wanted to see the place where a woman was found murdered. Sadly, I'd learned that murder was good for business, as long as the deceased hadn't died of food poisoning. People were curious. Besides, not much happened in a small town. A dead woman showing up at a bakery was probably the highlight of the day for a good number of people.

The blondies were a big hit, and I was grateful that Leroy had talked me into making some for sale and not just free samples.

By lunchtime, the crowds had thinned to the point that I felt comfortable leaving Leroy and Hannah to manage without me.

The Admiral wasn't convinced that I didn't need an armed bodyguard. However, I convinced him that he would intimidate Galina, and I'd never get a word out of her. So, we compromised. I agreed that he could come along with me to the Carson Law Inn and perhaps talk to Carson Law about attorneys. Then, we could have lunch together. I pretended not to notice the way his eyes lit up at the thought of seeing Carson Law again.

I drove to the inn. The Admiral went in search of the owner, while I had the front desk ring Galina and Elliott's room. She must have been thoroughly bored because she agreed to meet me in the dining room for lunch.

I wasn't surprised that I had to wait thirty minutes for Galina to join me. Her hair and makeup were impeccable. She was stunning but overdressed for New Bison in an iridescent lime bubble dress in silk faille.

Galina sauntered up to my table. "To what do I owe this honor?"

She had taken extra care in applying her makeup, but it was clear to me she had been crying. Her eyes were red, and there were dark circles under them.

"You look stunning. I've always loved Christian Siriano."

Galina paused for a moment, unsure how to take the compliment. After a few beats, she relaxed. "Thank you."

"His lines look great on someone slender like you." I piled on the compliments, and she unfolded and relaxed her mouth. Her lips hadn't moved upward into a smile, but at least they'd moved from their downward slope into neutral.

"You look nice, too," she said reluctantly. She narrowed her gaze and tilted her head to the side. "I don't think I recognize that designer."

"Monique Lhuillier." I leaned forward. "It's from last season, but I don't care. I love it." I glanced down at the sleeveless navy and floral-printed lace dress.

"It's lovely."

"Thank you. Please, have a seat. I'm supposed to meet my dad here for lunch, but I ordered some appetizers." I motioned to the charcuterie board in the center of the table.

Galina looked suspicious, but she sat and with only the slightest amount of coaxing helped herself to some of the cheese, meat, and other delicacies. A waiter filled her water glass and left to bring her a glass of white wine.

"Okay, what's this about?" Galina asked.

I rehearsed what to say while driving over, but one look at Galina's face and I tossed everything out. "I wanted to offer my condolences about Oliver Freemont's murder. I know you two were close, and I wanted to see if there was anything I could do for you."

CHAPTER 41

Unfortunately, Galina had just taken a sip of her wine. Her face went white. Her hand shook, and she started to choke.

Our waiter came back to see if Galina would need assistance.

Emergencies were not my strong suit, and I prayed that she wasn't going to need me to administer the Heimlich maneuver. She waved away the waiter, put down her wine, and took a sip of water.

Her hand was shaking so badly, she nearly spilled the water on her dress, but she managed to get enough of it down her throat to ease her coughing. She wiped the tears from her eyes and plastered on a fake mask of ignorance. "I don't know what you mean."

Boy, is she a horrible actress.

"Oliver Freemont met me at the beach yesterday. He must have been here when we were talking. That's how he knew where I was so he could follow me, right?"

"I don't . . . I don't understand."

"Look, it's okay. I liked Oliver Freemont, and I'm terribly

sorry that someone killed him." I thought about what I said and realized that it was true. I did like Oliver Freemont. Great-Aunt Octavia liked him. She trusted him with her secret package. Most importantly, Baby liked him. So, it was the truth. I liked Freemont, and I was sorry that he was murdered.

"But how did you know?" Galina whispered.

"He must have loved you very much. Your name was the last thing he said before he died."

Galina's eyes filled with tears. Her bottom lip quivered. And then the dam broke. Galina Forkin opened her mouth and wailed. If I thought her nearly choking caused attention, it was nothing compared to her sobbing and ugly crying.

I hadn't noticed Elliott until he came to the table. He had a dark bruise under one eye, and his nose was wrapped in gauze. I gawked for a moment and took a lesson from Galina and forced my lips into neutral. "Elliott, I didn't mean to upset her, but maybe you'd better take her upstairs to your room."

He scowled. At least, I think it was a scowl. It was hard to tell with the gauze. "Good grief, Galina. Pull yourself together. You're making a spectacle of yourself." He glanced around.

If he intended his words to bring comfort, he was sorely mistaken. Galina took one look at Elliott and wailed louder.

I stood, sidestepped Elliott, and helped Galina to her feet. "I'll help her. What room are you in?"

"She moved out. I don't know what room she's in. You'll need to ask her."

"I guess she's a lot smarter than I thought." I maneuvered Galina out of the dining room and toward the elevator.

Fortunately, we didn't have far to go. Once we were in her second-floor room, Galina flung herself onto the bed and unleashed the rest of the floodgates.

I let her cry for nearly thirty minutes. When I thought she was winding down, I got the box of tissues from the bathroom and sat next to her. "Galina, you're going to make yourself ill. Please tell me what I can do to help."

"Help? There's only one thing you can do to help me."

"What's that?"

"Find out who killed Oliver. I'm going to rip out their heart with my bare hands."

CHAPTER 42

I wasn't expecting anything quite that graphic. Her words were a reflection of her grief. She didn't mean it literally, but I still couldn't help staring at her pale white hands.

"Whoever did this will pay. The police will catch them. Trooper Bob—"

"Trooper Bob? That *edeot.*"

The more upset Galina became, the thicker her Russian accent, so I turned on an app on my phone to translate. Despite her accent, I recognized "idiot" when I heard it.

"Edeot! He will find Oliver's killer *kagda rak na gare svisnit.*"

My phone translator displayed "When cancer hangs on the mountain."

Okay, that has me stumped. "Galina, I don't know what that means."

She sat up. "It means, you must find Oliver's killer."

"Are you serious? You can't be serious. I can't find the killer. How am I supposed to find the killer? Heck, right now, the police think I killed him." *Oops. Maybe I shouldn't have told her that.* I watched her hands more carefully to make sure she wasn't going to make a move to rip out my heart.

"I know you didn't kill Oliver. He trusted you. He told me. Your great-aunt Octavia was a wonderful woman. She saved his life. He trusted her, and he trusted you. So, I trust you."

"But, I thought you hated me. I thought that was why you were with Elliott."

"I hated Brandy. She hated you."

I frowned. "This doesn't make sense."

"How did you not know? Brandy was jealous of you."

"Me? Why would she be jealous of me?"

"Because you're beautiful and smart and successful."

"Smart? Now I know you're making that up."

Galina shook her head. "No. You graduated from Stanford. Did you know that Brandy was rejected?"

"Lots of people get rejected. It doesn't mean she wasn't smart."

"You graduated with honors. You've traveled all over the world, and you speak multiple languages."

"Of course I've traveled all over the world—my dad was in the Navy! I was a Navy brat who never got to stay in one place long enough to make friends and have a hometown."

Galina waved all of that away. "You're beautiful and kind. Plus, you were engaged to a doctor. Brandy hated you because she wanted to be you. So, she set out to take Elliott. Leaving you at the altar was Brandy's idea, by the way. She wanted to humiliate you."

I don't know how long I sat there before I realized my mouth was open and closed it. "Okay, that sucks."

"Yes, but she really did you a favor. I mean, Elliott is not nearly as handsome as your sexy veterinarian."

I grinned. My veterinarian *was* pretty sexy. After a few moments, I came to my senses. "Whoa. Okay. So, Brandy hated me, but that doesn't mean I can figure out who killed Oliver, even if I wanted to."

"You don't want to know who killed him?"

She wrung her hands, and I stood up and walked farther away from her.

"It's not that I don't want to *know* who killed him. I don't want to *catch* the killer. Hey, big revelation here: *Killers are mean!* I've nearly died—*twice*! I don't want to go through that again. That's what the police are for. I want to stay here. Learn to bake. Live my life. I do not want to find myself in a situation where someone who has already killed two people is looking for me to be a third."

"But the police think you killed Oliver."

"And Brandy," I added.

"So, you have to find the killer, or you will be arrested. Do you really want to leave your future up to Trooper Bob?"

Galina could be persuasive when she wanted to be. And she definitely wanted to persuade me. I wasn't convinced, but I also wasn't ready to have my heart ripped out. So, I made a decision to play along. I needed to get out of her room. Once I was free, I could pass along whatever information she had to April and Trooper Bob.

"Okay, tell me everything you know about Oliver Freemont, and I mean *everything*! If you want me to find his killer, then I need to know the good, the bad, and the ugly."

Galina smiled, truly smiled for the first time today.

"Before you get too excited, I already know that Oliver Freemont was forging paintings. So, don't hide anything, or I'll back out."

Backing out was an idle threat since I had no intention of backing *in*, but it was all I had.

An hour later, I left Galina's room. My head was spinning, but I had a few more pieces of the puzzle. I didn't have all of the pieces, but an image was forming in the back of my mind.

CHAPTER 43

On my way out, I stopped by the dining room. The Admiral was sitting at a table with Carson Law. For a few moments, I stood in the corner and watched. Carson Law was talking, and she leaned forward and placed her hand on his arm. The Admiral said something, and then he laughed. Not just a modest snicker, but a full-out, eye-crinkling belly laugh. In that laugh, the Admiral was no longer the rigid, stuffed-shirt career military soldier. He was a man having a moment with a woman he obviously admired.

The Admiral hadn't lived the life of a monk after my mom died. He dated. But, there was something different about Carson Law. There was a spark in his eyes that hadn't been there before. I turned to leave. I wasn't hungry, and after meeting with Galina, I had a couple of stops I wanted to make before returning to the bakery. However, at that moment, the Admiral looked up and saw me. He waved me over.

"Madison, I had just about given up on you," he said.

"I'm sorry. It's been a crazy day. Would it be okay if I took a rain check on lunch? I'm just not very hungry."

"You're not coming down with anything, are you?"

"Just tired. I must be getting old. I can't pull all-nighters like I did in college."

The Admiral started to stand, but I motioned him back down. "No need for you to come. Stay and enjoy your lunch. I've got a couple of errands to run, and then I'm going home and straight to bed."

He frowned. "Are you sure?"

I nodded.

A moment of relief flashed across his face, but he cleared it quickly. "All right, but you be careful. Then, straight home."

I nodded and hid my hand behind my back with my fingers crossed. "Dad, stop worrying. It's broad daylight. I'll be fine."

Carson Law reached across and patted his hand. "Jefferson, I'm sure she'll be just fine."

He didn't look convinced, but he was outnumbered. "Okay. I'll be home shortly."

I kissed his cheek before leaving.

Once outside, I glanced at the time and then drove toward Lake Michigan.

The Beachcomber Hotel was a newly constructed building in downtown New Bison, and it was just a short walk to Lake Michigan. It was part of the development that Bradley Ellison had arranged with his Chicago investors who tore down the old, quaint buildings that once made up the village of New Bison in favor of the modernized tourist traps that lined the streets.

Inside, the Beachcomber was clean but dull. The pastel décor and furnishings took the beach theme to the max. The lobby was fitted with shell-patterned carpeting and wallpaper. The scones on the wall were shells. The chair backs were also shells, and the framed artwork continued the theme.

I was about to ask the bored teen behind the reception desk texting on her phone to ring Jessica Barlow's room when I caught a break. I turned as the elevator opened, and out she walked.

Jessica Barlow was a Southern Belle with an edge. She had big hair that would have made Dolly Parton drool with jealousy. She had gotten a nose ring and a few other piercings since I'd last seen her. She wore a black corset with a cinched waist, a flared skirt, and combat boots.

Jessica spotted me as soon as the elevator doors opened. She rolled her eyes and would have turned around, but she must have realized that resistance was futile. "Madison Montgomery. Fancy meeting you here."

"We need to talk."

"I've been answering questions all morning from Smokey the Bear, and I'm parched. I need a drink. So, if you want to talk, you better be buying." She walked toward the door.

I fell in beside her. "Fine. There's a great pub down the street."

We walked the few blocks to the Stray Dog Bar and Grille. It was still early for dinner, so there weren't many people there yet. We snagged a booth with no trouble.

I wasn't much of a drinker, so I ordered a Diet Coke. Jessica asked for a gin and tonic.

We sat in an awkward silence for a few moments until the waitress returned with our drinks and a bowl of peanuts. Before the waitress could leave, Jessica downed her gin and tonic and indicated that she wanted another.

"All right, what do you want?" Jessica asked. Her Southern accent made the words sound more drawn out. A casual observer might have thought that she was tipsy, but I'd seen Jessica drink a room full of fraternity boys under the table at a university fundraiser. It would take a lot more than a couple of gin and tonics to get her drunk.

"Why did Brandy really come to New Bison? And you can cut the reality television crap. I don't believe there was ever any rumors of me getting a reality show."

Jessica sipped her second drink. "Honestly, I don't know." I started to protest, but Jessica stopped me. "No. Really. I have no idea what the real reason was that she wanted to come to this gawd-awful place." She shivered. "I never imagined anything could get Brandy to come to a town that didn't have a Saks Fifth Avenue, but here she was."

"But she must have given some kind of indication why she came. Let's face it, I wasn't a threat to her. She humiliated me. She took Elliott. I left L.A. So, why follow me here?"

"Look, I was her drudge. Her P.A. I wasn't her confidant. All I know is that I used to open her mail. One day, she got a letter from someone. And before you ask, I don't know who. It was anonymous. Just a plain white envelope with her name and address typed on the front. I just know that the letter said if she wanted to complete her humiliation of you, then she should come to New Bison. And inside were twenty one-hundred-dollar bills."

"Someone paid Brandy Denton two thousand dollars to come here?"

Jessica nodded.

I'm not sure what I expected, but that wasn't it. "What did she do with the letter?"

Jessica shrugged. "Beats me. I never saw the letter after that."

"Is that it? There has to be more." I couldn't put my finger on it, but Jessica was holding something back.

"If there was more, she didn't share it with me. My job was to follow you around and see if I could catch you in an embarrassing position."

"So, you *did* record the argument Brandy and I had outside of the bakery and post it online."

"Yep. That was me."

"And you took the picture of me standing over Oliver Freemont's body?"

She shivered and took a sip of her gin and tonic. "That was horrible."

"Did you see who shot him? There must have been someone else there. You had to have seen something."

"I didn't see anything. I wasn't watching him. I was following you. I spent most of my time sitting outside your house, trying to make sure I was downwind of that horse you call a dog."

"How come I didn't see you?"

"Because I'm good at my job." She grinned.

I gave her a skeptical look, and eventually, she rolled her eyes and continued.

"When you came down the stairs, I hid in a cave." She tilted her head to the side and thought. "Funny, but there was a small dingy. I got the pictures, and then I took your dingy and got the heck out of there before the police came."

"What dingy?"

"I thought it was yours. I left it tied up on the dock. I was going to send you a note letting you know where to find it on my way out of town." She reached into her bag and pulled out an envelope addressed to me.

I glanced at the envelope. That's when lightning struck, and I figured out what she was hiding. "Okay, you said you never saw the letter again, but what about the envelope and the money?"

Jessica scowled, but she didn't deny that she took them. She reached into her purse and pulled out another envelope. She passed it to me.

It was just a plain white envelope with Brandy Denton's address typed on the front. I was sure there wouldn't be any point in turning it over to the police. It wasn't special or distinctive in any way. If the sender was stupid enough to have left fingerprints on the envelope, it wouldn't matter since it had likely been touched by at least a dozen people en route to L.A. I suppose there may have been some way for the police to check DNA if the sender licked the envelope to seal it, but I doubted it. Besides, as far as I knew, sending money to someone in the U.S. mail wasn't a crime. I looked in the envelope. Inside were ten one-hundred-dollar bills. I handed the bills to Jessica and kept the envelope.

Jessica stopped drinking and stared at the money. Then she looked at me. "You're not going to turn me in?"

"For what?"

That stumped her for a few moments. "For not telling the police."

I shrugged. "You have an envelope addressed to Brandy Denton and one thousand dollars. I don't think Brandy will miss the money."

The goth queen grinned. "Thanks. I thought I was going to have to sneak out of the hotel in the middle of the night."

"Brandy didn't pay for your room?"

Jessica shook her head. "Brandy Denton may have been rich, but she was also cheap. I had to pay my own travel expenses or stay at home. I could seriously make more money flipping burgers. If I didn't think I would have gotten grease on my clothes, I would have done it, too. My Papaw would say, 'She'd hold onto a nickel until the eagle grinned.'"

"Why'd you do it? Why put up with her? You're a talented artist. You didn't need Brandy."

She gazed into her drink, and her bottom lip quivered. But Jessica Barlow was tough, and she wasn't about to cry into her drink. She closed her eyes, batted her eyelashes for a few moments, and then took a deep breath. "Thanks. I appreciate that. It's nice to hear some positive compliments on my work instead of complaints."

"Brandy didn't—"

"Nothing but complaints. '*The shoes aren't centered in the shot. You should have adjusted the lighting better. That outfit looks ridiculous. I'm not going to be seen in public with you dressed like that.'*"

"No one deserves to be treated like that."

"Thanks."

"Why did you stay?"

"Good question." She paused and thought about the question. After a few moments, she sat back in the booth. "It's not easy breaking into the art or fashion world. All I've wanted to do since I was a little girl was to dress up in beautiful clothes and take pictures. I wanted to be an artist. I used to dream of seeing my photos in magazines and hanging in museums. I tried for years to just get a shot. I couldn't even get an unpaid internship with any of the top designers. I guess, after all of the rejections, I lost confidence in my art. I convinced myself that if I was any good, then I wouldn't get rejected. As Brandy's drudge, I got to be in the 'room where the sausage was made.' I attended fashion shows and after parties."

I took a good long look at Jessica. "You have a good head for hats."

She raised an eyebrow. "That's a weird compliment, but . . . thank you, I think."

"I was just thinking that I know this wonderful lady who's a milliner. I can't promise—"

"Are you talking about Carson Law? OMG! I love her hats."

"I don't know if she needs an assistant, but she might take a look at your portfolio and maybe—"

"Madison Montgomery, are you serious? Please don't string me along. Are you serious? Please, tell me you're serious. If you could get me a few minutes with her, I would . . . I don't know. I would scrub floors, wash dishes, clean windows. Anything."

I pulled out my phone.

Hey Dad. R U still with Mrs. Law?

YES

Can you deliver a message?

Sure

I mentioned that I knew a young artist who was looking for a job as a P.A. She would love to meet her.

I waited a few moments for his response.

Maddy this is Carson. I'd love to meet your friend.

Thank you!

Any friend of yours is a friend of mine.

"Okay, great. She'd love to meet you. She's really nice."

"Holy freakin' cow. I can't believe this is happening. You're serious? I'm going to meet Carson Law?"

"I can't make any promises, but she might be able to give you some advice."

"You're not the shallow, evil shrew that Brandy said you were."

"I don't know about that. I can be pretty shallow. At least I used to be. I didn't have much confidence, either. I thought the best I could hope for was to marry a doctor, Elliott, and let him take care of me. Thanks to Brandy, that didn't work out. The doctor I picked out dumped me. I inherited my great-aunt Octavia's house, bakery, and dog. I came to New Bison and met some 'real people.' I guess I owe Brandy a big thanks." I raised my glass. "To Brandy."

We drank to Brandy Denton and then talked about fashion and art. Carson Law told me to have my friend come by the inn tomorrow.

Jessica stressed out about what to wear for her meeting. She hadn't packed a lot of clothes, but her room connected to Brandy's, and she had brought two trunks.

By the time I left the pub, Jessica was practically skipping.

She threw her arms around my neck. "Thank you. If you need anything, just reach out."

"Thanks, I'm good. But if you think of anything that'll help figure out who killed Brandy Denton and Oliver Freemont, please let me know."

Jessica stepped back and took a deep breath. "Look. I don't know if this will help or not, but there is one thing that I thought was strange."

"What was that?"

"The day Brandy was killed, she was really upset about that tea thing. She went out, and when she came back, she was different."

"Different how?"

She pondered the question for a few beats. "If I didn't know Brandy Denton, I would have said she was scared."

"Scared? Brandy?"

"I know, right? That's so not like her."

"Where did she go?"

"She went to the Carson Law Inn. Then she went to that pet adoption thing."

"What happened to the kitten?"

"Don't worry. He's in my room. Your sexy vet came looking for it, but when he saw that I had it, he said it was okay if I kept it." She smiled but then got serious. "It is okay, isn't it?"

"He's the expert. If he said you could keep it, then I'm sure it's fine."

She released a sigh of relief. "I've gotten quite attached to the little rug rat." She took another breath. "Anyway, I don't really know where she went after that, but that's when she got all weird. She was fidgety and nervous. Then, she saw your post about the brownies and—"

"Blondies."

"You really have become all domesticated, haven't you? Blondies. After she saw that video, then she said we had to go to the bakery."

"That's when you came and recorded our argument."

"Yeah, sorry."

I waved away her apology.

"After that, then she got really scared. She told me to keep an eye on you, and she left. That's the last time I saw her."

"That's the last time anyone saw her . . . alive," I said. "Except the killer."

CHAPTER 44

I asked a few additional questions, but it was clear Jessica didn't know anything more than she'd already shared. I wished her well in her meeting with Carson Law tomorrow, and we parted.

I tried to make sense of everything I'd learned, but nothing seemed to add up. First, someone sent Brandy Denton a letter and money to come to New Bison. Who hated me enough to want to see me humiliated more than I'd already been? It had to be someone in New Bison, didn't it? My mind rushed back to the voice that I'd heard in Jackson Abernathy's office. The sinister voice of evil who said, "*If she gets in my way again, I won't miss next time.*" That voice was soft and quiet, but I knew he meant business, and it sent a shiver down my spine just thinking about it.

"Madison!"

An icy hand touched by arm, and I nearly jumped out of my skin. I turned and stared into the eyes of Chris Russell.

"OMG! You scared me."

"I've been calling your name for over a block. You must have been daydreaming."

"I'm sorry. I was a hundred miles away." I patted my heart.

"What are you doing?" Russell looked around.

I bristled at the idea of explaining myself like a teenager caught sneaking into the house after curfew. "I was just having drinks with . . . a friend. Did you need me?"

"I have some papers I need your signature on. Nothing to worry about, but if you have a few minutes to come up to my office, we can get the formalities taken care of."

Chris Russell's office was just a couple of blocks away.

We walked the short distance to the building where he had his office.

Russell, Russell, and Stevenson was a stuffy old firm that had been started by Chris Russell's grandfather and his brother-in-law, Joel Stevenson. Later, Chris's father and then Chris himself joined the family firm. The original location had been in a building that was more prominent with views of Lake Michigan. After the two elder Russells died, the remaining partner, Chris, reduced the staff and the firm's footprint by moving into the current location. I wouldn't accuse him of slumming, but the building and views weren't impressive or prominent. At least not from the outside. The inside was another matter.

Chris Russell's office was warm and luxurious in a subtle way. From the wood-paneled walls to the thick carpet and Aubusson rugs, he had invested quite a bit of money. One wall was fitted with floor-to-ceiling bookshelves filled with leather-bound books. I remembered the Victrola phonograph and antique typewriter from my first visit to his office. Antiques were casually placed throughout the room. I learned that Russell didn't just showcase the items, he used them. Most of them wouldn't merit a second look from the average client, but to an art history major who spent many wonderful days in some of Europe's finest museums, it was a wonderland. I couldn't be sure, but I would bet my favorite Jimmy Choo boots that the collection of vases on the bookshelves were from the Ming dynasty.

Chris Russell slid a folder in front of me and handed me a pen. "I need your signature."

"What are they?"

Russell flashed a smile. "Nothing important, but in light of your present situation, I think it would be wise to arrange for power of attorney in case you're arrested. This would allow me to manage your property, business, and other affairs. I would be able to make sure that your staff and bills are paid, and I can make other legal decisions until you're able to do them yourself." He smiled.

I started reading the document, but after a couple of paragraphs, I got lost in the parties of the first part, parties of the second part, heretofore, henceforth, and hereinafters. Part of me wanted to close my eyes and sign without reading. I could twirl my hair, bat my eyelashes, and put on the familiar persona of a silly female. But the Admiral's image came to mind. *Adults read documents before they sign them.* Ugh. The last thing I needed was my father's voice in my head. I put down the pen and shook my head like Baby to erase the Admiral's image.

"Are you okay?" Russell asked.

"Uh-huh. Yep. I'm fine."

He looked as though he wasn't sure and was waiting for me to explain, but I didn't have an explanation for the Baby head shake.

I picked up the pen. Before I could sign, my gaze drifted up to the wall of books. I knew there was a television on one of the bookshelves. I'd seen it the first time I visited Chris Russell. He used it to play an old tape that Great-Aunt Octavia had made for me. It was the first time I remembered seeing her. I remember thinking she looked smart and determined. She wasn't a woman who had trouble making decisions. I put the pen down.

"Mr. Russell, I'm going to need to take these papers home and read through them before I sign."

There was a flash behind his brown eyes, but it was quickly gone. He sighed. "Of course you can read through them, but time may be limited."

My heartbeat increased. "Have you heard something?"

"I did run into the district attorney at the courthouse earlier." He shook his head. "I didn't want to scare you, but I don't think it's looking very good. Trooper Bob hasn't found anyone else that has the motive, means, and opportunity that you did. I didn't bring it up because I didn't want you to panic. But I haven't been idle. The D.A. is a good friend, and I planted a bug in his ear that *if* charges were brought, I felt confident that we could work out a deal that would be acceptable." He patted my hand and handed me the pen.

"A deal?"

"The D.A. is very fond of Hannah's sweet potato pies and, of course, Octavia's Chocolate Soul Cake." He chuckled. "I think he might have said it would be a crime to deprive the community of those delicious baked goods."

"I'm not taking a plea deal. I didn't kill anyone."

"I'm not saying you did, but we have to be realistic. The prisons are full of people who claim to be innocent. Some of them probably *are* innocent. But, the problem is we have to be able to convince a jury that you're innocent. And, right or wrong, that might not be easy."

There was something in his voice that made me pry deeper. "Why not?"

He sighed. "This isn't L.A., where you have people from all different walks of life. This is a small town. Most people who serve on juries have lived here their entire lives. Their parents and grandparents lived here. Their children go to the same schools. They attend the same church. You're young, and you've been in New Bison less than a year. I'm just worried that people may be biased. You don't have deep roots in this community."

"You think people won't believe me because I'm young and from L.A.? Is that all? Or are you saying it's because I'm Black?"

"I didn't say that."

"You didn't have to." I put down the pen and stood up.

"Madison, I'm not saying that you won't get a fair trial. I'm just saying that we must explore all of our options, and a plea deal might be worth considering depending on what evidence the D.A. has. That's all. It's common in cases like this to consider a plea deal, but we don't have to worry about things like that now."

I scooped up the papers and shoved them in my purse. Then, I hurried out of the office before I embarrassed myself by bursting out in tears and blubbering like a baby.

CHAPTER 45

I rushed out of the office and hurried down the street toward my car. Blinded by tears, I didn't realize where I was going until I hit a wall.

"Maddy, what's wrong?"

I looked up into a pair of soft brown eyes. Michael's brow was furled, and his voice was gruff from the concern I saw in his eyes. I threw my arms around his neck and cried.

He wrapped his arms around me and held me close while I sobbed. The stress from the past few days released into a flood of tears. When the flood slowed to a trickle, I pushed away.

"I'm sorry."

Michael took my chin and lifted my head so I could look into his eyes. "You don't ever need to apologize for needing a shoulder to cry on."

"I'm supposed to be strong. I'm an adult. I shouldn't be crying like a two-year-old." I hiccupped.

"Madison, you are strong, but that doesn't mean you don't have feelings or that you have to shoulder everything by yourself. You're human. Humans cry."

I don't think I've ever loved that man more than I did at that moment. I reached up and kissed him. "Thank you."

He grinned. "You don't have to thank me, either, but feel free to kiss me whenever you want."

I giggled.

"Madison, are you okay?"

I turned around and saw Constantine Papadakis's concerned face.

"Hi, Mr. Papadakis. I'm fine. Thank you."

"I saw you crying, and I was worried, but it looked like Dr. Portman had everything in hand." The florist chuckled. "But, it made me so sad that I wanted to give you something to put a smile back on your beautiful face." He reached behind his back and handed me a bouquet of flowers.

"Oh, Mr. Papadakis, these are beautiful. Thank you so much."

"Ah, that smile. That's what I want to see. Your baked goods make me happy, so I'm glad I can bring a smile to you, too. Now, I will go back to my shop and leave you in the capable hands of Dr. Portman." He grinned.

"That was so sweet of him to make me such a beautiful bouquet. I love Asiatic lilies." I sniffed the flowers. "I should pay him. This bouquet is huge and had to cost a small fortune."

"He wanted to do it, but I'm sure he won't say no to a dozen thumbprint cookies. Now, do you want to tell me what—"

"Madison." A soft voice caused me to look up.

"Hello, Mrs. Hurston."

Alma Hurston was a petite woman with white downy hair and blue eyes. She was also Candy Rivers's mother and my next-door neighbor.

"Are you okay? Kay Lillie was driving down Main Street, and she said she saw you crying and wanted me to go and make sure you were okay. She would have stopped, but she was late for work."

"I'm fine, and please thank Mrs. Lillie for checking on me."

"Are you sure?"

I nodded. "Yes, ma'am."

She looked into my eyes and must have determined that I was telling the truth because after a few moments, she nodded. "Well, if there's anything you need, you just let me know. I lived next door to Octavia for over forty years, and if she thought we weren't taking care of you, she'd roll over in her grave." She patted my arm.

"Thank you. I'm fine."

Her phone rang, and she glanced down at her cell. "This is Kay calling for an update. I better take it before she has a fit. Now, you're sure you're okay?"

"Yes, ma'am. I'm fine. Please tell Mrs. Lillie I said thank you."

"I'll stop by your house later and bring a casserole and a ham bone I've been saving for Baby." She walked away talking into her cell phone.

"That was nice."

"A lot of people in New Bison care about you," Michael said. "And I'm at the top of the list. Do you want to tell me what happened?"

"People do care." I looked at my flowers. I thought about the people I'd met in the six months since coming to New Bison. I'd received a lot of love and support from the people in this small town who knew that I wasn't born and raised here. I can't trace my ancestors here beyond Great-Aunt Octavia, and yet they embraced me. They supported Baby Cakes. And I had no reason to believe that if selected to serve on a jury, they wouldn't be fair.

"Do you want me to take you back to Baby Cakes?" Michael asked.

"No. I want to go home."

CHAPTER 46

Michael helped me into my car and followed me home.

I sent a text to Leroy. He and Miss Hannah had everything under control at Baby Cakes and would swing by the house when they closed up for the evening.

April's car was at the house along with a silver vintage car.

"It can't be," Michael said as he got out of the car. He strolled past me and around the classic with his mouth and eyes open in awe.

I opened my door and walked over. "Nice car."

"Nice? That's like saying Niagara Falls is a nice stream of water. This is the most amazing car ever." Michael shook his head, practically salivating.

"I didn't think you were a huge car enthusiast. What's the big deal?"

He gave me a side glance that indicated he questioned my sanity. "Big deal? This car is beyond big. It's an Aston Martin DB5."

"Okay."

"It's a DB5," he repeated.

"I heard you the first time. What's so special about it?"

"James Bond drove an Aston Martin DB5."

"Oh." I headed for the door.

"You don't get it."

"I get it. James Bond drove a car just like this, so—"

"No. James Bond didn't drive a car just like this. James Bond drove *this* car. When I was a kid, I had a poster on my wall of Sean Connery driving this car in *Goldfinger*. Plus, Daniel Craig drove it in *Skyfall*."

"Really? *Goldfinger* was before your time, wasn't it?"

"My grandmother was a huge fan of Sean Connery. I think she had a crush on him." He chuckled. "Anyway, she watched every 007 movie and any movie that Sean Connery made. She loved his voice. She used to say she would pay money to listen to Sean Connery read the phone book."

"Who would have thought Miss Hannah was so romantic." I laughed.

"I don't know about 'romantic.' She said the same thing about Barry White, but the point is I studied everything I could about that car. It had machine guns, an ejector seat, and all these cool gadgets, and this is that car."

"Hmm. I wonder who's visiting. I seriously doubt that Daniel Craig is inside. Maybe we need to go take a look."

We went inside and found the Admiral, April, and Carson Law sitting at the island, drinking tea and eating thumbprint cookies.

Michael gazed at Mrs. Law. "That car. Is it . . . ?"

"That's mine." Carson Law sipped her tea. "Do you like it?"

"It's . . . I mean, it looks exactly like the one . . ."

Carson Law smiled and nodded. "That was my big splurge when I finally started making money as a milliner. My dad used to love 007 movies and the cool cars that James Bond drove."

"But, that's the real car?"

"No. Sadly, it's not the original. Apparently, the authorities frown on people driving around town with built-in machine guns. However, it's almost an exact replica." She leaned forward and grinned. "I did get the ejector seat, but I've never been brave enough to try it out."

Michael and the Admiral both raised their hands and said, "I'll do it."

"Men," I mumbled.

Baby was curled up in his dog bed, gnawing on a bone, and barely looked up at me.

"Now, what's this I hear about you crying in the street?" Carson Law gave me a long caring look and reached out a comforting hand.

"How did you hear about that?" I asked.

"News travels fast in a small town. I think Claude, my maître d', told us that he'd heard from one of the cooks or something like that." Carson Law waved her hand. "Your father was going to go down there with guns blazing, but I assured him that your young man had the situation well in hand."

A moment of sadness flashed across the Admiral's face, but it was gone as quickly as it came.

Before I could explain, there was a knock at the back door.

Baby sat up and gave a quick bark. He rushed to the door, but his tail wag told me the visitor was a friend.

Michael opened the door.

Alma Hurston was holding two casseroles.

Michael relieved her of the dishes.

"I made casseroles," she said. "I hope you're feeling better, dear. Comfort food. That's what you need." Her cell phone rang. "Oh dear, I better go."

Tyler, Leroy, and Miss Hannah came in as Alma Hurston left.

Tyler placed a large bucket of chicken on the counter. "Sorry we're late, but Miss Hannah insisted we had to stop at Love's Soul Food Kitchen to get fried chicken."

"Nobody fries chicken like Dru Ann," Hannah said, "plus, I had a couple of emergency pies in the back of the freezer."

"Emergency pies?" the Admiral asked. "What's that?"

Miss Hannah looked at him as though he'd suddenly grown two heads. "It's exactly what it sounds like. It's pies that I put away in case of an emergency. And Maddy crying in the street is definitely an emergency. That girl has the spirit of Octavia, and she don't cry easy. Sister Sylvia told me Maddy was crying and Alma was bringing a casserole, so I figured we best get some chicken to go with the casserole."

"Sister Sylvia saw me crying and called you?" I asked.

Leroy held up his cell. "The way my phone's been blowing up, half of New Bison must have seen you."

I picked up my cell phone and saw that I'd missed a ton of messages. Some were left to my personal account and others to Baby Cakes.

#Hugs #NobodyMakesMyFavoriteBakerCry #WhoDoWeNeedToTakeOut? #LoveYouMaddy

"Wow! I can't believe so many people saw me." At one point in my life, I would have been humiliated, but after getting dumped during my livestreamed wedding, it took a lot to humiliate me.

"People care about you," Hannah said. "Now, you go in the dining room and sit down. We'll get everything set up, and then you can tell us what's bothering you." She pushed me out of the kitchen and got busy arranging things.

It didn't take long. Leroy and Tyler arranged the food on the dining room table while Miss Hannah gave orders and set each place setting. Within minutes, we were all seated at the table.

Miss Hannah looked at the Admiral. "Would you like to bless the food?" Her voice was firm, and it was clearly an order and not a question. Fortunately, orders were something with which the Admiral was well acquainted.

He quickly bowed his head and said a blessing over the

food, and we all filled our plates. For several minutes, the conversation revolved around food and had nothing to do with murder or me crying in the street, but that didn't last.

"Maddy, what happened?" Miss Hannah asked.

What did happen? It had been a long day. I started with Galina and then moved into my conversation with Jessica.

"Wait, Galina Forkin was dating both Elliott and Oliver Freemont?" the Admiral asked.

"She said she was in love with Freemont. They broke up when he went into hiding in Greece, and she started dating Elliott, but then Freemont came back and—"

"She admitted that he was forging paintings?" April asked.

I nodded. "Apparently, Oliver Freemont was great at copying the style of famous artists like Vermeer and Rembrandt. He was paid a lot of money to copy them."

"Isn't that illegal?" Tyler asked.

"Only if he sold them as originals, which he wasn't. She said he was told that he was just copying the originals for restaurants and businesses."

"And he bought that?" April asked skeptically.

"According to Galina, he did. He couldn't imagine how anyone would take his paintings for the real thing. After all, the Mona Lisa is hanging in the Louvre, so why would anyone mistake his painting for the real thing?"

"But, how could his paintings fool experts?" Carson Law asked. "Wouldn't it be easy to tell that his paintings weren't made hundreds of years ago?"

"That's the rub," April said. "The forgeries were painted on old canvases with authentic stretchers from the period. He had to know what he was doing was illegal."

"According to Galina, the commissions started off simple, but as time went on, the requests got more complicated," I said. "They wanted him to use certain canvases, paints, even providing the water he was to use for dipping his brushes."

"That's one of the ways forensics teams are able to identify forgeries," April said. "Scientists can determine where a painting was made by looking at the chemical composition of the water. I don't understand it."

"Well, that makes sense," Hannah said. "I'm sure they weren't adding fluoride to the water in Italy back when that Leonardo fella was painting that Mona Lisa woman."

April stared at Miss Hannah as though seeing her for the first time. "That's right."

"I don't suppose Galina knew who paid him?" Leroy asked.

I shook my head. "She claims he never told her, and I believe her."

"Why?" April asked. "She's probably lying. I'll bet if we take her to the police station and have the experts question her, she'll break down."

"I don't think so. She was hysterical when I talked to her. I can tell you that she believes whoever paid Freemont also killed him. So, she wants me to find them. She wants them to pay for murdering him."

"How does she expect you to figure that out?" the Admiral asked.

Something was swimming around in my brain. When I reached out to grab it, it floated away. Experience told me that the best way to catch a missing thought was *not* to focus on it. So, I let it slip away and focused on the conversation at the table.

"Did she tell you where he hid the package Octavia sent him?" Hannah asked.

"How did you know about that? I never told anyone about it."

"You didn't have to. Octavia told me when she sent it," Hannah said.

The Admiral and I exchanged a look.

"Did she tell you what was in it?" the Admiral asked.

"She said it was the evidence of who was causing all of the problems in town. I told her to put it in a safe deposit box, but she didn't want to do that." Hannah shrugged. "She said it would be safer out of New Bison."

"Galina knew Freemont had a package he wanted to give me, but she swears she didn't know what it was or where he hid it."

When we'd exhausted the topic of Galina, I shared my conversation with Jessica Barlow and passed around the envelope that had brought Brandy Denton to New Bison.

"I'm looking forward to meeting with your friend tomorrow," Carson Law said.

"I don't know that I'd go so far as to describe Jessica as a friend. We got off to a rough start, but I think we could be."

"That's all good, but I don't see how any of that left you crying on the sidewalk," Hannah said.

"That was because of my conversation with Chris Russell." I shared the details of Russell suggesting I accept a plea deal.

"Poppycock," Hannah said. "First, you didn't kill those people, so pleading guilty would be lying. I don't take with lying. Second, I've lived in New Bison for nigh on forty years. There's good people and bad people everywhere. *If* you ended up on trial, then we're going to pray and leave it in the Lord's hands. I don't believe He would put racists on the jury." Hannah pursed her lips and frowned. "Nothing but poppycock. That's what that is."

Carson Law reached over and patted Miss Hannah's hand. "I agree. I grew up in New Bison, and I believe you'd get a fair trial in the unlikely event that things went that far. However, I am firmly of the belief that we will find the killer and none of that will be necessary."

"I just grabbed the folder, shoved it in my purse, and ran."

"Can I see those papers?" the Admiral asked.

I pulled the folder out of my purse and passed it down. "I

was overwhelmed. That's why I was crying." Michael reached under the table and squeezed my hand.

We talked about everything I found out—everyone except the Admiral, who was scowling at the envelope I'd gotten from Jessica Barlow, only to scowl at the papers Chris Russell had wanted me to sign as he read them.

"What's the matter, Dad?"

"This power of attorney is a pile of—"

"Jefferson Augustus Montgomery!" Hannah said.

"Sorry, but either that attorney is an idiot or a crook, and my money is on the latter."

CHAPTER 47

"What do you mean?" we all asked.

"This isn't just a document giving him power of attorney to act on your behalf if you were convicted of a crime," the Admiral said. "If you'd signed this document, you would have given him authority to act on your behalf in all matters in perpetuity."

"But, it can't be. I mean, he's an attorney, and he represented Great-Aunt Octavia for years. She trusted him."

"Where'd you get a cock-and-bull idea like that?" Miss Hannah asked.

"What do you mean?" I asked.

"Davis Russell, Chris Russell's father, was Octavia's attorney. Davis died about six months before Octavia, and that just left Chris Russell. She barely knew that prune-faced man and didn't like what she *did* know." Miss Hannah sipped her tea.

A puzzle piece fell into place, but I didn't like the picture that was unfolding in my mind. "Why not? I mean, he did her will. Why didn't she like him?"

"His father did her will. Chris Russell was all about making money, and he didn't care how he did it. Driving around in that fancy sports car and always buying expensive antiques." Miss Hannah sucked her teeth. "Octavia didn't like him, but she said she'd made sure he couldn't touch her money."

"How did she do that?" I asked.

But it was too late. Miss Hannah had zoned out.

"How did who do what?" Miss Hannah asked.

CHAPTER 48

April helped Miss Hannah to the guest room to lie down.

Michael stood up. "Maybe I should take her home."

Baby barked and ran to the back door.

Candy Rivers burst into the house. "Help! Daisy's lost, and I've called and called until I'm hoarse. I'm so worried about her."

The Admiral and Carson Law agreed to stay with Miss Hannah. The rest of us split up and went in search of Daisy.

According to Candy, Daisy had been playing on the beach. Candy's phone rang, and she took her eyes off the dog for a few minutes. When she looked up again, Daisy was nowhere to be seen.

Leroy took the road. Tyler and Candy took the beach toward the Hurston house. Michael, Baby, and I went down the stairs and searched the beach in the opposite direction. I was so nervous about Daisy that I barely remembered going down the rickety stairs.

Michael grinned. "Not bad, Squid."

"I didn't have time to think about the stairs."

We called for Daisy and scoured the beach. It was slow going because the heels of my Jimmy Choo sandals kept sinking into the sand, and Michael had to help me wrench my feet out. Eventually, I gave up and took off my shoes.

Michael must have noticed that my gaze kept drifting to the waves of Lake Michigan.

I finally worked up the courage to ask, "Can all dogs swim?"

Michael squeezed my hand. "No. Bulldogs and breeds with short legs aren't really built for swimming. I wouldn't call mastiffs water dogs, but they are powerful and can be powerful swimmers."

I swallowed the fear that had made its way to my throat and continued searching. For a moment, I looked away. When I looked back, Baby was gone.

CHAPTER 49

"*Baby!*" I screamed.

Michael rushed ahead and around a large rock that protruded from the bluff. After a few moments, he came back around and beckoned for me.

I ran around the rock and noticed a cave.

Michael pointed to two sets of paw prints in the wet sand that went from the beach into the cave.

"Maddy, I'm going to get Daisy and Baby. You wait here and— "

I was shaking my head before the words left his mouth.

"Listen, soldier. I told you at Baby Cakes that I wasn't going to fall for that *You-wait-here-while-I-go-face-the-bad-guys-alone-routine* again. We go together or we don't go at all." I folded my arms across my chest and glared.

"Maddy. There's likely spiders, maybe even rats and bats."

I shivered but didn't balk.

"There may even be snakes."

My resolve faltered for a moment, but I put my shoes back on and looked around until I found a large stick.

Michael must have seen that arguing was useless. After a few moments, he shrugged. "Is it okay if I go first?"

I moved behind him and clutched his shirt as if my life depended on maintaining my grip.

He pulled out his cell phone and sent a text, and then he turned on the flashlight and headed into the cave.

"Who're you possibly texting?" I asked, but then I heard a chime. One glance at my phone told me he had sent a text to the Admiral notifying him of our location using longitude and latitude that a sailor would be sure to understand.

Following paw prints into a cave

Hope U won't need this

"Are you sure you—"

"You're wasting time," I said.

"Okay, let's go."

CHAPTER 50

It was still daylight, but the deeper we went into the cave, the darker it became. From time to time, Michael had to crouch, pointing his cell phone at the ground to see the tracks.

The cave smelled dank, moldy, and earthy.

From time to time, we heard something scuttering around that was way too small to be Baby. I clutched Michael's shirt so tightly, my fingers ached.

As we tramped through the wet sand, I wished over and over again that I had taken a few extra moments and changed out of my cute strappy sandals and into my Sculpts. My lovely Jimmy Choo sandals were ruined. I focused on my shoes to keep my mind from thinking about everything else. After walking for what felt like an hour, I was ready to scream.

Michael stopped, and I bumped into his back.

"What?"

"Listen."

In the distance, I heard a whimper that made my heart skip a beat.

"Baby!"

Baby barked, and I rushed forward.

In a few moments, we were met by the smell of wet dog and a barking, jumping mastiff.

I dropped to my knees and hugged my dog. "Baby, you were a bad dog. But Mommy loves you. You know better than to run away like that." He planted doggy kisses all over my face.

I wasn't the only one being covered with dog kisses. Michael got his fair share. I noticed that his petting wasn't just comfort, but he was checking Baby for injuries. Satisfied, he patted him. "Okay, buddy. Where's Daisy?"

Baby barked and headed back where he came from. Deeper inside the cave, and through a tunnel, we saw Daisy lying on her side licking her paw.

Michael examined the dog and whispered soothing words while he checked her out. The grateful dog licked him until he touched her leg. Then she screamed.

"It's okay, girl. I'm sorry. You're such a good girl, but this is going to hurt a little."

"Is she okay?" I asked.

"She's got a broken leg, and she looks dehydrated, but otherwise, I think she's okay. I won't know if she has any internal injuries until I get her to my office. Let me have your stick."

I handed him the stick I had been clutching since we entered the cave. I quickly sent a text to Candy.

Michael broke the stick and ripped his shirt into strips. "This is going to hurt, and she may bite me, but it's just because of the pain. So, don't panic."

"Can I help?"

"Cradle her head and keep Baby nearby. He might help to steady her."

I carefully cradled Daisy's head in my lap and petted her and muttered soothing words while Michael worked.

Daisy let out one loud scream and a howl, but that was it, and she didn't bite either of us.

He worked quickly and set her leg. Then he petted her. "You were such a good girl." Then, he lifted Daisy, careful not to move her leg more than necessary. Fortunately, Daisy was a female and considerably smaller than Baby. But at one hundred and sixty pounds, she was no lightweight.

We turned around to head back the way we came when we heard squeaking and voices.

"Maddy!" Tyler yelled.

"We're down here."

Tyler and Candy came around the corner. Tyler was carrying a flashlight. The squeaking was the wheels of a wagon that Candy was pulling.

"Oh, my poor baby!" Candy cried, and she hugged Daisy.

Michael gently placed the dog in the wagon. "How'd you know to bring this?"

"Maddy sent me a text," Candy said. "She said bring blankets, a wagon, water, and any medical stuff in the back of your truck."

"That's my girl." Michael grinned. Then he turned back to his patient. He opened a bottle of water, and Daisy lapped up nearly all of it. Then, he reached into his bag and pulled out a syringe with a needle. He gave Daisy something for the pain, and within moments, she was asleep in the wagon and covered with a blanket.

Candy hugged Michael and me and then Michael again. She was shivering like a leaf. "Thank you. I don't know how to thank you. You saved her."

"We found her because of Baby," Michael said. "He's the hero in this scenario."

"Baby gets a lifetime supply of pup cups. And his owner gets a lifetime supply of cortados."

"Great," I said, "but let's get out of here. This place gives me the creeps." I glanced around. "Where's Tyler?"

"Not again," Candy said. "Tyler!"

"Right here." Tyler came from around the corner. "Do you know what this is?"

"It's a cave," I said. "It's dark. It's smelly. I've ripped my dress, and my shoes are ruined. Plus, there are all kinds of creepy-crawly things in here."

"I think this is one of the tunnels that was used by the criminal underground," Tyler said enthusiastically.

"Yeah, well, you can have the town council put up a marker and give tours to school children," I said. "But it's icky, and I want to go back. Let's go."

"Wait," Candy said. "What's that behind your back?"

Tyler showed us a plastic paint box. "I found this propped behind the wall back there."

I stepped forward and looked at it. "It can't be."

"Only one way to find out," Michael said.

I took the paint box and opened it. Inside was a plastic envelope addressed to me. I recognized the handwriting. "It's Great-Aunt Octavia's."

"Are you going to open it?" Candy asked.

I paused. "Not here. Let's get out of this cave. Let's go back to the house where it's warm and dry and doesn't smell like dead fish. Then, I'll open the envelope."

Tyler looked disappointed, but it passed quickly when Candy clasped his hand and said, "Good idea. I want to get Daisy out of here."

We turned to leave, and that's when we heard the sound of the slide of a gun moving back and forward to get the bullet into the chamber.

We looked up and were staring into the barrel of a revolver.

CHAPTER 51

Holding the gun was Chris Russell. "I'll take that."

He snatched the envelope from me. "You couldn't leave well enough alone, could you? You just had to meddle in things that don't concern you. You're just like that crazy aunt of yours."

Michael took a step forward, but Russell reached out and grabbed me. He pulled me close to him and pointed the gun at me rather than Michael.

A rumble started in Baby's belly and grew louder until it came out of his mouth. Drool dripped from his jowls in threads. His eyes were cold, and his body was wound up like a spring. In a few moments, he would pounce.

My mind went back to when he attacked before to protect me, when I was being held at gunpoint. Baby had been fierce, but he had still gotten shot.

Chris Russell clutched me closer and slid back so that I stood between him and Baby, and he leveled his gun at my dog. My best friend.

"No, please," I said. "Don't hurt him." I turned to Michael. "Please."

"Baby, sit," Michael ordered.

Nervous energy and fury made it challenging, but after a few false starts, Baby put his butt on the ground. His gaze never wavered from Chris Russell's face. One word, and he'd pounce. But for now, he was sitting.

Chris Russell grinned. "That's better. I should have killed that beast when I did away with Octavia, but I wanted it to be an accident. If the beast was shot, that would have drawn attention to Octavia's death, and I couldn't have that."

Candy gasped and quickly clamped her hand over her mouth.

Tyler Lawrence pulled her close and sidled around so that he was standing in front of her.

Michael was inching closer. He moved so slowly and quietly that it was barely noticeable.

Keep him talking. I need to distract him so he doesn't notice Michael.

"I'm surprised Baby let you get close enough to hurt her," I said. "How did you manage?"

"It cost me twenty bucks for a T-bone steak and a handful of tranquilizers." He chuckled. "I misjudged his weight. I put enough tranquilizers in that steak to take down an elephant. It should have taken him out, but instead, he was just groggy."

"Why did you have to kill her?"

"Because she was nosy. She blocked my plans to take over the lake shore real estate market and develop it. She demanded soil samples, which caused the developers to get nervous. They bailed out, and that cost me millions."

"She was smart," Candy said. "She outsmarted you."

Michael inched closer.

"Actually, her meddling worked in my favor. If she hadn't been so adamant that we needed to test the soil, we never would have found these tunnels."

"We?" I asked.

"The town council—Abernathy, Rivers, and I. We found the tunnels and realized that we could put them to good use."

"Paul?" Candy asked.

Michael inched closer.

"Oh yes, your late husband was heavily involved, although a bit worthless. Thanks to me, that Witless Wonder managed to get elected mayor. His job was to convince Octavia and your parents to sell. Then, with the entire city council in on the plan, we could push through any zoning changes needed without any issues. But, that incompetent fool couldn't even get that done."

"When did you start forging and smuggling works of art?" I asked.

Chris Russell laughed. "I guess you really are related to Octavia. Always figuring things out. Freemont used to come here in the summers to paint. I stumbled across a painting he did and realized he had talent. Not for his original works. Those were unimaginative and dull. But, he could mimic the works of the masters, and I doubt if the artist himself would have been able to tell the original from the forgery."

Michael inched closer.

"How did you make the swap?" I asked hurriedly.

"As an attorney, I've made the acquaintance of some of society's most skilled criminals." He threw his head back and laughed. "I helped them evade justice, and they used their finely honed skills to help me. It was a win-win situation."

"So, you hired Oliver Freemont to forge paintings, but why kill him?"

"I had to when I learned that Octavia had sent him a package. I couldn't count on the fact that he hadn't opened it and learned who was behind the forgeries."

"What do you mean? You hired him."

Russell grinned. "Ah, but that was the key. No one at the . . . shall we call it the bottom of the pile, knew who was calling the shots at the top. Freemont's contact was Abernathy. Abernathy and Rivers knew about me. They were both weak. Rivers was so head over heels in love with you"—he pointed his gun at Candy—"that he was about to throw everything away to try and win you back."

Candy gasped.

"Fool! And I heard Abernathy, the sniveling idiot, in the kitchen at Baby Cakes. He was so afraid of going to jail that he would have sung like a canary."

"So, you killed him," I said.

"I had to. Surely, you see that."

Michael inched closer.

"Why did you kill Brandy? I didn't like her, but there's no way you can convince me that she was one of your minions and involved in your dirty business."

"Ah, yes, Brandy. That was one of my few failures. She was merely the bait that I used to trap you."

"Me?" I felt an ache in the pit of my stomach.

"Yes, you. I wrote to Brandy to get her to come to New Bison. She really despised you and was only too glad to come. My plan was that if Brandy died, then you would be blamed and would be out of the way. I could then get the property and level it to the ground."

I saw spots in front of my eyes, and for a moment, I was afraid I would pass out. "Are you telling me that the only reason you killed Brandy was so you could frame me for her murder?"

"Yes. Ingenious plan, I thought. Who else but you would have hated her enough to want her dead? And that argument you two had was perfect. It should have worked. It would have worked, but then you went into your Nancy Drew routine and started digging up other suspects with motives and opportunities." He shook his head and then shrugged. "I feel confident that in the end, I would have been able to convince my D.A. friend to prosecute. Defending you would not have been my best effort, but then even the great Perry Mason lost one case." He laughed.

"You're a monster," I said.

Russell laughed. There was something in the laugh that was off. Chris Russell was insane. "And here I thought you were just a flighty airhead."

My heart skipped a bit, and my blood went cold. *Flighty airhead*. I had been called that name once before. Chris Russell was the voice. He was the one I'd overheard threatening me. His was the voice I wasn't able to identify. He was the one who had said, *If she gets in my way again, I won't miss next time*.

"You're the puppet master."

CHAPTER 52

"What?" Chris Russell asked.

"It was you. I overheard you talking that day."

"Aw, I told that fool someone had been in the office, but he swore it was empty. So, you overheard that? You are much smarter than you look. The puppet master? I prefer to think of myself as the conductor of the greatest criminal network in the world. I'm the Conductor. Or, better still, I'm the Maestro."

Michael inched closer, but his toe hit a rock.

"Stop right there. Now is not the time to be a hero. Someone might get shot." He pressed the gun to my head. "Now, enough talking."

Baby growled louder.

"Enough talking." Chris Russell was getting impatient.

"Just one more question," I said. "How did you manage it? How did you kill . . . I mean, the official cause of death was anaphylactic shock. How did you—"

"Aw. That was one of my finer maneuvers. I knew everything was botched up when I heard that the police were descending on your house. It was too much to ask that the mutt would have taken him out. Then, I could have had him put down. But, I always believe in being prepared. This time, all it took was a small dab of peanut butter on a business card. I could tell from the look in his eyes that he knew what I'd done, but within seconds, he was in anaphylactic shock. The mutt even licked the evidence off." He grinned. "If I were kinder, I might let him live out of gratitude, but . . . I can't start getting soft now."

Michael squared up. In seconds, he would make his move. Our eyes locked. He mouthed one word. *SING.*

I gave a slight nod.

He tapped his right hand against his leg. One. Pause. Two. Pause.

From the back of the cave, I heard a whistle that I recognized from years onboard Navy ships.

Michael tapped three.

I wished I was wearing my Louboutins. The heels were taller. But I put everything I had into those Jimmy Choos when I kicked Chris Russell's *shin*. The heel snapped, but I had punctured his flesh. Then, I put all my weight on his *instep* and impaled the broken heel into his foot. I used the heel of my hand and punched his *nose*, turned, and kneed his *groin*. When I heard the air leave his lungs, I dropped to the ground.

Michael and Baby flew through the air and there was a vicious battle. It sounded as though flesh was being ripped apart.

Chris Russell screamed.

The Admiral burst through the tunnel and joined the fray.

Within seconds, a bloodied Chris Russell lay on the ground.

"Oh my God, is he dead?" Candy whispered.

Michael reached a hand down and checked Russell's pulse. "No. He'll live."

"Darn," Candy said.

The Admiral hugged me.

Michael asked, "Are you okay?"

I flew into his arms.

The Admiral and Michael had their backs to Russell, so they didn't notice his hand, which had lain limp moments earlier, grasp the gun and point. But I did.

I shoved Michael aside moments before the gun exploded, and then the lights went out.

CHAPTER 53

When I opened my eyes, I was lying in my dad's arms, and Michael was kneeling over me. He pressed a cloth onto my shoulder.

Baby whimpered and then licked my face.

"I'm okay, Baby. You were such a brave boy."

Baby lay his huge head on my stomach, and I ignored the drool that soaked through my shirt.

"Ouch."

Michael swore and then pulled me into an embrace. After a few moments, he released me. "Are you crazy? Don't ever scare me like that again."

"Don't worry. I don't plan on getting shot again, but he was going to shoot you. I had to do something."

"Did you think about dropping to the ground?" Michael asked.

"I guess that would have been better." I winced.

"Come on. Let's get out of here." Michael looked up at my father. "With your permission, sir?"

The Admiral saluted.

Michael returned the salute. Then he gently lifted me and carried me out of the tunnel.

I don't remember riding to the hospital in an ambulance, but Michael assured me that I did. Apparently, Michael and Baby refused to leave my side. Both were crammed into the back along with my gurney. Michael said it was a tight fit, and the EMT may never be the same, but we all made it in one piece.

Getting shot hurt like Hades, but the hospital gave me good drugs, so I slept through most of the extraction. Initially, the emergency room doctor wanted to keep me overnight. That was until he learned that an overnight stay for me would involve keeping Baby, too. Suddenly, they had the bullet out and my shoulder stitched up, and I was released in record time.

When I got home, there was a mountain of flowers, plants, cards, and dishes.

I refused to go to bed and made myself comfortable on the sofa in the living room.

April hovered like a mother hen, bringing pillows, tucking blankets, and making sure that everything I needed was within arm's distance.

Miss Hannah was one of the first people who came calling. Her eyes filled with tears when she hugged me. "You scared the living daylights out of me."

"I'm sorry. I didn't mean to scare anyone."

"Well, don't go getting yourself shot no more. It was bad enough when Michael and Baby got shot. But, Baby's strong as an ox, and Michael's tough as leather. He's a soldier. You're soft, and I don't care what they say. I don't believe God intended for a woman to be getting shot like that. I'm not your blood like Octavia, but I've come to love you 'bout as much as she did, and I don't know that my heart could take it if something happened to you, too." Miss Hannah wiped her eyes with a handkerchief.

I cried at that, too.

Miss Hannah pulled herself together and stood tall. "Now, I need to bake something to relieve my feelings." She marched into the kitchen.

I chuckled. "She and Leroy both bake when they're stressed."

"They've both been baking nonstop," April said. "Baby Cakes will have enough baked goods to last a month."

The Admiral sat in a chair nearby.

Michael came in. I thought he would come and talk to me, but instead he went to the Admiral. "Sir, may I have a word?"

The Admiral stood, and the two of them left.

"I wonder what that's about?"

April shrugged, but a smile tugged at her lips. The drugs that kept the pain at bay were strong, and my brain wasn't firing on all cylinders. So, I didn't pursue it. Instead, I glanced over at Baby, who had climbed on the sofa and was lying at my feet.

Seeing Baby reminded me to ask, "How is Daisy?"

"She's fine. Dr. Howard said Michael set the broken bones perfectly."

"Of course," I said with pride.

After a few moments, Michael came back.

"Will you excuse me?" April said. "I have to go and . . . get something from the other room." She hurried out.

Michael sat on the sofa and looked into my eyes. "How are you feeling, Squid?"

"Good. Great, actually. I don't know what drugs they gave me, but they're working." I smiled.

He smiled, too. "This is probably not the best time for me to do this, but when you were lying on the ground in that cave, I made a vow, and I intend to keep it."

"Before you tell me about your vow, I have a question for you."

Michael tilted his head to the side. "Okay, what's your question?"

"Michael Portman, will you marry me?"

I have rarely managed to shock him, but he wasn't expecting that.

"Ah . . . shouldn't I be the one proposing to you?"

"Why? Why can't the woman propose to the man?"

"No reason, but I don't know that I should answer that question right now."

My smile fell. *I was wrong. I thought he loved me. I thought he seriously cared for me, but I was wrong.*

"I see." It took all of my effort and energy to keep my lip from quivering and not to cry. I refused to cry. One tear fell. *Darn it.*

"Hey, please don't cry. I just don't—"

"I'm fine. You don't have to explain. I get it. You don't love me." Several more tears came.

"That's not it. I—"

"Michael, really it's okay. I'm a terrible judge of people. I thought you felt the same way about me that I felt about you, but you don't, and it's okay. I get it. I think it would be best—"

He kissed me. "Will you stop talking for a minute and let me explain?"

"I don't want an explanation. You don't want to marry me. I get it, and that's all I need to know. It's okay." I sniffed.

"I do want to marry you. In fact, I was about to propose to you, but—"

"But, you realized that you don't want to marry me after all."

"I realized that you're on drugs, and this probably isn't the best time to ask you an important question like that. I don't want you to say yes because of the medication. I want you to have a clear head and to be sure that you do want to marry me because if you say yes, there's no backing out. I don't think I could stand it if you changed your mind."

"I think you're just saying that because you feel bad, but it's okay. I'll get over it. Why don't you tell me about your vow?" I asked.

"I'm not just saying that. I mean it. I love you, and I want to marry you. When you were shot and lying on the ground in that cave, I prayed. I vowed if God would let you be okay, then I would do what I should have done weeks ago."

"What's that?"

Michael got down on one knee. "Madison Renee Montgomery, will you do me the honor of accepting my hand in marriage?" He pulled out a box from his pocket that contained an engagement ring.

"No."

"No?"

"No."

"You won't marry me?" Michael asked.

"No. I'm drugged, so obviously I can't make good decisions. Besides, you don't really want to marry me, and you're just doing it now out of . . . guilt."

"I can't believe this is happening," Michael mumbled. "I'm not proposing out of guilt. I'm proposing because I love you, and I want to spend the rest of my life with you."

"Then why did you cancel so many dates with me over the past few weeks? Be honest. You're bored with me, right? That's why you didn't invite me to go with you to Chicago when you went."

"No, I'm not bored with you. I canceled dates because I was working, and I was working because I wanted to earn extra money to buy your engagement ring. The reason I didn't invite you to Chicago is because I wanted to look at engagement rings at Tiffany's." He held up the Tiffany blue box with the engagement ring.

I stared at the ring, a large heart-shaped diamond. It was dazzling.

"That's why I asked your father for permission to propose to you. That's why I'm here on one knee, pleading for your hand in matrimony. I love you!"

"You're serious?"

"Yes. I'm serious."

"What about Dr. Howard?"

"Maddy, anything I felt for Alliyah was over long ago. I am madly and hopelessly in love with you."

"You are?"

"I am."

"So, back to Dr. Howard."

He growled and rolled his eyes.

"Do you think she would cover the practice so we could go away on a long honeymoon?" I grinned.

He lifted his head. "Does that mean you're accepting?"

"Yes."

"That sounded decisive. You don't want to think it over?"

"I don't need to think it over. I know exactly what I want."

"What's that?" he asked with a devilish grin.

I whispered in his ear and saw the blood rush up his neck. He swore and pulled me into his arms.

"Did she accept?" Miss Hannah yelled from the kitchen.

Michael pulled away and swore softly. "If I didn't love that woman, I think I could strangle her right now."

I giggled and held out my finger.

He slipped the ring on and then held my hand to his lips and kissed me.

"Well?" Miss Hannah yelled.

"We both said yes!" I yelled.

There was a cheer from the kitchen before our friends and family descended to congratulate us.

The celebration didn't last long. Because of the drugs, I

couldn't drink Champagne. I swallowed two yawns before one escaped.

"That's enough," Miss Hannah said. "Party's over. You need your rest." She rushed everyone out of the house.

The Admiral kissed my forehead. "I'm really proud of you. You've blossomed into a beautiful, intelligent, kind, and loving woman. You remind me so much of your mom."

"Thanks, Dad. Will you give me away?"

"I would be honored. You couldn't have picked a better man." His eyes filled with tears.

Michael and the Admiral shook hands, and then Michael lifted me from the sofa and carried me to my bedroom.

I rested my head on his shoulder.

He gently placed me on the bed and then pulled the blankets up around me. He kissed me tenderly and much too briefly. "When you recover, I'm going to take you to La Petite Maison and propose again. That one didn't go exactly the way I imagined."

"Because I'm drugged?" I grinned.

"Let's not go into that again," Michael said.

"I know exactly what I agreed to, and don't think you're going to get out of holding up your side of the bargain. You proposed, and I have witnesses and a ring to prove it."

"Haven't you figured it out yet? I don't want to get away. I'm here to stay. For richer or for poorer. For better or worse. In sickness and in health. Till death do us part." He kissed me. When he pulled away, he said, "I do have one request when I propose next time."

I raised an eyebrow. "What's that?"

"Wear that blue dress you had on the other day."

I laughed. "I have one I think you might like better."

This time, he raised a brow. "I can hardly wait."

Later, I awoke to Baby snoring next to me. On the nightstand was the envelope from Great-Aunt Octavia. In all of the excitement, I had forgotten to open it.

Great-Aunt Octavia had sent me soil reports that showed the land near the Lake Michigan shoreline was not stable enough for heavy development. She had included other documents, but I put them aside and read a handwritten note addressed to me.

Madison,

If you're reading this, then I'm dead, and you're living in my house and running Baby Cakes. I hope you will love it as much as I have. I've stumbled across some shady business here in New Bison, and I think they're on to me. Just like Sherlock Holmes and Moriarty grappled at Reichenbach Falls, I have been grappling with my very own Moriarty. I've known for some time that I've had a spy in my camp. I finally figured out it was Chris Russell. I never did like the man, but I didn't want to believe he was as evil as it looks like he really is. His father, Davis Russell, was a good man, and I'm glad he didn't live to see what his son has become. So, if I'm dead, chances are good he's responsible. I don't know if April will find enough evidence to convict him of my murder, but the information in this envelope proves that he and the city council are involved in deceiving the public. I'll rest easy knowing that he will spend some time in jail.

Don't be sad. I have lived a good long life, and I am ready. My only regret is that I didn't get to spend more time with you. And, I will miss Baby more than anyone (but don't tell Garrett and Hannah I said that).

I love you, and I know that you will take good care of Baby. He's a good boy.

Love,

Octavia

I looked out the window as the sun set on Lake Michigan. I said a silent prayer of thanks. I was thankful for Great-Aunt Octavia. Thanks to her, I had a home, a business, a dog, and love. I glanced at the ring on my finger and smiled. I reached for my phone and snapped a picture.

#ISaidYes!

Acknowledgments

Special thanks to my editor, John Scognamiglio, at Kensington, and literary agent, Jessica Faust, at BookEnds. Thanks for believing in and supporting me.

Thanks to Ellery Adams for helping to make two of my dreams a reality. I will be forever grateful.

Thanks to Alex Savage for the military expertise, Alexia Gordon, for medical expertise, Abby Vandiver for pushing me through sprints, Christopher and Carson Rucker for your fashion expertise and suggestions.

Most of all, I want to thank Debra H. Goldstein for listening and for the pep talks, moral support, brainstorming, and legal advice. You're the best.

Recipes from Baby Cakes Bakery

Old-Fashioned Pound Cake

Ingredients

4 sticks of butter, softened, plus more for the pan
3 cups sugar
3 cups cake flour, plus more for the pan
8 large eggs, room temperature
1 cup heavy cream
2 tablespoons vanilla

Directions

1. Preheat oven to 350 degrees F. Butter and flour a Bundt pan.
2. Beat butter until soft. Gradually add in the sugar and beat until light and fluffy.
3. Add the eggs one at a time and beat well.
4. Add the flour 1 cup at a time and alternate with heavy cream and beat at low until just blended.
5. Add the vanilla and mix.
6. Pour into the greased and floured Bundt pan. Bake on the center rack until golden brown, approximately 1–11/2 hours.
7. Remove from oven and allow the cake to cool. Loosen the edges of the cake with a sharp knife.

Note: This is great with a scoop of vanilla ice cream, fresh strawberries, and whipped cream!

Blondies

Ingredients

1 cup melted butter
2 cups dark brown sugar
2 eggs
2 teaspoons pure vanilla extract
$1^3/_4$ cups flour
$^1/_2$ teaspoon baking powder
$^1/_2$ teaspoon salt

Directions

1. Preheat oven to 350 degrees F. Spray an 8" x 8" pan with cooking spray or coat with butter.
2. In a large bowl, mix melted butter and brown sugar.
3. Add eggs and vanilla and stir vigorously until smooth.
4. Add the flour, baking powder, and salt and stir until well incorporated.
5. Pour the batter into the prepared pan and smooth out.
6. Bake for 45 minutes until the edges are golden and a toothpick comes out mostly clean.
7. Cool completely, then cut into squares.

Sweet Potato Pie

Ingredients

(2) 9-inch pie shells
2 cups cooked sweet potatoes
8 tablespoons butter
1¾ cups sugar
1 teaspoon ground nutmeg
1½ teaspoons vanilla extract
2 eggs
1 cup (8 oz.) evaporated milk

Directions

1. Preheat oven to 350 degrees F. Place sweet potatoes in a five-quart saucepan and cover the potatoes with water.
2. Boil over medium heat until the sweet potatoes are soft when poked with a fork (approximately 30 minutes).
3. Drain potatoes and remove skin and beat with an electric mixer until smooth.
4. Cream butter and sugar together and add to sweet potato mixture and beat well. Add nutmeg, vanilla, eggs, and evaporated milk.
5. Mix ingredients thoroughly and pour into unbaked pie shells.
6. Bake until the pies are set in the center (approximately 35–40 minutes).

Naturally Dyed Easter Eggs

Ingredients

1 dozen eggs
1 cup shredded purple cabbage (Blue)
1 cup red onion skins (Lavender)
1 cup yellow onion skins (Orange)
1 cup shredded beets (Pink)
2 tablespoons ground turmeric (Yellow)
1 bag hibiscus tea (Lavender)
1 cup water for each color
1 tablespoon white vinegar for each cup of dye

Directions

1. Boil the eggs over medium high heat for 17 minutes. Then, remove from heat and fill with cold water to stop the cooking process. Let the eggs cool.
2. Fill a saucepan with 1 cup of water and add ingredient for appropriate color (i.e., turmeric, beets, etc.) and boil. Then, reduce heat to low and simmer for 15–60 minutes until the color is a couple of shades darker than your desired color. The longer the dye simmers, the darker the dye.
3. Let the dye cool to room temperature. Then, strain through a mesh strainer.
4. Add vinegar to the strained dye and stir.
5. Place eggs in the dye and refrigerate for 2–12 hours.
6. Dry with a paper towel. If you want a darker color, return to the dye and repeat until the color is as dark as you want. Multiple dips will produce darker colored eggs.

Notes:

- White eggs will have more vibrant color, while brown eggs will have a darker, earthy color.
- For lighter pastel colors, rinse and dry after removing from dye.
- Create new colors by dyeing in multiple colors (i.e., after a few hours in turmeric, dip in purple cabbage to get a green color).

Visit our website at
KensingtonBooks.com
to sign up for our newsletters, read more from your favorite authors, see books by series, view reading group guides, and more!

Become a Part of Our
Between the Chapters Book Club
Community and Join the Conversation

Betweenthechapters.net

Submit your book review for a chance to win exclusive Between the Chapters swag you can't get anywhere else!
https://www.kensingtonbooks.com/pages/review/